The Living Past

DONALD MACLEOD

acair

Contents

Contents

Preface

These letters are published with the author's express permission and with only minimal changes, the main one being that I have eliminated most of the personal references to myself. Some of the letters obviously grew beyond the size of any normal correspondence, and I did seriously consider either reducing them in length or breaking them into smaller units. But I decided in the end that this would have amounted to a kind of literary vivisection. They are published, therefore, as I received them.

Jacqueline Quessaud
Quebec, September 2005

2 August 2020

Dear Mme Quessaud

I am sure you will understand when I say that your letter came as something of a shock. I was distressed to hear of your dear mother's death. It seems hard to believe, but I hadn't seen her since the summer of 1962. There was nothing romantic about it: at least, not overtly. It was on the *Loch Seaforth*, the steamer which carried us Hebridean unfortunates to and fro across the Minch. We were both students, she returning home from college in Aberdeen, I from college in Edinburgh. It must have been a better day than usual because I distinctly remember being able to engage in something like rational conversation. Normally, the very smell of 'the boat' made me seasick. Not that the rational conversation amounted to very much: at least, not on my part. At that time she was undergoing her post-graduate training as a teacher and still relatively close to her own schooldays. She didn't say much about her experience of placements. In fact, the one thing that seemed to strike her (and not very favourably) was that all the children were driven to school by their parents. I remember too that she mock-solemnly rebuked me for using the construction 'after having ... '. I had, it seems, once corrected her for using it. The original conversation still haunts me. What on earth was the point I had been trying to make?

To you 1962 suggests, I suppose, prehistory. To me it is still a powerful presence: defining me, but lost beyond recovery. I have seen myself grow old, but not her. She remained always, and remains still, what she was that day: a young twenty-two year-old girl, with long, shining dark hair, a slim, lithe figure and a smile that lit up the whole of her face. I never knew what life did to her, or what she made of it, but I can still walk through a door to that moment: to the smells of the ship and the rolling of the sea; to the teasing smile; and to a fated friendship, because she would never have allowed it to come to anything. In her own judgement (and it had to be decisive), I was a Christian and she was not.

I can understand perfectly well that your mother's death should trigger off an interest in your own roots and in her background, and particularly her early schooldays. I shall be glad to help if I can. Maybe your mother knew that I was a temperamental antiquarian. The obsession becomes worse with age. As you run out of future, you tend to buy more and more into the past.

The parish of Uig, where your mother was born, was as remote from me and my childhood as Canada is today. It was only fifty miles away; it might as well have been a thousand. My world extended only as far as I could walk between meals - except that once a year we could take a bus to Ness at the northerly tip of the island for a couple of weeks' holiday. It wasn't that Ness was a recognised resort or anything like that. But it was where the whole battery of grandpas, grannies, aunts, uncles and cousins lived; and Maggie, the horse (we didn't know she was a mare). We had no aunties in Uig. Your mother came from a world of which I knew nothing. She was a girl, which made her different (and terrifying) enough; she was a fluent Gaelic speaker (which I certainly wasn't) and therefore superior; and she came from a place where they had salmon and deer and fishing-boats and other things which to me were the stuff of romance.

It would have been in August 1953 that we both enrolled at the Nicolson Institute in Stornoway: two among some one hundred others from all over Lewis who had just passed the Scottish equivalent of the 11-plus: 'the Qualifying', as we called it. It involved two IQ tests in successive years, plus two sudden-death examinations in English and Arithmetic. It effectively defined your life, which was pretty grim if you were one of the eighty per cent who 'failed' it. From that point onwards, you had no academic future, especially if you were a boy (girls could become nurses). Your options were limited to being a shop assistant, a sailor, a postman, a bus driver, a bricklayer or a docker. These were all honourable trades. Indeed, in our early years we had no greater dreams. School-leavers usually became petrol boys, grocers' message boys or telegraph boys. My ambitions were higher: I longed to be a bus driver. But why should a boy's choices be so narrowed by the age of twelve?

However, on that particular day such things were far from our minds. Those who had failed were the lucky ones. They were back in the familiar surroundings of our old schools. In Laxdale, where I had come from, they were probably engaged in the age-old ritual of the daily (and daylong) football match between Laxdale and Marybank (the two ends of the parish). Today, sadly, I can't even go back to visit the site. It's been re-engineered beyond recognition. In those days you could have told at a glance it was no place for football. There was a one in three gradient, the surface was a mixture of gravel, outcropping rocks and endless rivulets: an environment to deter even a moon-buggie. On one side was the river, fast flowing and swollen; on another, a busy main road; then the front of the school with its massive fragile windows; and worst of all, on the west, the headmaster's (or 'the Master's', as we called him) garden. Every game of football was an accident waiting to happen: cuts and bruises, broken windows, falling in the river, being struck by a bus or being caught in the garden. But while we were all more or less sane as individuals, we were not sane as a group. We played all day, every day.

Even the tinkers played. Nothing remarkable about that, you might think, but there was: they had no boots. Many of us had horrendous boots, the soles covered in tacks or studs to prolong the life of the leather, and the toes and heels tipped with steel plates. They were probably designed for miners, but they would have done for divers. It was hazardous to be involved in any tackle involving such footware. To be involved barefoot would seem suicidal. But the tinkers thought nothing of it. They were brilliant and fearless footballers and had a precociousness which always puzzled me because it never came to anything. Many years afterwards, when I visited Australia, I heard similar stories about the Aborigines. In their schooldays they excelled as athletes and sportsmen. In adulthood they lost it. But that's a problem for psychologists and sociologists, not for geriatric theologians. Maybe travelling folk and aborigines are driven by a deep-seated belief that grown men shouldn't play.

Once we went to the Nicolson, the tackety-boots and the tinkers were behind us. I shouldn't put that so glibly. The travelling people (that's what we have to call them now, but the change of name has done little to improve their condition) were trapped by social classification, and the schooling did little to help them. It wasn't the fault of any individual teacher but of the system. Now, almost eighty years later, I find the thought of it well-nigh unendurable. We had progressed to the National Health Service and even to free school meals, but the classroom was no place for those at the bottom of the social pyramid. Instead, Scottish attitudes to travelling people differed little from the attitudes to gypsies which I saw in Hungary and Romania towards the end of last century.

One particular injustice I remember with special aversion. Travellers' children were late for school every morning, simply because they had no clocks. It was in no way the children's fault, yet they were belted for it (by the Headmaster) every day as if it were a capital felony.

Why? The only reason I can think of is that it was a legacy of the authorities' attitude to school attendance after the introduction of compulsory schooling following the Education Act of 1872. The Act was certainly not welcomed with enthusiasm in crofting communities, and for generations afterwards children were absent from school on every pretext

12

imaginable: especially cutting peats, lifting potatoes and herding cattle. In such a context, ensuring regular attendance became a daily personal challenge to the head teacher. The real culprits, of course, were the parents, but since he couldn't belt them he did the only thing he could: he belted the children.

The only other anti-absenteeism strategy I remember was the dispatching of the school janitor (on his bicycle) to ascertain the circumstances (or, more likely, to 'explain', in the children's hearing, the gravity of the situation: if they weren't in school tomorrow they would be sent to the Ragged School). In a few instances, the Master would get into his car and make the journey himself. That was really serious.

By the time such children left school they could barely write their names. Nor were they the only victims. Anyone with learning difficulties was simply stuck in the back row of the class and ignored (disruptive children were punished by the opposite procedure: placement in the front row, under the teacher's nose). Of children with serious learning difficulties there was scarcely a trace. In all my schooldays I never saw a Down's Syndrome child. Yet there must have been some. In later years I had a nephew, a niece and a cousin who suffered from this disorder, and delightful children (and, later, companions) they were. But until the Seventies of last century such children were simply hidden away, sometimes in institutions, but as often as not in the home itself. In the latter case, they would be known (at least to other adults) as So and So's 'Poor One' ('*am fear bochd aig ...*'). I suppose this was simply a literal Gaelic translation of the euphemistic description of illness as 'being poorly'.

It always puzzled me that as Scottish society became less and less Christian it also became more and more compassionate towards those with learning difficulties. I put it down to two things: first, greater understanding of the nature of these problems, particularly those due to genetic malfunction; and secondly, mounting evidence that, given the opportunity, people with Down's Syndrome, Spasticity and other highly visible limitations could actually make considerable progress in cognitive and communication skills and even greater progress in their ability to form deep, lasting and highly rewarding relationships.

But enough, or you'll be regretting you ever followed your mother's advice.

Yours sincerely
Donald Macleod

2. Upward mobility

13 November 2020

Dear Mme Quessaud

Thanks for being merely amused by my rambling so dramatically off the subject in my previous letter. Of course your mother never went to Laxdale school. I just got kind of carried away, perhaps because my memories of Laxdale are more vivid than my memories of the Nicolson. For both of us the transition to secondary school was traumatic, but it would have been particularly so for her, since it meant leaving home and staying in a hostel. There would be occasional weekends at home, but since her home was almost fifty miles away, they would have been very occasional indeed: probably only once in a term. I never heard her complain, and I suppose it contributed to that annoying kind of maturity she had while I was still only a child.

Quite apart from the sudden uprooting from parents, siblings and friends, the culture shock alone would have been considerable. For one thing, the whole of rural Lewis in those days was Gaelic speaking. It was the language of the playground as well as of the church and the home. Stornoway was quite different. There (and in the Nicolson) English had for generations been the local tongue. The day had passed when children would actually be belted for speaking it, but there was still strong social and peer pressure against it. Social climbers, if asked, would deny that they spoke it.

There were also subtle pressures within the education system itself. Your mother was on Class 1B, because she took Gaelic; I was on 1A, because I took Latin. This was another life-defining choice forced on us at the age of twelve. Goodness knows why I took Latin. It certainly wasn't because of any formal advice.

Parents didn't feel qualified to give you advice about school; and teachers thought their responsibility ended with teaching the lessons. I suspect I took Latin because some of the local worthies told me as we filled the peat lorry that it was very good for your English or that many words used by doctors and vets came from Latin. It may also have been on my mind that it would be very handy if I ever went to a country that spoke Latin: an experience which, unfortunately, I never had. In those days we had little sense of the intrinsic value of any subject. Everything had to be good for something.

In the event, I received unforgettable instruction. To this day, gerunds and gerundives, ablative absolutes and deponent verbs taking the ablative haunt my sleep. On the other hand, I was never introduced to the glories of Classical literature. It was as if Livy and Ovid, Virgil and Cicero, existed only to be parsed. I met the same attitude later in connection with the teaching of the biblical languages. Time and again I was told that you couldn't use a language unless you could parse it. I used to think, 'You should have heard my mother! She couldn't tell a verb from a preposition, or a phrase from a sentence. But she could certainly use language!' But I shall drop that subject (grammar, I mean) for the moment.

The most ridiculous feature of the arrangement was that it debarred generations of Lewis students from doing Honours in Celtic at University, Higher Latin being an essential prerequisite for such a course. Of course the universities were as much to blame as the school, but the effect was to deprive Celtic scholarship of the greatest single pool of talent available to it. By the time the mistake was discovered it was too late.

But language wasn't the only difference between your mother and myself. They might have been only fifty miles apart, but Stornoway and Uig were different worlds. In Uig, if you met someone on the road, you said 'Hello!' and stopped. In Stornoway, people walked past each other as if they weren't there. Sociologically, too, it was very different (although we'd never heard of sociology then). Even in suburban Laxdale my classmates were all the children of weavers, dockers, bus drivers, joiners, bricklayers and labourers (mothers didn't 'work' in those days). Even after eighty years their faces still remain with me: Bobby, Chingie, Peavey, Jackie, Fagan, Bondo, Davie Murdo, Murdo Kai, Murtie, Jean Ann, Dolly Mary, Cathie, Cathie Bheag, Stella ... It's odd, isn't it: for seven years they fill almost every waking hour of your life. Then, one day, it's the end of term, the summer holidays, and you never see them again. You stay in touch only through the grapevine.

None of them came from professional homes. Their fathers were all men who in the camaraderie of communal crofting would speak scathingly of those who had never done a day's real work in their lives. They had 'minister's hands' - white, smooth and clean. No such disgrace marked *their* hands. They were rough, calloused and dirty, the grime of soil, mortar or oil permanently ingrained in the skin: hands of which men could be proud.

The only professional in the village was the Headmaster; and he, if he had been allowed, would have lived in the town. But once we went to the Nicolson we mixed with the great and the good. Such people lived in the great posh mansions of Goathill and Matheson Road. You used to pass them on your way to football matches or if you had to visit someone in hospital (beside the football park). Occasionally, you might walk up there or go for a spin on your bike, just to see them, and you might feel a special bond with those your father had helped to build. They had gardens, even lawns, and occasionally, if you were lucky, you might see someone using a lawnmower. They had bulbs and roses, cars and garages. One or two had greenhouses. Rumour had it they even had pianos. One, according to legend, had countless souvenirs and mementoes from all over the world. Another had a boomerang. They played golf and bowls and bridge. They fished for salmon and even ate it. They would be doctors or mill managers or shopowners or car-hire operators.

They could be councillors or even the Provost. They would walk about the town with huge elegant dogs on leads. If anyone (especially a middle-aged woman) suddenly came out of such a house, you wouldn't know what to do or say. You would either freeze or run.

And now, suddenly, their sons and daughters were on your class. There was Margaret Maclean, for example, who was a genius, scoring a hundred per cent in every exam. Her father was headmaster of one of the biggest island schools and very high up in the Comunn Gàidhealach and the Lewis Football Association. For years she would have to soak up the pain doled out by our inverted snobbery. Beside her was Jean Harthill. Her very name was enough. Her father managed one of the local mills and she would turn out to be the real brain in the class. We, country Free Church folk, assumed as a matter of course that none of these townies went to church. In fact, Jean's family were Exclusive Brethren: an affiliation for which she paid a high price. They decreed that she couldn't become a graduate since that would place her on a list with unbelievers. This left Jean with no option but to give up her course at Glasgow's Royal Institute of Science and Technology at the end of her first year. I'm not going to call it a waste. There's more to life than graduation or even academic brilliance, and Jean survived without bitterness. But it was a cruel price to pay for being part of a group duped by control-freaks.

Among the boys, sitting right beside me, was Willie MacTaggart. His father was manager of the local cinema, the Stornoway Playhouse. I didn't tell him that I wasn't allowed to go to the pictures; or that it was a dreadful thing that they had had the cinema painted on the Sabbath; or that my minister had had a dream that it would go on fire and everyone inside would be burned to death except one little boy. We became friends. What else could you do, sitting beside a guy seven hours a day, five days a week? But my old pals from Laxdale took a dim view of it. Already, I was a traitor, showing clear signs of snobbery and a distinct taste for upward mobility. They were probably right, and I reacted by becoming a recluse.

Willie owed some of his importance to his father's friendship with the school Rector; and I suspect that this friendship itself owed something to the latter's attitude towards the church. The Free Church clergy disapproved of the cinema; the Rector, therefore, would be all for it. But that wasn't the whole reason. The school had no Assembly Hall, or indeed a hall of any kind. It had a couple of impressive Victorian buildings, but for the rest it had to use an assortment of scattered pre-fabs and temporary huts, and Mr MacTaggart was most obliging in making his very comfortable and commodious cinema available for school functions.

William (as the teachers called him) was a distinguished member of the Nicolson team which won the BBC's *Top of the Form* competition in 1953/54. Even Kaney, our Maths teacher, was impressed. When he came into the class the day after the Final, he walked straight up to Willie and congratulated him most warmly. We had never seen the like: a teacher shaking hands with a pupil! Willie was suitably embarrassed, but the incident made it very difficult for Kaney ever to find fault with him afterwards. Willie solved the problem by leaving the island early in his second year. I never knew whether winning *Top of the Form* was the greatest moment in his life or merely a prelude to greatness.

At playtime (called 'intervals', now that you had moved up to the Nicolson) you might see (perhaps only in the distance) pupils even more distinguished than Willie. You might, for example, see Ronnie Uggie, who owed both his name and his nickname to his father, Mr Alex Urquhart, the Deputy Rector and the real driving force behind the school. Ronnie was the school dux and captain of the *Top of the Form* team. Then there was Alasdair Maclean, who was not only the most brilliant boy who ever lived (according to my friend, Donnie Murray, who lived out the road and had actually been to his house) but also played the piano, bowled spinners and held high office as a

Patrol Leader in the Scouts. You could see Murdo Alick, later to be Free Church minister of Stornoway, but at that time more famous as the mischievous son of the Minister of Back and star inside-right of the School football team. You might even get a glimpse of Bill Cameron, a science teacher who had played for Scotland's amateur football team and now graced the School forward line with an economy of effort and movement of which Andy Ritchie and John White would have been proud. No one had ever told him that running was part of the game.

I have no idea what your mother was thinking as she lined up for school that first day in August 1953: boys and girls were lined up separately. Teachers of that era were like army NCOs, firmly believing that it was either them or you, and thoroughly convinced that the only way to survive was to put the fear of death into the little b...s. To adapt an old management distinction, it was very efficient and hopelessly ineffective. The teachers had no problems and we (in some departments) had no education. I never learned anything from anyone I feared. I simply opted out. It had nothing to do with classroom regimentation and that kind of thing (four rows of twelve, facing the teacher and the blackboard). That could be effective enough. The problem was the thugs and psychopaths who held the chalk. After the educational revolution of the 1960s, I often heard people lament the passing of 'the good old days'. They were good only for teachers. The problem later was that society never accepted that the new methods required far higher staffing levels than the old, and by the 1990s we had moved from a situation where life was a misery for pupils to one where it was a misery for teachers.

To your mother and me, that fateful day in 1953, some of the teachers were already legends and these legends cast terrifying shadows. That first morning we kept a wary look-out for them. There was one particular Maths teacher, Harley (that name will do for now), who, according to playground mythology, was on his last warning. In one memorable fit of rage he had thrown the blackboard compasses at a girl in his class. I doubt it (it was probably only the blackboard duster), but all the lies about that man were true. I never saw him throw the compasses, but I saw him give many a shaking, I saw him call one poor, rather dumpy girl 'a cow', and I saw him once storm out of the class knowing he had lost control, but having just enough sense to realise that in that mood he was a menace to himself and others. Fortunately, I had but little of him - just enough to lose all respect for him and his subject.

We had another Maths teacher who, without being a danger to children, certainly regarded raging, shouting and bawling as the first rules of pedagogy. He erupted the moment he received the answer to his first question and stayed erupted to the very end of the class. It was quite a feat, and very bad, I am sure, for his health. He never threw anything but he had one most delicious habit. Instead of using the standard issue duster to clean the blackboard, he licked his hands and smeared the writing off the board as best he could.

He was a Free Presbyterian and, as it happened, one of the sons of the Free Presbyterian manse was on my class. He came from a family of able, affable, athletic and well-rounded boys, all of whom later achieved distinction, but this particular one had a slight problem with punctuality. The situation wasn't helped by the fact that the manse was just beside the school. This particular year, the Maths class was at 1.15, immediately after the long lunch. Every day the class began with the words 'We'll wait for James Tallach!' And almost every day he was greeted with the words 'The late James Tallach!'

On the other hand, there was another occasion when we had Maths in the morning and we Laxdale boys happened to be delayed by well-nigh impossible road conditions. We reached school twenty minutes late and meekly explained that the bus was late. 'Very convenient!' he said, every syllable separately emphasised. Which, of course, it was.

There is no doubt that these teachers had two personalities: or at least one plus a mask. I met the said teacher once or twice outwith the class and he was as nice as pie. On one occasion he even gave me five shillings for singing to another of his classes. Even if I had been Caruso (which I wasn't), that would have been an extravagance. In my world pennies, let alone shillings, were scarce; my normal daily budget was one penny for either an ice lolly (made and marketed by an old Free Church deacon called 'The Cando'), a penny-toffee or a gobstopper. Five shillings amounted to sixty pennies: a year's revenue in one day.

The curious thing is, I haven't the slightest recollection what I did with it. I certainly couldn't have spent it without advice. Years later I came to link my windfall with the story of a little girl from a slightly earlier Lewis generation. One day, probably during the Great War, left alone in the house by her mother, she found half a crown (twelve and a half pence), sufficient in those days to buy ten loaves. What could you buy with such a fortune? It had to be something edible and sweet. She knew nothing of toffees, lemonade, chocolates, lollipops, crisps or gateaux. She knew only one form of treat - gingerbread - and even that she knew only in Gaelic. Clutching the coin in her hand, she ran to the shop and brightly asked the shopkeeper for 'half-a-crown's worth of aran-cridhe', enough gingerbread to sink a fleet. He laughed, gave her a couple of pieces, kept the coin and eventually returned it to her mother. In those days half a crown was as rare as meat in Kruschev's Russia.

Another teacher later became a Free Presbyterian minister. I never had him, but he did leave one outstanding memory. Remember I told you we had no Assembly Hall? Well, we acquired one with the new building (long since demolished) on Springfield Road in 1956, and for the remainder of my time in school every day began with Morning Assembly. I'm not sure whether this was always taken by the Rector, but it certainly was on important occasions. On one Founders' Day (27 February) we had a specially invited guest, Mr Roderick Smith, a well known local pharmacist and an ex-Provost of the town (and grandfather, as it happened, of the last Provost, Sandy

Matheson). To the best of my recollection, Mr Smith wasn't asked to speak: he was there to listen to good things being said about himself. Unfortunately, the Rector, Mr C J S Addison, decided to address Mr Smith from Ecclesiasticus: 'Let us now praise famous men!' (Ecc. 44.1). This public endorsement of the Apocrypha was too much for Edward. He rose, erect and immaculate in his dark suit, and strode up the length of the aisle in a quite magnificent walk-out, the heels of his spotless Oxford shoes clicking in flawless and ominous rhythm on the parquetry of the Hall floor. There was a deadly, petrified silence. The aftermath, whatever it was, exploded in private.

But it would be invidious to suggest that all the teachers of the day were bawlers and belters. We tend to remember only the eccentrics, the misfits and the bullies. The decent, normal ones weren't legends then, and they aren't particularly memorable now. In retrospect you realise that those who were least qualified academically were often the best teachers, presumably because they had more sympathy with the pains of the learning process. Unfortunately, these were the very teachers who remained unpromoted, and one or two of the heads of department were truly awful. But we learned invaluable lessons nonetheless, although it's odd what stays with you: things like the sage observation of our history teacher that no one could curse like a bishop. We also had the benefit in my last year of an English teacher who had come straight from the class of Professor Peter Alexander at Glasgow University and who disabused us of the fatal flaw theory of Shakespearean tragedy. According to this theory (expressed definitively in A.C. Bradley's *Shakespearean Tragedy*), the reason that Hamlet failed to avenge his father was that he suffered from the fatal flaw of indecisiveness. Mr Scott (I'm sure that was his name) had little patience with it, pointing out the devastatingly simple truth that hesitation to kill is a strength, not a flaw. This is not the place to explore where the germ of tragedy does actually lie, but it is hard to believe that the core truth about Hamlet, Macbeth, Othello, Coriolanus or even

Lear is that they were fatally flawed. There is no single key to tragedy, factual or fictitious. Shakespeare's heroes are victims of a potent mixture of ambition, manipulation, circumstance, virtue, self-doubt and (particularly in the case of Coriolanus) a stubborn refusal to play by society's rules.

I've no doubt that many teachers, particularly in English and history, influenced us deeply, without our being able to trace that influence in any detailed way. The one I remember best is the Latin teacher, Mr William Macleod. He died, a comparatively young man, almost sixty years ago, yet I can see him still: tallish, with greying and thinning hair, a slight stoop, an expressive hunch of the shoulders and a smile which could suddenly appear from nowhere. When about to express disapproval, he took a very deep and very audible breath and let the rebuke out very slowly, and even more regretfully. The mannerism was easily mimicked, but he gave us enough knowledge of Latin grammar to last us several lifetimes.

He's often fascinated me since, not least because he was the most effective disciplinarian in the school and yet never resorted to the belt. There was something in his presence and in his bearing which for some inexplicable reason brooked no defiance. I've never been able to understand it. It would be tempting to put it down to his Christianity, but there were one or two other men in the school who were also Christians and they had nothing like the same effect. Yet Christian he certainly was.

You may think such language odd, particularly if you've heard from others that in these days the influence of the church was all-pervasive. I don't agree at all. In Laxdale school, not one member of staff would have claimed to be what in the 1990s used to be called a born again Christian. In the Nicolson, with a much larger staff, Willie Macleod was the only one who was a Free Church elder; and so far as I can recall, there was only one other male teacher who was a Free Church communicant. But the demography of Lewis religion is for some other time, perhaps.

I'd better stop. I know that all you young things find it easy to 'write', simply speaking your profundities into voice-recognising computers. But I still have to type it all out laboriously on an old-fashioned keyboard. It's painful for the keyboard too. I first typed on a machine made in Stalin's Russia and it required a right old thumping. The habit has stayed with me and now my wrists's turning blue and the keyboard's a wreck. Sorry for being such an old crock.

Yours from the Dark Ages
Donald Macleod

16 March 2021

Dear Mme Quessaud

I thought my last letter might have convinced you that, despite your mother's recommendation, I wasn't your man. It's kind of unnerving too, writing to someone you've never met about things that are curiously intimate. But I'll do my best to answer your questions, although I'll probably have to compose the letter by instalments. There's no truth, sadly, in the observation that men improve with age. Nowadays I can sit at the computer only for limited periods. I hope the breaks won't be too obvious.

Unfortunately, I have no personal memories of life in the hostel and your mother never said much about it. Even the goings on in the Boys' Hostel were a closed book to the rest of us. We knew that there were some dreadful initiation rites when boys were given nicknames to the accompaniment of cold duckings (or worse); occasional stories of boys being drunk; and other equally occasional stories of teachers being drunk. Above all, we heard constant complaints about compulsory church attendance on Sundays. It didn't take Free Church and Free Presbyterian boys long to figure out that the shortest services (and by far the shortest sermons) were in St Peter's (the Episcopal Church, known as 'Meaden's' after a Canon of that name who gained immortality as founder of the local sea Scouts) or Martin's Memorial (where the minister was an eccentric, anglified dignitary by the name of Dr de Lingen, who caused a more than minor sensation by joining the Roman Catholic Church immediately after he retired). The standard requirement in the Boys' Hostel was that they attend church once a Sunday, but at one time a particularly zealous regime insisted on twice a day. Rumour had it that this caused something not far short of a riot, but the facts never entered our domain. Lewis had not then attained the saturation levels of media coverage it came to enjoy towards the end of last century, when it had more reporters, journalists, broadcasters and independent television companies than any comparable community on earth. In the fifties the only news gathering agency was the *Stornoway Gazette,* and its interests didn't extend beyond trials in the Sheriff Court. A riot in a school hostel was not the sort of thing any decent newspaper would talk about. All we knew then was that several toings and froings were taking place among the staff.

From a practical point of view what we were most aware of was that 'the hostel boys' and 'the hostel girls' had a distinct, close-knit identity. At that time, the usual teenage activity in Stornoway of an evening was to walk up and down Cromwell Street (the main street) either as part of a group or to find a group. Occasionally you stopped in a shop doorway, and ideally a group of boys would be joined by a group of girls. At least, I think that's how the system worked: I could never find a pack. Hostel boys always went about in packs, often ranging widely in age. Whether or not they had leaders I never knew. The packs were impenetrable, but the thing became a nuisance only when the hostel monopolised such things as the football teams. But that was never much of a personal threat. I was too small to play football (except in my dreams).

Sorry for rambling on. Your mother would have something to say if she heard that you asked for information about her background and were fobbed off with a dissertation on the Boys' Hostel. But she knew the routine well. She covered every inch of Cromwell Street every night.

I'm probably equally useless when it comes to shedding light on the kind of education your mother would have had in earlier years. I never heard her mention her local school; and although it may seem strange to you, I have never actually set foot in the village where she was born. Nor did I ever meet her parents. As far as I know, she went to a one-teacher school; her teacher was one of her aunts and there were about 15 pupils altogether. That school would have been her world for seven years, and her experience wouldn't have been much different from my own, although my school was much larger (about 200 pupils).

I can still remember the first day I saw it. It was about a mile from our house downhill on the way there, but seriously uphill on the way back. To me at the age of five that was as far away as Mars, but somehow my little legs had once made their way in there in the company of Callie Sos.

Seventy years have passed since I last saw Callie Sos. He owed his name, I think, to the fact that somewhere in his ancestry there had been a butcher who gloried in the name Sausage King. You'd need to be very careful in trying to work out how on earth a man could come to have such a name. It could have been a compliment: the man was famous either for the quality of his sausages or for inventing them (or at least being the first man to bring them to Lewis; it amounted to the same thing). On the other hand (and I think this is more likely), it may have been an insult. I suspect the gentleman had made claims a little above his station and was quickly reminded that all he was fit for was making sausages.

Anyway, Callie Sos's links with Sausage King were pretty remote as far as we were concerned. He was a hero: grown-up, and the closest I knew to the cowboys other boys could see at the pictures. He could ride a bike with his two hands above his head or with his feet on the handlebar. He could speak to old men as if he were old himself. And he was the best whistler in the world, able to make up the most fantastic tunes as he went along, and able to do so when he was breathing in as well as when he was breathing out. Rumour had it he could even drive.

I'd never really met Callie before, except that one day shortly after we went to live in Laxdale he came to our house to ask my father if he could have one of his caps (a Naval Petty Officer's cap). Whether he was given one or not I don't know. But one thing I do know (at least, I know it now, though I didn't know it then): Callie had not enjoyed school, and the day he showed it to me he made it very clear that I was not going to enjoy it either. The building itself, as it stood that day in 1945, was different from any other building in the world (remember at this time I had never so much as heard the word 'village'. I knew only of the world). To my wee eyes, enlightened by Callie Sos, it was huge, with two rows of grim windows and a long forbidding perimeter wall. And it was white. I don't know why this made such an impression on me but it did. It was, I suppose now, only some kind of lime-wash, but for me it seemed to be part of the definition of a school; so much so that when on holiday in Cross (my father's native village) a couple of years afterwards, I caused complete bewilderment in a group of little men gathered at the gable-end of a similarly whitewashed house by announcing, in tones of great solemnity, 'This house is as white as a school!'

But Callie Sos wasn't interested in its colour. What mattered to him, as he towered above me seven feet taller and a lifetime wiser, was that inside the school there was a creature called 'The Master' and a group of lesser monsters known as 'teachers'. Their job was to belt, and according to Callie Sos they were very good at it and they loved it.

No Muscovite boy ever surveyed the Lubianka, or Parisian the Bastille, with greater foreboding than filled my little heart that day. When the dreaded moment came and I had to be enrolled myself, it confirmed all my worst fears. My mother was told not to bother waiting. 'His kind will be all right,' said the Master. For some reason I hadn't enrolled with the others. Perhaps I was ill. As a result I had the privilege all to myself. It's difficult to be sure now whether what I have are genuine memories or mere impressions, but certainly what lives with me is this: that when I was taken to the Master's room he was already busy at his work dealing with boys who had been absent the previous day. Each was asked for his excuse and each replied, 'Please, sir, I had no boots.' The Master was totally unimpressed, not because he thought they were lying (some at least, weren't) but because, as he told them, he himself had gone to school without boots many a day. There, before my very eyes, he belted them. I now realise that the action was part of a long (and misguided) personal campaign against skulking and truancy. For me it was a decisive, unforgettable statement as to what school was all about. For the next twelve years (I went late and left early) it would be my life. The initial impression never wore off. In retrospect, I suppose I spent a good deal of my childhood working out legal ways of being absent.

The first three years were horrendous. The best way to describe them is to imagine three middle-aged women who start work at 9.30 in the morning and regard it as an indispensable element in their professional skill to be convulsed in paroxysms of rage by 9.45. I don't know which College had taught them that, but they had been apt pupils. Maybe it went back to the days when only the frustrated (particularly frustrated ministers, unable to find congregations) became teachers. Every day things began normally enough. They took the register quietly. They collected the lunch-money ('our canteen', as we called it) quietly. They had us say prayers quietly. Then they turned to reading or counting or singing (it varied from day to day). That's when reality was abandoned. The routine was simple. A question would be asked; hands up with the answer. First answer, OK! Second answer, OK! But the moment there came the first non-OK answer, all hell broke loose. It was as if their anger instantly developed critical mass and exploded in moral nuclear fission, sucking us into a mushroom cloud of wrath and keeping us in it for the rest of the day. It wasn't merely a case of individual teachers and their quirks. It was a system.

It's a curious thing, looking back. In some respects it's like yesterday. A child has no past, only a future. He's full of hopes, dreams and ambitions. We never seem to lose that. In my own case, anyway, I seem to have spent most of my life in a kind of ante-room preparing for life, as if everything were a mere training and what we were training for never arrived. Age modifies it but never entirely eliminates it. We simply can't help assuming a future and the need to prepare for it.

Yet at the same time these early schooldays are light years away: another world geographically, socially and culturally. I carry it with me every day, and yet I can never reach it. In darker moments I get angry with time. It's much more uncompromising than space. We can always go back (or forward) to other places. But time is rigid and unyielding. We can never revisit it; we can never put down roots in it; and we can never get it to wait or to hurry up.

You must remember that these days of our early schooling were in 1946. The Second World War had ended just the previous year but its effects were everywhere, not least in the scarcity of resources. I was never entirely sure whether it was economic stringency that left us using slates rather than paper exercise-books in our first two years, but whatever the reason, that's the way it was. These slates were roughly 12" x 8", with wooden frames, and you wrote (or scratched) on them with what we called slate-pencils, which left a kind of chalk-coloured impression behind. The advantage, of course, was that you could re-use them ad infinitum, or at least until they broke (not that they were always thrown away even when they broke; we often used broken ones). You simply wiped them clean, and to do that you used a damp cloth.

It's a trivial detail hardly worth mentioning. The only reason I do mention it is that these cloths became a formidable weapon in the Infant Teacher's armoury. One of the first things she checked every morning was whether you had your 'cloot'. If you didn't, the eruption occurred there and then. If you did, the cloot was deposited with the rest in a bucket containing disinfected water. In moments of mega-explosion it became a missile, snatched from the bucket in an instant and hurled at the face of the little monster who was threatening your peace and security. In moments of mega-mega explosions, it would be the blackboard ruler, 3 feet long and 3 inches wide, across the knuckles. When control was completely lost, the pupil was grasped by any available attachment and shaken till nearly choked. I remember one girl caught by the neck of her newly knitted jumper and shaken so violently that when she went home her neck was a mass of weals. Her father was furious, but not with the teacher - with the mother. He didn't bother removing the jumper slowly. He simply cut it furiously with the scissors and gave his wife a piece of his mind for making the child wear something so dangerous. It would never have occurred to either of them to make a complaint. Parents were as much in awe of their children's teachers as they had been of their own.

I realise now that there was nothing personal in it. The rantings, ravings and furies were a professional strategy. After I left the infant class I often met the teacher concerned in the playground and elsewhere. She was positively charming; treated you like a grown-up and even took you into her confidence. Curious things stick in your mind. In those days it wasn't unusual for altercations between two boys to develop suddenly into something more formal. Other boys would quickly form a ring, the two quarrellers would square up to each other and fists would fly until one or the other had a bloody nose. On one such occasion Morag, the demon infant teacher, came on the scene. "Is this a scrap, boys!" she said, and sauntered on.

But while she had you in her class she conducted a reign of terror. The violence also had its by-products. She would question you closely on the happenings in your home. Was your mother making jam (almost every house had rhubarb and many had soft fruit and, of course, sugar was rationed), and could she have some? Within days you'd be carrying a jar or jars to school. One day she decided that the hair of every boy on the class was too long and announced that she was going to cut our 'dossans' (from the Gaelic word for our forelocks). We were duly lined up and subjected to a few quick clips. Not a word of protest from our parents. They were probably mortified that the teacher had had to do it. Ministers and even doctors could be criticised freely and openly. But not teachers. The fear bred in classrooms stayed with my parents for the rest of their lives.

It's little wonder that on Monday morning (or even Sunday night) the week spread before you interminably. Friday afternoons as you walked home were bliss: no school tomorrow. The summer holidays were paradise. We knew their duration precisely: seven weeks and one day.

Many children, I'm sure, never recovered. Even when you knew the right answer you choked with panic. The successful were either favourites or children with quick reflexes. Indeed, for the rest of my life I found it hard to stop and think before answering a question. Speed was of the essence. I hid as invisible as possible somewhere near the bottom of the heap. The best I could hope for was that I might emerge after ten years able to whistle like Cally Sos and perhaps get a job as a petrol boy.

But enough. So many pages I may not get them into the envelope.

Good wishes
Donald Macleod.

14 June 2029

Dear Mme Quessaud

Your very welcome letter reminded me of a reply I once received from an elderly hypochondriac when I asked him, 'How are you?' 'Do you really want to know?' he replied, with the air of a man long resigned to the fact that few people were as interested in his health as he was. But you did ask whether I learned anything during these early years in school, and I shall flatter myself that you really do want to know.

After three years I could write my name, tell the time on the clock, read out loud at a furious rate (in these reading lessons everything was sacrificed to speed, with disastrous consequences for the rest of my career) and probably do the multiplication tables. We had to write these out daily on our slates and I remember having something of a disagreement once with the teacher as to whether my tables were 'straight'. All the " = " signs had to be in an absolutely perpendicular column. I was sure they were OK. She wasn't, but that day, for some obscure reason, there was no explosion. She was probably right. Eighty years on I still have difficulty writing addresses in straight lines on an envelope. They seem to insist on veering upwards. But a couple of years passed before another teacher told me that my handwriting was as if a spider had been dipped in ink and forced to walk across the page leaving a trail. She was even more right than the first one, and that particular spider has had a long life.

I should add that by the end of Primary 3 I had also learned to put a comma before 'but', but not before 'and'. Very useful rules, I'm sure, but unfortunately there are different kinds of 'buts' and different kinds of 'and', and such rules could be something of a nuisance. We also spent a day learning to use the ending '-ing' to combine our sentences. I think this was fun, although it almost hurts to admit it was probably because it was simple. You started off with two sentences; for example, 'John walked down the road. He carried a pail of water'. Then you joined them into one. 'John walked down the road, carrying a pail of water'. That was probably the first time I actually managed to do something in school. It was also, I suspect, the beginning of a lifelong fascination with words. Why were they sometimes similar and sometimes different? How many ways were there of saying this? And why was it one way in Gaelic and another in English? Not much use, but enough sometimes to keep you awake at nights.

There was something else which never occurred to us at the time but should have been blatantly obvious to all concerned. All the books we used came from a culture totally alien to our own. The heroes were Pat and Tom. We didn't know anyone called Pat and Tom. We knew only Dolly Mary and Angus. Besides, when Pat and Tom walked to school, they passed traffic lights. When they went on holiday they went by train. When they went to the garden they played under apple trees. In the autumn they played conkers. We knew none of these things.

On the other hand, the things we did know were never mentioned. Pat and Tom never went to the fank or to the loom shed or to the peats; and they never seemed to wear bobbin jumpers and tackety boots. The real world (the world which had won the War, presumably) was the world of London and the Home Counties. Our world wasn't in it.

This tension spilled over into all kinds of things. In Primary 3 we were introduced to history, not only a new word but a new world. We even met a king who had some affinity with ourselves, Malcolm Canmore. 'Malcolm with the big head,' explained the teacher. It didn't need a book or a teacher to tell us that. We all knew that *ceann mòr* meant a big head. But just imagine that! A king who spoke Gaelic! But then we were introduced to St Margaret, Malcolm's wife. She, we were told, had come from

England to Scotland, a very backward country where she found it hard to teach her husband English and good manners. In those days, the book assured us, houses were very different from ours. How? Well, for example, they didn't have paintings on the walls. Neither did ours. The closest we had was Mummy and Daddy's wedding photo and another of Mummy and Daddy with the little one (*an tè bheag*, our dead sister). Paintings were part of wonderland, like having a mother who was a teacher or a father who owned a sweet shop. But if every ordinary decent house had paintings on the wall, we were clearly very odd. Fortunately, we were all in it together. All of us were odd.

As you moved up the classes in primary school, things improved. I suppose the thinking was something like the military. You broke the spirit of the recruits in the initial stages and then you started treating them reasonably. Things never reached the stage where you actually wanted to go to school, but we reached a plateau where we didn't dread it. Even so, you could still encounter monsters like Long Division. He lurked in Primary 4. In those days it would never occur to you to ask your teacher to explain something. That would have meant admitting there was something you didn't know: a high-risk strategy. You either picked it up the day she did it on the blackboard or you didn't pick it up at all. If you were absent that particular day, then, of course, you'd had it. But eventually, somehow, the monster was tamed and I learned to divide 36,789 by 174 (paying special attention to the Remainder). We even learned to divide by Long Division sums of money in pre-decimal sterling. Could you do £27,934 10s 3d (maybe with a farthing thrown in for good measure) divided by 139? We then proceeded to fractions, vulgar and decimal.

We also did what were called Intelligence Tests. Two of these, one at the end of Primary 6 and one at the end of Primary 7, were official in the sense that they were part of the Qualifying Examination. How people could ever have expected to measure intelligence, whatever that is, I don't know. They assumed, I think, that they could test not only performance but potential, a forlorn hope surely. In any case, the whole thing was rendered doubly useless by the fact that you could practise these things, so as to improve your performance. We were tutored in them every morning, becoming short-term experts in the techniques appropriate to codes, odd-man outs and assorted verbal and numerical puzzles. I have no idea even yet whether such things proved anything about your powers of verbal reasoning, but I've known many a Classical scholar who could never have been trained to change a tap-washer and many a plumber who has had to laugh at the stupidity of a surgeon. Intelligence is job-specific.

One incident from my last year in primary school still lives with me. Forgive me if I come at it indirectly. Whatever the defects of early years' education in these days, the later years of primary had one great merit - they stressed the importance of written English. We had to extend our vocabulary by noting unusual words; we were drilled in the meaning of words of ever increasing difficulty and obscurity; we were taught to identify opposites and synonyms and we were encouraged to look out for interesting phrases and store them up for future use. Above all, we had to write essays ('compositions' we called them), sometimes two or three a week. These were usually on fairly hackneyed topics: describe a scene; recount a dream; write a sketch of someone you know; relate an adventure. If we had a choice, we never described scenes: these were far and away the most difficult compositions (it never occurred to us to go and look at a real scene and then try describing it. We thought you had to imagine one). We always chose adventures. I suspect, now, that that was because they gave greater scope for plagiarism. In those days the whole educational system not only frowned on 'comics' but thought that all comics consisted of cartoon-strips like the *Beano* and the *Dandy*. The teachers never caught up with the fact that we very quickly graduated from these childish things to the very much more substantial, un-illustrated boys' papers. There were four of these every week: the *Wizard* and the *Adventure* on Tuesdays, the *Hotspur* and the *Rover* on Fridays. My father brought them home faithfully every week (along with goodies on Fridays) and we devoured them. The layout was Spartan: almost identical in fact, to the *Monthly Record* (the official magazine of the Free Church of Scotland) when I edited it between 1977 and 1991 - unrelieved double columns of print. Every week each episode ended in suspense: Will Tom escape? See what happens next week. There were school stories, like 'Smith of the Lower Third'; westerns such as 'J K Slade'; football stories ('The Cannonball Kid'); athletics ('The Tough of the Track', who beat the world's finest on a diet of fish and chips); and above all, war stories, most notably 'I Flew with Braddock'. These last were excellent source material for writing adventure compositions. I became an expert at getting Lancaster bombers home from Berlin without wings or engines, tail or fuselage: so much so that one perceptive teacher in my first year in the Nicolson marked one of my efforts 'Excellent although incredible!' I couldn't understand then, and I can't understand still, how something could be excellent and incredible at one and the same time. But it wasn't ours to wonder why. Nor did it occur to me to work out precisely the minimum number of bits a Lancaster would need to stay in the sky. Some wing was obviously essential.

In the late 1940s another genre began to appear in these comics - science fiction. Oddly enough, I can't remember the titles or the heroes of any of these, probably because no one series ever really established itself before that whole world was overtaken by a new generation of illustrated papers such as the *Tiger* (these had serial cartoons with text underneath). But they gave us new materials for our compositions. Unfortunately, our teachers had cut themselves off in principle from this new realm of the imagination, and one day mine was most put out by something I'd referred to - a space-ship. She asked me where I'd found this word. What could I say? I thought the whole world knew this word, and if they didn't I really couldn't tell her she should read the comics (which is what my son, John, would have told her twenty-five years later). She contacted the Assistant Head (a male, of course, and a graduate), but he obviously didn't read the comics either. She probably concluded that I'd invented the whole thing myself; and she may even, for all I know, have taken the further step of concluding that I was a genius.

Her name was Catherine Macleod. She was a brilliant teacher even though she knew nothing about space-ships. She threw no tantrums, used no violence and yet maintained perfect discipline. She caught me day-dreaming once in the Geography class and asked me a question, to which I replied, sleepily, 'Geography!' Another time in a similar situation I answered, 'Orange!' I don't know why I remember and I don't know why I got off with it. She probably thought my embarrassment was punishment enough. But in my waking moments she enthused about words in all their subtleties and combinations, poured out from memory the great poems, stories and parables of the world and strode the floor in ecstasy teaching us the mysteries of General Analysis: clauses beginning with 'if', clauses beginning with 'although', clauses beginning with 'that' (there are two kinds of those).

I would like her to be immortal.

Good wishes
Donald M.

19 September 2021

Dear Mme Quessaud

Please forgive my delay in replying to your last letter. The community here has been shrouded in gloom these last two weeks, and even at my age, having seen so much of death, it still gets to me. This time, as so often before, it was a fishing tragedy. The weather here the last month has been atrocious, but the fishermen are in such dire straits that they venture out notwithstanding. To make matters worse, the boats are getting smaller. Men can no longer afford the trawlers that were in vogue thirty years ago. All we have is prawn-boats and crab-boats, and these little things are venturing further and further out, often against all reason. The inshore waters, they say, were scraped and sucked clean years ago.

The vessel that foundered a fortnight ago was one of these small crab-boats, with a crew of three, two men and a woman, all of them in their early twenties. The mother of one of them (the owner and skipper) had been watching them through binoculars earlier that day as they lifted the creels in worsening conditions. She had lost sight of them as they set off along the east coast to land their catch at Stornoway. When conditions made that impossible, they decided to seek shelter in Broad Bay, but the boat must have caught a heavy sea beam-on and capsized. One man was cast ashore but the other man and the woman (his wife) were lost. Her body turned up a few days ago on the other side of the bay. His has not yet been found although the search is renewed every day, urged on by the frantic father.

Forgive me rambling on like this. The sea is in my blood, but only as a fascination: I am a hopeless sailor. I love looking at it, I love fishing it, I love sailing it and I love reading about it, but it doesn't like me and I could have been a seaman only vicariously.

Anyway, for one reason or another I've never known what it is to steer a small lobster boat far beyond sight of land or to bait hooks with frozen fingers or haul in creels when soaked to the skin. I've never known the sea in inky darkness, tossing a tiny boat from crest to trough like a dog playing with a ball. I've never found myself utterly at its mercy, powerless and rudderless and totally at a loss as to where I was or where I was heading. And I suppose, in a way, I feel guilty about it. I liked to pretend, once, that I would have loved to do it; and even that I could have done it. A hundred years ago, of course, I would have had no option. It would have been the only way to earn any kind of livelihood. My grandfather, a great giant of a man with steel-blue eyes, enormous hands and the stamina of an ox, was a fisherman all his days. He asked me once in Gaelic, "Do you get seasick? ('M bi 'm muir a' cur ort?). "Yes!" I said. "Oh, well!" he replied, "That was in our people." He was sick every day he ever spent at sea. That didn't always make me feel better.

The funeral of the man whose body was found took place here last Friday and Stornoway Crematorium was full. There was no religious service, of course, but the Chairman of the local Fishermen's Co-operative read a tribute, a local bard recited an elegy, there was some strident piped music and a Celtic shirt draped the coffin (Celtic is one of Scotland's cult football teams, closely identified with Roman Catholicism. John was a Protestant and ought to have supported Rangers, but like many other Lewis Protestants he was an ardent Celtic supporter. We could never see the connection between football and sectarian religion).

And that was that. Tonight the weather is as bad as ever and out there some other poor souls are fighting for their lives. Whatever the catch, most of the money will go to the auctioneers and the salesmen: only a pittance to the men who take the risks. Many of these boats are tragedies waiting to happen: old, poorly maintained and regularly pushed far beyond their limits. Even the larger ones are so unregulated that scarcely a day passes without an accident: snapping hawsers, electrocutions, men being dragged overboard by flailing lines and tangled nets, men maimed and mangled by unguarded machinery. Part of the problem is the code among the men themselves. They think it sissy to wear any kind of lifejacket. Unless they all wear it, none will wear it; and no one will wear it till one man gives the lead. So far that one man hasn't come forward.

Fishermen have always been given to pessimism and nostalgia. By the time of my childhood the halcyon days of the herring fishing were already over. Only the memories remained. My grandfather spoke often of the time when you could walk across Stornoway harbour from one side to the other, stepping from drifter to drifter. In the 1940s there was still a fair number of drifters, although by this time the seine-netters were taking over. These seine-netters never seemed to have the romance of the older boats. In those days memories were still alive of the last of the sailing drifters, the *Mùirneag* (named after a hill near the village of Back. It's only a few hundred feet high, but against the low-lying moors of Lewis it was a clear landmark to those out at sea and came to have the mythical status of a mountain). But the relic I remember best was the *Windfall*, the last of the steam drifters. We always thought she was far and away the best boat of the lot. Long, squat and made of steel, she stood out among the others as a symbol of speed, strength and space. We weren't to know that she was hopelessly unprofitable. Coal couldn't compete with diesel.

There's no use my pretending to know much about either fishing or the sea: at least, not from the inside. Laxdale was an inland village and none of us had any real experience of boats. When Charlie came from South Lochs to live next door to us, he was something of a phenomenon. He pined for the sea.

He could row. He had shot seals. To us, although we lived within sight of the sea, that world was as far away as Nelson's.

What we knew of the sea was Stornoway: not the wind and the waves but the landing, the repairing and the trading. For the first five years of my life I lived within the harbour area. There's no danger of the site ever becoming a shrine. The house we lived in has been demolished long since and the last time I visited the place I couldn't be quite sure whether I had lived on the nightclub or on the vacant gap-site. It was impossible to get my bearings. But it's not at all difficult to recall the atmosphere. I say 'atmosphere' advisedly because, even across the years, I can still smell it. At that time access to the wharves was unrestricted even for small boys, and the harbour was our daily playground: an adventure playground, I suppose. One of the highlights was the weekly landing of huge bales of wool for the local mills. These would be about ten feet long, I suppose, and five feet in diameter. When they were stacked high, you could climb up to the top and jump from bale to bale with perfect safety, or you could hide between them, or you could just touch them and feel the fragrance: a unique mixture of sheep, oil and jute.

The other unforgettable smell was from the timber. In small quantities you don't notice it, but stacked high on the quay week after week, it etched itself into your nostrils and stayed there for ever. Its destination and purpose baffled me as a child. Where could all that wood be going? But as the end of the War approached, so, too, did the end of the black- house and from that day to this Lewis has enjoyed a building boom. It would puzzle economists, I suppose. How could building be the main industry of a declining island community? It still puzzles me, but the two main builders' merchants were a central part of our childhood, as every visitor seemed to feel bound to discuss with my father the best place to buy this, that and the other. Was it at the locally-owned Bain and Morrison's? Or at *Stòr a' Bhùird* (a store run by the Board of Agriculture? As far as crofters were concerned, that was *the* Board: the one and only.

Such was the demand that there was a similar store in Ness at the north end of the island). But I can't imagine that the building habits of Lewis would be of much interest to a sophisticate in Quebec.

Wood in one form or another was always around, although I was never too skilled at it. It was probably just a case of a child imitating his father. We had a stool in our house, made by my father. It was a thing of considerable solidity and substance, but for some extraordinary reason (extraordinary, because my mother was a strict disciplinarian) I was allowed to use it as a test-bench for my woodworking ambitions. I drove nails and tacks into it day after day until at last there was scarcely a space to put them. I also sawed it, not with a saw (saws were too precious) but with a bread-knife which had a bright yellow handle and a serrated edge. Some of these cuts went very deep, but the stool soaked up the punishment with exemplary courage and survived till I was almost sixty. By that time, I suppose, the hardships it had suffered in its youth had caught up with it. It was probably a symbol of my destructive, not creative, skills. In different circumstances I would have been a demolition contractor.

So much hammering and hacking obviously carried some risks and there were inevitable mishaps. Ever since the age of four I've carried on my left thumb the scar of an accident with a tenon-saw. But the incident that lingers in my memory is the day I broke the Admiralty's circular saw. Cars, even more than wood, fascinated us. We dreamed of nothing but driving, and as a child I would sit for hours with a cushion on my knees supporting a round tray more or less the same diameter as the steering-wheel of a bus. I would then make all sounds appropriate to all the movements and gear-changes: move off in first, change into second and right up to high, slow down, double de-clutch and change into third, stop and say goodnight to the passengers who were disembarking or good morning to those who were coming aboard. If you were driving a lorry full of sand, you'd be labouring up a brae, changing down and down until at last you were struggling up the last few feet in bottom gear (in those days what worried you wasn't a vehicle's speed but its 'pull'). In later years after we moved to Laxdale, we could find steering-wheels and gear-boxes and dashboards in the local dump (the rubbish from Mitchell's garage: every time we saw a lorry heading for the dump off we went in pursuit), and I managed to set up a simulator in the cellar below the house. The cellar also had a swing suspended from the floor joists and altogether it was a godsend in the rain that bedevilled our Lewis climate.

But in my early years in Stornoway such treasures as a real steering-wheel were in the distant future. All I had was the tray - until the day I found the circular saw.

My father, like most men of his generation, was always reluctant to talk about the War. In common with almost all his Lewis contemporaries, he had joined the Royal Naval Reserve in his late teens, needing the money and little thinking that one day it would mean being involved in real hostilities. It's odd, isn't it, that they hadn't learnt the lesson of the First War, in which hundreds of Lewis reservists died? Or did they believe the propaganda about 'the war to end wars' and think that joining the Reserve was just money for old rope? Anyway, domestic conversations in Laxdale were frequently punctuated by references to 'the first crisis'. It was a kind of chronological marker: '*Àm a' chiad chrisis*'. I still think it a peculiar form of words. Munich was the first crisis, the War itself the second. I would have thought the War was a little more than a mere crisis. In any case, that's when he was called up. At the time he was working in one of Glasgow's shipyards (probably as a rigger) and living with my mother and their daughter at Greenfield Street, Govan (the street was obliterated in the 1970s). One evening shortly after he got home from work the door-bell rang: a policeman with his call-up papers. He took the train for Chatham that night and ever afterwards had a total contempt for those in charge of the early war effort. The ineptitude was summed up in one fact: they had scarcely a rifle between them. The reservists drilled using broom handles and anything else remotely resembling the geometry of a musket. He never forgot that the powers-that-be had left the country utterly defenceless. Had Hitler pressed home his advantage after Dunkirk, there would have been no hope.

After Chatham it was minesweepers, then destroyers (the most wretched life in the Navy) and then the cruiser *Glasgow*. The trouble with cruisers, I gathered, was that they carried so much top brass: a 'four-ringed Captain', at least, and too much humbug. Most of the time was spent worrying and waiting. The *Glasgow* appears to have had a fairly undistinguished war. She was involved, peripherally, in the hunt for the *Bismarck*, but then, so was the whole Royal Navy.

Never was there the remotest suggestion of heroics, even though I used to boast, 'My father killed five men in the War. How many did yours?' Individuals, I gather, had no such significance. His role, when it came to action stations, was that of a powder-monkey: locked in a tunnel between decks and passing shells from hand to hand towards the gunners. If the ship sank, hopeless ...

Three years of this broke his physical health for ever. He was given a shore job, promoted to Petty Officer (Joiner) and posted to, of all places, Stornoway. That's not as crazy as it sounds. Stornoway was never used for the assembling of Atlantic convoys (these gathered at Aultbea, where the surrounding mountains guaranteed immunity from air attacks), but it was used as a repair and supply depot and the Admiralty had a workshop around Quay Street, near the Custom House and beside a place which we knew simply as Cruelty's. 'Cruelty' was a Stornoway worthy (and the son of a worthy) and 'Cruelty's' was an engineering shop which did to metal what joiners did to wood (although the smell could never rival the aroma of the woodworker's). There my father spent the rest of the war, his repair work alternating with lifeboat duty.

There would be nothing unusual about his being posted to Stornoway. To the vast majority of navy men Stornoway was at the North Pole: the last place to which anyone would want to be posted. A man actually volunteering for it would be seen by the Admiralty as going far beyond the call of duty and would probably be drafted before he changed his mind. Central authorities never get the hang of these things. To this day people are given special Islands Allowances for agreeing to work up here, even when they're natives and wouldn't want to be anywhere else. I had a friend once who worked in the Stornoway office of what you would call the Welfare Office and we called the National Assistance Board. All his colleagues were receiving the Islands' Allowance, but not Donnie, because he had been recruited locally and this was his first posting. He applied for a posting to Birmingham, got it, then immediately applied for a posting to Stornoway. That too he got, and with it his Islands' Allowance.

Sorry this has been such a long story. The Admiralty workshop on Quay Street became my den: normally, I suppose, under strict supervision. The circular saw, a whirring, screeching, whining thing, was an object of dread. But it had one feature I couldn't resist - a wheel. This wheel was about the same size as a car steering wheel and its function in an adult's world was to adjust the height of the saw-bench up and down. I knew nothing of this. All I knew was that you could turn it and say 'bbbbrrrrh' like a car. And so I turned and turned and turned it. But a point came when I could turn it no more; a point, indeed, when no one could turn it any more. I broke it, I think.

I never knew the exact extent of the damage. I wasn't charged with sabotage. And I never went back to 'the Base', as we called it, any more. But the Captain came for tea once after that, and 'Stokes' remained on good terms with my father, even though I can't understand for the life of me why a repair base in Stornoway needed a stoker.

After the War, of course, that whole world disappeared overnight, and when we moved to Laxdale the beloved quay was nearly three miles away. Still, we visited it frequently. I think we were gradually corrupted by the Stornoway boys, because we spent much of our time around the fishing boats with less than exalted intentions. The fishermen, particularly if they had large catches, didn't mind if you helped yourself to a few herring. I remember one particular day when there was a glut (more herring than the market could cope with) and you could take as many as you wanted. I put my haul into what I thought was a strong carrier bag and set off for home. As usual, we sat in the back of the bus for the ten minute journey. When we reached the terminus, I picked my bag off the floor. The bag came no bother, but not the herring. I had forgotten that the herring would soak through the paper in no time. They slithered, a slimy, elusive mess, all over the floor. The conductress (whose duty it was, of course, to clean the bus) was mightily unimpressed. She was also extremely eloquent. I managed somehow to catch them all and lay every last one of them by the roadside (but not, alas! to clean the bus). In those days we had a twenty minute walk from the terminus to the house. I ran all the way, jumped on my bike and dashed in to reclaim my catch. Not a bone or even a scale remained. All the world's seagulls had got the message, and twenty minutes was more than enough.

Doesn't it break your heart, the thought of the poor wee boy who had lost his fish?

Good wishes
DM.

6. Wakes and bundlings

8 October 2021

Dear Mme Quessaud

I hope your thesis is coming on OK. It's always important to select a topic you're really interested in, and I think it's a great idea to capitalise on your own natural connection with the community you want to study. The only problem is that there have been so many of these studies in the last fifty years that it's hard to find a niche. I don't think I ever actually asked what your precise topic was. That wasn't due to any lack of interest. As you get old you become wary of asking personal questions. Besides, when you first wrote I imagined we would exchange one or two letters and that would be it. Now this correspondence is generating a life of its own. Be sure to tell me when you've had enough. And don't tempt me into autobiography. I don't mind sharing impressions of the outside world as I've seen it. But the inside world (myself as object): that's beyond me. Anyway, what would it be worth? There's not much point in putting your soul into a bottle for posterity.

Yes, I'm afraid it is true that nowadays virtually every funeral here is a cremation. I have no particular objection to it, but I do regret the passing of the old rituals of grief. People no longer face up to the reality of death. Very few die at home, and even those who do are promptly whisked away to the mortuary or the funeral parlour as if we couldn't get rid of the dead quickly enough. We also try to disguise death. Corpses are embalmed, made-up in rouge and other grisly cosmetics, dressed in their best suits and propped up in their coffins as if they were film stars on couches. I remember on one of my first visits to Canada being told that the funeral business was such a rip-off that if you died in Toronto it was cheaper to be buried in Lewis. I'm afraid that's no longer the case. Things began to change at the turn of the millennium. The trouble with a place like this is that once one person goes for an extra special funeral, people begin to compete with each other, until at last the elaborate and extravagant becomes the social norm. This happened with weddings fifty years ago. Then it happened with kitchens. Now the same thing has happened with funerals. Not only are the funeral director's charges high, but money is wasted on such ridiculous things as lining the graves with concrete. As a result many families are now having to borrow heavily to pay funeral expenses.

Probably the most obvious change in the ritual was the passing of the wake. In my earliest memory the wake was an all-night - indeed, an all-day - affair. By today's standards there was certainly a degree of liturgical overkill. Typically, relatives, neighbours and friends would gather in the early evening, and at around 8.00 pm worship would begin. This would consist of several singings of Gaelic psalms, interspersed with several extempore prayers and readings from the Bible. The person presiding would normally be a local elder. In those days ministers never attended wakes. In fact, their presence wasn't deemed necessary even for funerals. When my sister died in 1940, the funeral service was conducted by my mother's uncle, one of the local elders.

After this, the first part of the evening rituals, was over, people gradually drifted away leaving the family more or less by themselves. Later in the evening there would be the normal family worship ('taking the books'). By about 11.30 the next wave of visitors would begin to arrive. This would consist not of the religious but of what was called 'the young' (*an òigridh*, in Gaelic). They would come in relays throughout the night, in effect turning the bereaved home into the village's temporary *taigh-cèilidh*. The occasion would be totally sober. No alcohol ever appeared and the hours would be whiled away in reminiscence, conversation and, no doubt, occasional argument.

I suppose religion would be one topic but it might equally well be politics, the seasons' work, the fishing, the War; or it could be the deceased or his relations, the state of the cemetery, genealogies or who died when and who was buried where. This would go on throughout the night till breakfast time.

In retrospect it all seems extremely civilised. Later on I heard many discussions as to the origin of such wakes. Some suggested they began as a safeguard against body snatchers; others that they were to ensure that the corpse wasn't bitten by rats - a real risk, I suppose, in the old black houses. There's no way any of these theories can be verified. My suspicion is that wakes had their origins in the bacchanalian instincts stimulated by bereavement in so many communities all over the world. In the late Sixties of last century when I was a minister in Lochaber, whisky was always in evidence at funerals, particularly in the more remote glens. According to oral tradition, the justification for this was that men often had to walk many miles to the cemetery. They would stop at intervals for a rest, laying the bier on specially prepared cairns, and fortify themselves with alcohol before resuming the journey. By the time they reached the burial ground they were often in an advanced state of inebriation.

Many many years ago, at the Free Church College dinner-table (a raconteur's paradise), I heard tell of one burial party which set off from some remote village in Wester Ross for the churchyard in Gairloch. After many rests they eventually reached the summit of a hill commanding a magnificent view and paused for yet another refreshment. Weary, disorientated and legless, one of the party made a suggestion. Hadn't they gone far enough? Why not bury him here? There was a chorus of objections: "He wanted to be buried in Gairloch!" "Well," said the Ideas Man, "he can see Gairloch from here."

Funerals seem to have been a frequent topic of conversation at College dinners. The setting of another such story was Glenurquhart (east coast near Inverness), native parish of three of my original College colleagues. A group of men (so went the story) were returning from a funeral. The usual thing on such occasions was to discuss the virtues of the deceased. This time they had buried a rogue - more than a rogue, indeed. The man was what we in Lewis would have called a *troc*: not only a useless but a nasty character about whom, even dead, no one could think of anything good to say. At last, in the leaden silence, one of the men took out his pipe and began to fill it. "Och, well!" he said, "one thing about John. He loved a good smoke."

The Lewis wake as I knew it was probably no more than the Christianisation of the age-old bacchanalian gathering. It certainly had no connection with rats or body snatching. Nor was it simply a useless relic of the past. It had an essential function: it meant that the family were never on their own, day or night. To you and me that may seem an intolerable intrusion: we'd be screaming for space. But that's not how these people saw it. There was a genuine awe in the presence of death, and probably some reluctance to go to bed and put the lights off. Some primal instinct probably suggested that while death was in the house (the coffin would normally lie in for two days) someone should keep watch. If the house were full of animated young people, the older folk could go to bed with peace of mind and sleep soundly. In fact, very often members of the family would go and sleep in neighbouring homes, leaving visitors to look after the house where the coffin lay.

It was the same instinct which demanded that in a case of grave illness someone should keep watch by the bedside all night. If the situation were protracted, relays of relatives and neighbours would share the burden. In the older Gaelic culture there was a specific word for this - *caithris*. To say of someone '*Thathas ga chaithris*' meant that you were keeping an all night vigil and expecting an imminent demise. Curiously enough, the same language could also be used of a very different rite of passage - courting. I assure you I have no personal experience of this, but it seems to have been an accepted practice that when a couple were courting the young man would enter the young woman's house after the rest of the family had gone to bed and they would spend most of the night on (but not in) a bed together. The practice (still well remembered in my younger days) was honoured with the designation *caithris na h-oidhche*. The proximity of parents and siblings (and probably grandparents, uncles and aunts as well) was probably enough to prevent any real shenanigans. Matters became critical only when the man persisted after his cause was lost or when the residence of a family of eligible sisters became the simultaneous target of all the young men in the village. Maybe the old folk put up with it not only because they had done it themselves, but because they were happy to know that at least their daughters were all under their own roof.

Yet, as with many of these customs, this was by no means unique to Lewis. Exactly the same practice was current in New England in the first half of the 18th century. I stumbled upon this fact many years ago while reading a biography of Jonathan Edwards. Most people know of Edwards only as the man who preached the sermon 'Sinners in the Hands of an Angry God', but all of us Free Church people revered him as a magisterial theologian and about thirty years ago Americans had re-invented (and canonised) him as America's greatest ever philosopher. During his time as minister of Northampton, Edwards had considerable trouble with the local young people (particularly those with wealthy parents) and one of the practices he tried to put an end to was 'bundling'. This was the exact equivalent of *caithris na h-oidhche* in Lewis: young people spending the night together, partly clothed, in bed, in parents' homes. In New England it seems to have led to a fair degree of promiscuity. There's no evidence that it had any such consequences in Lewis, though I doubt if this reflects any superior morality. We can put it down, I think, to the fact that the old black houses didn't afford much privacy. But it's fascinating that social conditions in Ness in the 1920s bore such a resemblance to early colonial America. There were also striking similarities in religious practice, but that's another story.

Even in their most solemn moments, these older generations seem to have been fascinated by romance, and courtship often provided preachers with their illustrations. One such preacher, expatiating on the dangers of spiritual self-deception, commanded the rapt attention of his audience by telling a story about a young 'Eskimo' couple who were deeply in love. The girl's father would have none of it and the young folk decided that the only solution was to elope: not an easy matter if you live in an igloo in the middle of a frozen waste. The plan was simple enough: the suitor would tunnel into the igloo in the dead of night, throw a sack over his beloved and run off with her. It was duly put into operation and off the young man ran carrying his strangely subdued prize. Once he'd put a safe distance between himself and the igloo he stopped and pulled off the sack. "*Murt!*" he cried, "*am bodach!*" ("Oh, no! and blue murder! It's the old man!")

But back to wakes. The last real wake I remember was when my grandmother died in 1959. My father and I left the house some time after midnight and went to spend the night with the Gunns next door. After that date things began to change and the practice of people keeping watch throughout the night quickly ceased. That was a real social loss because it put an end to one of the most lively (pardon the pun!) meeting-points in the life of the community. It's easy enough to think of reasons for the change. Housing improved greatly and the advent of electricity made it easy to light every room in the dwelling. At the same time, work patterns were changing even in the rural communities. The old days of the self-employed crofter were gone, and people had to be at their places of work in Stornoway by eight or nine in the morning. It was no longer practicable to be up most of the night.

At the same time other changes were radically transforming community life. Everything was becoming more individualist.

For generations many crofting activities had been communal: taking home the peats, for example, and lifting the potatoes and going out fishing. But in the Fifties families began to acquire their own tractors and to plant potatoes and take home the peats with no outside assistance. By that time, of course, white-fishing (using great lines from open boats) had long ceased to be a commercial option for most villages. It's easy to lament such a change. But such fishing was hazardous and every district had experienced its own *bàthadh mòr* ('Big Drowning'). The men of Ness, for example, were fearless and sometimes foolhardy seamen. But they had no proper harbour and every time they tried to negotiate the entry they were taking their lives in their hands.

The revolution in transport also contributed to the breakdown in community interaction. In the days before motor-cars people had no option but to walk; and very often they walked in company. Going to church on Sunday morning, for example, was almost like a pilgrimage. People spilled out of every house to join the procession. My maternal grandfather's house in Habost (Ness) had its gable-end at the very edge of the road. When we were on holiday there we used to go upstairs to watch. The road would be black with people (the black wasn't a theological, Calvinist statement. It was partly due to there being no options and partly due to the fact that after two Great Wars a large number of women were in mourning). I can still hear the clip-clop of hundreds of feet striding along on their way to church. These were lively, animated walks, the old women often arm in arm, teasing, sharing and questioning. No doubt the whole of human life was there: births, deaths and marriages; fishing and harvest; gossip, malevolent and benign. But there would also have been such religious and theological discussion as would have graced the table at any seminary.

The advent of buses didn't have any significant impact on this aspect of community life. Buses were conversation-friendly, and in the 1940s the 27-mile journey from Laxdale to Ness could take over two hours. In fact, improvements in transport, then and now, enhance rather than impoverish human life. But I need hardly tell you that. It's very well to dream of the age of the horse and cart: very leisurely and idyllic. But by the same token it meant that people in different villages saw very little of each other. If you married and settled in Stornoway, you might see your parents (in Ness) only once a year, and even that needed careful organising. If you emigrated to Canada or Australia, you might never see them (or your native island) again. So, no romanticising of the world before buses, telephones and airliners! Modern technology has annihilated distance. Otherwise we wouldn't be writing. Let's be thankful!

The Lewis buses of the 1940s moved slowly and uncertainly and usually to the smell of something burning. They must have been very heavy on batteries because whenever they were moving the driver switched off the interior lights. We travelled in darkness, the lights coming on again only when someone was getting off. And any sheep on the road were a hazard. Brakes were such that anything fifty yards in the distance required an emergency stop.

I remember too the ritual when waiting for a bus, particularly at night. Motor cars were few and far between. In fact we played football on the roads knowing we'd have ample warning of any approaching vehicle. At night, if your visitors were waiting for a bus, the adults told you to look out while they continued their conversation. You simply looked for reflected lights in the telegraph wires and then shouted (or whistled) to inform folk that the bus was coming. The lights seldom heralded any vehicle save the bus and your visitors had abundant time to make a leisurely journey up the path to the road.

The buses themselves carried everything: prescriptions from the chemist, bags of biscuits (from Ness Bakery), warps to be delivered to weavers, finished tweeds, assorted bits of ironmongery and bags of wool. Accommodation for humans was seldom a priority. Various legends also circulated as to the drivers themselves. One of them (Ruairidh Ròigean, who also owned and ran Ness Bakery) was said to drink a whole bottle of Navy Rum on the 27-mile journey to Ness (a variant on this theme suggests that he was very unsteady on his feet when approaching the bus, but was OK once he got behind the wheel. I have a vague memory of once checking this out and having the first version confirmed as authentic). Such legends are marginally funny. Only the fact that the roads were empty and the buses trundly prevented disaster.

Ruairidh, tragically, bequeathed his habits to his sons and the flourishing business collapsed soon after his death. But it's surely more than an historical curiosity that in the inter-War years the village of Habost (about fifty families) had no fewer than three bakeries. I remember Ness Bakery's biscuits well. We used to buy them hot out of the oven for a penny each and consume them instantly. They were about two and a half inches in diameter and half an inch thick: very like what we in Scotland now call high baked water biscuits, but much thicker. Each had a stamp: 'Ness Bakery: Famous Biscuits'. I doubt if they went all over the world as was sometimes claimed, but they certainly went all over Lewis and probably even as far as Glasgow. Of course, we being Scots and having 'kent his faither', there would be local mutterings every week that the biscuits weren't as good as they used to be. The bakery itself was just across the road from my grandfather's house (my birthplace) and I was in it once or twice as a very little boy. But all that are left are vague impressions. I remember the smell of paraffin (presumably the oven was oil-fired) and I remember the sense of wonder as a man opened a large black box (like my father's large toolbox, still sitting in my shed to this day) and lifted out this huge white lump. This, I learned afterwards, was dough, and it was pushed through a succession of rollers till the enormous block was almost as flat as a pancake. Then my grandfather (probably the last job he ever had) attacked it and cut it into circles. He had an implement which they called (in Gaelic) a 'saw': totally illogical because it had neither teeth nor a sawing action, but it did cut.

Only two men knew the recipe (by this time old Ruairidh himself had died): the eldest son, Roddy; and Tormod Ruadh, our neighbour two houses along, who worked all his life in the bakery. Whether the 'Famous Biscuits' baked on a Lewis croft ever had the market potential of Coca-Cola is a moot point, but the formula was certainly jealously guarded. When these two men died, the biscuit (and part of my childhood) died with them.

It was natural, I suppose, that your mother should speak to you about Lewis religion. It would be interesting to know what she herself thought of it. Her observations would be at least as interesting as mine. She never seemed hostile to it, but like many young folk of her generation she was probably terrified of '*getting the cùram*': an experience which, as they saw it, cut you off forever from all the pleasures of life, if not, indeed, from life itself. Did her attitude change towards the end? Of course I know nothing of the circumstances of her death. Did she know she was dying?

The wrists are creaking. I'd better stop.

Take care
Donald (Macleod)

17 November 2021

Dear Mme Quessaud

Sorry for the delay in replying. I've been laid low for a couple of weeks with pleurisy, my lungs feeling as if they were being scraped with sandpaper. It will carry me away one day as it did my father and grandfather ('Chronic airways disease,' said the death certificates). It's strange how unrealistic we remain, even in old age. I remember once hearing a 98-year-old woman being asked on the radio whether she had any remaining ambitions. "Yes," she replied, "I would like to live to a good old age!" She opined, further, that the reason she had already put a fair number of years behind her was that she consumed huge quantities of vegetables, throwing them into the pot straight from the garden, soil and all. She was English, of course.

Thanks for sharing with me some of the background to your dear mother's death. In the days when I was active myself it never ceased to amaze me how people coped with the knowledge that they were terminally ill. I do indeed remember a senior medical person once telling a conference that he had never seen anyone come to faith while in a hospice, though he had see many abandon it. But only once have I seen anyone collapse into a total depression: a young woman diagnosed with a particularly aggressive leukaemia. She came from a dysfunctional family headed by a world renowned expert on the psychology of relationships. His one contribution to his daughter's struggle was to breeze into her ward and brutally disabuse her of any illusion that she might recover. She was living with a prosperous and decent young Glasgow fellow, and when they discovered that she was dying they were both possessed by a compulsion to marry. They had absolutely no church connection, but one of her nurses happened to be a member of my congregation and he approached me asking if I would be prepared to marry them. By this time all treatment had stopped and she had left hospital. I visited them in their home a day or so later. She was stunningly beautiful, in her late teens, a classical blonde, but certainly no bimbo: articulate, aggressive, angry and without a trace of self-pity. I arranged to marry them on the earliest possible date and left. I never saw either of them again. Two or three days later she literally turned her face to the wall and never spoke another word.

I was deeply moved by what you said about your mother's closing days, and not just because it answered the question I posed at the end of my last letter. Her words have been going round and round my head: 'Dying is a full-time job!' And linked to that her thankfulness that she hadn't left it to her deathbed to sort out her spiritual affairs. The Last Enemy leaves little strength for other battles. But when you mentioned the almost merciful weakness of her closing hours, my thoughts turned to a little boy also the victim of leukaemia. 'Daddy,' he said, 'I want to be alive when I die.' Not for brave men like him the gradual drift into oblivion under the influence of sedation and medication. Instead he wanted to be there at the End: if not at his own funeral, then at least at his own dying.

It's hard to arrange, but it resonates so well with what we're told about the Cross of Christ: He 'tasted death'. Who knows?

It was remiss of me to use the word *cùram* without clarifying it. For a moment I suppose I thought I was writing to your mother, who would have understood it instantly. Every religious tradition creates its own specialist vocabulary, but this one is further complicated by the fact that it's been transported from Gaelic and suffered some changes in the process. The core idea is simple enough. The Gaelic word *cùram* is the same as the Latin word *cura*, care. An Anglican curate, for example, is someone who cares for the flock. In Gaelic religious usage, the stress moved more towards the idea of concern. A new convert would be described as being '*fo chùram*' or '*fo chùram anaim.*' Literally, she was 'under concern' (for her soul). Such a form of words was common enough in the theology of the Puritans, where 'soul concern' had a clearly understood meaning. Someone who had previously given no thought to life after death or to her relationship with God or to the importance of spiritual things would come to be possessed with a sense of the primacy of such matters. This was often linked to a particular view of the conversion experience: first, conviction of sin, then weeks or months of more or less intense concern, followed by eventual deliverance and peace.

When the phrase was carried over to English, a subtle change occurred. It was no longer 'coming under' *cùram* or concern, but getting it: 'getting the *cùram*'. It was coined, I think, by Stornoway folk (English-speakers, as alienated from the religion of rural Lewis as they were from its language and culture). It was a term of insult, disparagement and mockery. I well remember on my own return home after my first term at university being approached by a group of former school-mates, led by a loud-mouthed coward and bully who demanded to know whether it was true that I now had the *cùram*.

The assumption behind such language is that religion is some disease or contagion. You get it as you get measles. But the change in wording also had theological implications. It reflected, and perhaps even encouraged, a kind of spiritual fatalism. Religion was something that God either gave you or didn't. I remember at a wake, once, people praying most earnestly for the unconverted members of the family. The form of words, unvaryingly, was that 'Lord, we pray that they would receive what the other members of the family have received': not, you will notice, that they would do what the other members of the family had done. The preaching fortunately laid more stress on responsibility, but Celtic fatalism was always adept at turning the doctrine of predestination into 'whatever will be will be'.

The religion of Lewis had a very specialised in-house vocabulary, and if you didn't know it, it would sound like gobbledy-gook. Many, many years ago I attended a conference in England where two ministers from Lewis were asked to give an account of the revivals then taking place in the island (this was in the 1970s). The two brethren spoke in the language natural to themselves, but their English and Welsh hearers were completely nonplussed. "Stop!" they said. "Tell us what these expressions mean!"

I'm not sure it's altogether easy. In Lewis in those days the first (and usually definitive) sign that one was 'born again' (not an expression we used) was that one went to the midweek prayer meeting. In many ways this step had the same confessional status that baptism had in the early church or that coming forward to the front of the auditorium had in the Billy Graham crusades of the 1950s. It was a public declaration of a change of spiritual and, indeed, social allegiance. You were deciding against the temporal, and for the spiritual, world; for the prayer meeting against the football match. It was a spiritual Rubicon, more important even than your first Communion; and remarkably few who took this step ever went back on it.

Various words were used to describe this step. At the conference I referred to (it was in Leicester, I think) the Lewis ministers could report, for example, that 'fifty came out that week' or fifty 'started' or they 'began following'. This last form of words was shorthand for 'following the means of grace' and this was both the strength and the weakness of Lewis Christianity. On its good side it reflected a hunger for biblical preaching and Christian fellowship. On its downside it could lead to a neglect of the practical, ethical side of religion. A 'zealous' Christian was one who attended an incredible number of meetings not only in her own parish but beyond. It was a kind of spiritual hedonism. Such meetings could be hugely enjoyable, but they created the risk of allowing Christianity to degenerate into an endless quest for 'blessing'. It's curious how easily a kind of Protestant monasticism can develop and a man come to have no contact with the world even though he has a regular nine to five job. His real life consists of meeting after meeting after meeting. But I'd better stop. Too much theology.

The other critical moment in spiritual experience in Lewis was your first Communion. As your mother probably told you, comparatively few people actually became communicants: about a third of adult church attenders in those days. For many people their first Communion seemed to be a traumatic experience. Various phrases were used to describe it, the two most common being 'going forward' and 'professing'. In many ways it was a step almost as momentous as conversion itself. I know that it was often said that people in the islands were discouraged from becoming communicants, but what I saw was the reverse. The Sunday before Communion the local minister would often use his sermon to urge upon believers 'the duty and privilege' of becoming communicants. Apart from all else, at the level of human vanity, the greater the number of new communicants, the greater the tribute to his own ministry. A minister who went years with few new members (or none) would feel extremely dejected, at least in my young days.

He might even become the butt of bothan humour. Bothans were primitive bothies which served as ceilidh houses for men who couldn't socialise without alcohol. One night, so the story goes, the men in the Habost bothan decided to turn their ceilidh into a dream-telling session. One after another spoke, relating his visions and nightmares with all the eloquence and frankness that whisky and chasers could produce (quite a lot!). But then one man announced that his dream was about all the ministers in the parish. He saw each one going to the Throne of Judgement, proudly leading his converts. First, the Free Church minister, followed by a multitude (the dreamer was Free Church); then the Church of Scotland minister, followed by a respectable crowd; and lastly, the poor Free Presbyterian minister. In the dream he cut a sad, lonely figure, followed by not a single convert but looking forlornly over his shoulder and exclaiming, 'Fhearaibh, am faca sibh Seumas?' ('Friends, has none of you seen Seumas?' Seumas being his one and only elder). Even the FPs would have laughed (and got their own back the following week).

These sermons urging people to 'go forward' had an almost evangelistic fervour: a far cry from the common perception that folk were discouraged from coming to the Lord's Table. For the people being addressed it created, often, an acute tension. They wanted to go forward, partly because it was an act of witness, partly because it was the final seal on their identification with 'the Lord's people' and partly because they had heard so much about the blessing or spiritual pleasure which others had experienced through Communion. On the other hand, they shrank from it. The reasons for this were complex. Some might not be sure they were genuine Christians at all. Some might be afraid that after such a public step they would lapse and bring disgrace on themselves and their families. Some might hold back because being a communicant put you under a special pressure. This was particularly true of the men. There was probably a subconscious idea that so long as you weren't a communicant less was expected of you. But there was also a fear (and sometimes sheer terror) of the duties and responsibilities involved. In the Highlands and Islands every male communicant was expected to be able to pray in public; and not only to pray, but to pray eloquently, in sentences, extemporaneously for ten to fifteen minutes, skirting the margins of profundity while remaining within the borders of orthodoxy. That could be a daunting prospect because these prayer meetings were no little huddles: sometimes (even among expatriate Gaels in Glasgow) the attendance could run to hundreds.

The astonishing thing was that in the event every man was able to do it. This always struck me as just about the most remarkable feature of Highland evangelicalism. Many of these men had little or no education and even less experience of public speaking. Yet the language would flow out of them, moving coherently from topic to topic, laced with appropriate biblical quotation and coming from the depths of the heart. The very excellence of their predecessors must have been a deterrent to young men. How on earth could they ever get up on their feet in a crowded meeting and pray like that? But they did, almost without fail.

There was one other deterrent to becoming a communicant which I haven't mentioned: the fact that one had first to appear before the Kirk Session and be examined as to one's fitness to be received into the membership of the church. There was nothing in strict canon law to require this. In most other parts of Scotland the practice had been, for generations, that a new communicant would apply to the minister and he would recommend him to the Session. In some others they were interviewed by a small group of elders (two or three) along with the minister. But in Lewis and throughout the Highlands generally they had to appear before the whole Session. In the Highland Free Church in Glasgow where I was minister in the 1970s this meant having to walk in and face a dozen men, each looking more formidable than the next. It always seemed to me an utterly overwhelming ordeal, particularly for women. I asked one once how she had found the experience. She hadn't been able to lift her eyes. "All I saw was boots!" she said (thirteen pairs, if I remember rightly). But women had their own way of coping. They broke out in a flood of tears at the first question. That was usually enough to unman both ministers and elders. It certainly unmanned me, but I never cared for the practice anyway. All my instincts pushed me towards making the path to Communion as easy and as natural as possible.

These instincts were not universal among Highland ministers. Some of them felt it their duty to make the examination before the Session as intimidating as possible. One of the first stories I heard around the professorial table at College related to one such case. A certain minister by that time long dead hadn't seen much blessing on his labours and the congregation hadn't had a new communicant for years. This particular Communion weekend, however, there was an applicant, but the congregation had grown so small that there was only one elder (to form a quorum for a meeting of the Kirk Session there had to be two). The custom in such cases was to ask the visiting minister to sit in for the interview. This he duly did, and listened with growing horror while the applicant was subjected to the most fearful grilling. The man was eventually admitted and the meeting of Session closed. "Were you no glad to see him?" enquired the shocked visiting minister of the local one. "What, maun! I was never so glad in my life!" But it was important not to show it.

The practice which grew up in the Highlands in connection with new communicants was to ask those appearing before the Session for a narrative of their conversion experience. To a degree this was unnecessary because the elders already knew the applicant well - inevitably so in a small, closed spiritual community. Even the details of their conversion would often be a matter of general knowledge. No doubt it was reassuring to hear them tell the story in their own words, but it created an obvious danger. It was all too easy to assume that a verbal facility on matters religious was somehow a sign of mature spirituality. That was, in effect, a hypocrites' charter. What saved the situation was the elders' prior and general knowledge of the applicant. From this point of view the interview by the Session didn't really matter. It gave the elders some satisfaction (perhaps sadistic), but no-one was ever accepted (or turned down) on the basis of an interview alone.

Many years later I discovered that there was a remarkable similarity (yet again) between these Highland procedures and the practice of New England Congregationalism. There, too, admission to church membership was preceded by a conversion narrative. But I don't suppose that's of much interest.

Much of this is perplexing, at least to me, particularly because from a New Testament point of view it's off the wall. Where can one find a suitable text for a sermon urging Christians to become communicants? For the New Testament it simply wasn't a problem. On the contrary, it was the most natural thing in the world for a believer to be baptised and for the baptised to break bread. We should have left it that way. The underlying thrust in attempts to safeguard the Lord's Table was twofold: first, an endemic Christian unease with the idea that God requires nothing but faith in Christ; secondly, a persistent idea that we must keep the church pure. Both these ideas are borne on the stock of legalism, which means they are fatally incompatible with Christianity.

The paradox is that from my recollection virtually everyone who should have gone to the Lord's Table did eventually go. The problem was that church leaders (not always the ministers!) made it appear so difficult. Sometimes it was even dramatised. People were warned not to let 'the day' past. A few were convinced that they had. And sombre stories were told of people who had been strongly drawn to 'going forward', had not done so and had died before the next Communion. Opposite stories were told too of people who had gone forward and mercifully so, because that was their last opportunity. They died before the next Communion.

This did not fit into any New Testament pattern that I could see. St Paul's word about coming to the Lord's Table unworthily was, I suppose, always in the air, but I doubt if it really operated as a practical deterrent. People had enough theological sophistication to know that no one was worthy; and everyone knew the story of 'Rabbi' Duncan (an eccentric 19th century Edinburgh theologian), who, seeing a woman hesitate to take the bread immediately, approached her and said, "Tak it, woman! It's for sinners." But in the event, as I said, few of the born again stayed away.

As you probably gathered from your mother, the Highland churches were non-liturgical. They had no set forms or prescribed rituals. Yet there were often unwritten rituals particularly linked to the celebration of the Sacrament.

In my early days, for example, it was *de rigeur* that when the presiding minister stood up to begin the administration of the sacrament he always used the words "We now come to the most solemn portion of the service of the day." In the late Fifties and early Sixties of last century men began to question this. Rev Murdo MacAulay, the forceful and very able minister of Back (a parish on the east side of Lewis), began to point out that such a form of words elevated the sacrament above the preaching: a betrayal, he rightly argued, of the Reformation's insistence on the primacy of preaching. Nothing, said Mr MacAulay, was more solemn or more important than the Word: a fact emphasised by the very architecture of the old presbyterian churches, where the Communion Table was always under the pulpit (and dwarfed by it). By the time I was ordained (1964) this particular issue was more or less settled and I was never under any pressure to use the aforementioned formula.

Another intriguing piece of ritual involved the precentor. A Highland Communion in these old days was a very elaborate affair. I well remember an old minister, highly stressed over his responsibilities one Communion Sunday morning, telling me the service involved no fewer than thirty-two steps. For some reason which I was never able to understand, the bread and wine ('the elements') were never on the Table at the commencement of the service. At a particular point the elders went to the vestry and returned in procession carrying them and depositing them on the Table. Just prior to this the minister would announce, "We shall now sing some verses to God's praise while the elders bring in the elements, symbols of the broken body and the shed blood of the Lord. And we shall continue singing till the elements are on the Table." He did not announce the number of verses to be sung, but when he was satisfied that the elements were safely on the Table he would lean over the pulpit and tap the precentor's shoulder with the Psalter. That was the signal for the singing to stop. For us as children it was a kind of magic moment, which happened only at Communion, and we used to await it as an item of special drama. It was repeated minutes later when communicants were invited to come forward to the Table 'while some further verses are sung'. Again, no number of verses was specified, but when everyone was seated the tap on the shoulder was repeated.

Another peculiar practice was drawn to my attention only many years later. In the Highland Presbyterian churches communicants partook of the sacrament sitting in their pews. This was a clear breach of the rule laid down by the old Scottish theologians that communicants must be seated around a Table, but we'll ignore that for the moment. A proportion of the pews was marked off with white linen, to demarcate the area to be used as a 'Table'. I was discussing these things once with a friend, the late Flora Macleod, who was both a keen observer of such matters and also well versed in theology and church history. She told me of her own disconcerting experience at her very first Communion. She went to the Table, no doubt in a state of high trepidation, following everyone else and sat down. As she did so she placed her Bible on the book-board in front of her. The woman beside her immediately removed the Bible and placed it behind Flora's back. Apparently it was a rule that the Bible must not be on the book-board during the Communion. I'm not sure how widespread this practice was, but it certainly prevailed in Stornoway (although I doubt if even the local minister was aware of it). Whence and why? I haven't the remotest idea - not yet anyway, and time is running out.

Linked with this was something equally odd. In Lewis churches the practice prevailed of men walking into church in front of their wives and families, finding a suitable pew, standing at it and ushering them into it, first the children, then the wife (there would also be a predetermined arrangement to ensure that the youngest members of the family did not sit next to each other. They would be separated by someone 'adult' enough to see to it that they didn't torment or provoke each other; or, what was worse, induce fits of giggles). When it came to

Communion, however, this practice was abandoned. Not only did the husband not usher his wife into the pew, he went in before her. I have a vague memory of once asking for an explanation of this and I think the reply was linked to Jesus's words in Matthew 22.30: "In heaven they neither marry nor are given in marriage." It was definitely connected with the idea that the Lord's Table represented a temporary suspension of natural relations: as if in Christ a man's wife were not his wife but his sister. There was probably a parallel to this in the fact that when a woman died the plate on her coffin always bore her maiden name, not her married one.

There were other peculiarities too about a Lewis Communion Service: for example, the use of tokens and the practice of fencing the Table. But I've wearied you already and it's time I went and opened a tin of something or other. We used to think that when this new millennium came we'd be far beyond the use of tins and even beyond such antiquated nonsense as cooking. But the human body imposes its own limitations and doesn't take kindly to the notion of living on vitamins and supplements. My mother used black pans. I use stainless steel ones. But they're still pans, and what comes out of mine doesn't taste half as good as what came out of hers.

Once more, I've talked too much. It's bad enough when men love the sound of their own voices; infinitely worse when they love the sound of their own keyboards. What old age and loneliness will do to a man!

Good wishes
D.

8. The chain of events

22 January 2022

Dear Mme Quessaud

You're quite right about Evangelicalism being a relative upstart in Lewis. At the beginning of the 19th century such religion as there was in the island appears to have been a mixture of Paganism, Catholicism and Moderatism. The Moderates were a school of Presbyterian ministers more interested in their glebes than in their people and more familiar with the poems of Burns than with their Bibles. They found preaching a real chore and had no compunction about using other men's sermons: even less about regularly re-using old ones of their own. A story circulated once about one of them who had only one sermon. It was about Nicodemus (do I need to tell you who he was: the man who came to Jesus by night? Read all about about him in the third chapter of the Gospel of John). The people, thoroughly fed up with it, pled and pled and pled with him to preach on a different text, but the thought made the good man blanch. Finally he relented. Next Sunday he had a new text: Genesis 1.1. Solemnly and sonorously he read the words 'In the beginning God created the heavens and the earth'. The people sat up, expectant as journalists at a Prime Ministerial press conference. 'We know next to nothing about this man Nicodemus,' began the preacher.

Sorry for the digression. If it's not the pleurisy, it must be the dementia. I've had it for fifty years now. It's bound to go away some time.

The man usually credited with bringing Evangelicalism to Lewis is the Reverend Alexander Macleod, a native of Stoer in Sutherland, who came to the parish of Uig in 1822. The precise spot where Macleod was born was the village of Balachladaich, near Culkein, some fifteen minutes' drive north of Lochinver. It wasn't a place with which Laxdale boys were familiar, but in May 1962 I was posted to the parish of Stoer for my first placement as a young divinity student. I had to look up a map to see where it was and then plan my route, starting from Lewis. As the crow flies it was about twenty-five miles, but I wasn't a crow and I couldn't fly, and although I could see the mountains of Assynt from my Laxdale window, the journey would take almost twenty-four hours. It began at half past ten on Friday evening and ended around eight o'clock on Saturday: Stornoway to Kyle by steamer; Kyle to Dingwall by train; Dingwall to Lairg by train; Lairg to Lochinver across the Sutherland moors by bus; Lochinver to Stoer by van (the most magnificent scenery in Scotland, one of the worst roads and, I was told, a blind driver). I was met by two women of the congregation. You could class them as 'young elderly' and also in good Presbyterian-speak as 'discerning'. To say they were horrified would be an under-statement. Who on earth could have sent them this - and for eight weeks? I was aged twenty-one and looked seventeen. I was green (and probably some other colours as well) after pitching and rolling on the Minch. I was built like a needle, weighing-in at about eight stone. And to crown it all, when they asked, "Do you preach Gaelic?" I said, "No!"

They couldn't send me back: there was no way out till Monday morning. Mrs Macleod, whose recently deceased husband had been the only male communicant in the Free Church of Assynt, took me home and I spent eight unforgettable, formational weeks in the hospitality of the home she shared with her daughter Joan, a strikingly beautiful and terrifyingly efficient girl whose golden hair, unblinking blue eyes and noble bearing I can see still. She made no profession then of being a Christian, but her name was in the Book of Life. She married shortly after I left and died before she reached middle age.

The Macleods lived in an area known locally as 'The Glacin'. I think the word derives from Gaelic *glaicean* and means 'hollows', and the spot took its name from the fact that the houses were set in relatively fertile (and sheltered) hollows in the craggy, hummocky land adjacent to the shore. Within hours of reaching Assynt I was introduced to the Clearances (a concept I had never met in Lewis); to the Vesteys, the detested local landlords; and to the story of the sufferings of previous generations driven from their fertile inland holdings onto the very edge of the Atlantic and forced to live on the limpets they could gather from the rocks: rocks pounded even in summer by ferocious seas.

I was also introduced to a story far closer to home: yet another reminder of how fragile are the ties of kinship even among such a people as the Gaels, whose first question is neither the Glasgow one "What do you do?" or the Edinburgh one "What school do your children go to?" but the simple, direct "Cò leis thu?" ("Who are your people?").

In the Glacin I was living within a few yards of my cousins. In fact, in the parish of Assynt there were three sets of them. The nearest, Jean Brown, lived beside me in Balachladaich. In Stoer village lived Dolly, Mrs MacKenzie. In Lochinver lived another Mrs MacKenzie whose first name I forget (not that she was at all unfriendly, but I was too young to be on first name terms, and since she didn't live in Stoer her name didn't circulate in local conversation).

What's the story? So far as I can put it together, it's as follows. My grandfather, Murdo Macleod (one of the *Piobairean* associated with North Rona and Piper's Rock), had a sister whose name, I think, was Peggy. Like many others, she left Lewis as a young girl to go to the fishing in Wick. Remember I told you about my own journey to Stoer. In those days (probably late 19th century) it would have been even more awful: first the long sea-journey from Stornoway to Glasgow, then north by train to Wick. From what I heard she was never able to face the return journey and never again saw her parents or any of her siblings. At the fishing she met a man from Stoer, married him,

73

made the journey from Wick to Balachladaich and never left it. In old age she used to sit on a rock outside her house gazing across the Minch, seeing the flash of the Tiumpan Head lighthouse and remembering, weeping and wondering. For her, Stoer might as well have been Canada.

But Stoer had something else to boast of: it was from the rocks of Balachladaich that the gospel had come to Lewis. Alexander Macleod was our St Columba. Lewis was not slow to acknowledge the debt, acclaiming Macleod as '*Alasdair Mòr an t-Soisgeil*' (Alexander the Great of the Gospel), but this veneration of Macleod, I suspect, is less a reflection of the truth than of the tendency of the clergy (who, after all, write most of the ecclesiastical history) to assume that all good things began with a minister. Having said that, I must add that Macleod was an interesting guy in his own right, and he was good enough to leave us a brief diary which records his first impressions of Uig. Your mother may already have shared with you some of the best-known stories, like the one about the elder who, when called on to pray, referred to the death of Christ as a grave misfortune and strongly deplored the fact that it had ever occurred, stopping just short of condoling with the Almighty in his loss; or the one about the other elder, who having had 'frequent experience of the material benefit accruing to them on the occurrence of a wreck on their dangerous coasts', publicly prayed that the Lord would bless them with such a catastrophe yet again.

But other details of Macleod's life are less well known. During his student days Macleod came under the influence of another Macleod, the legendary Norman. This Macleod, himself a son of Assynt, seems to have embodied in his person all the vices of Highland Separatism without any of its virtues. His original intention was to become a Church of Scotland minister. He became, instead, a scourge of all ministers, Evangelical as well as Moderate, and a scathing detractor of all Christians except himself and his fiercely loyal followers. He boasted once that he had toured the whole Highlands and found only one other born again Christian. But whatever his vices, he was a born leader of men, and twice persuaded his flock to follow him across thousands of miles of ocean in ships built with their own hands. The first voyage with some two hundred followers was from Lochbroom to Pictou in Nova Scotia; the second, bordering on the incredible, was from Nova Scotia to Waipu, in New Zealand.

It was natural that Macleod and Macleod should be associated during their time together in Aberdeen. It was also natural that when young Alasdair Macleod came to be licensed by the Presbytery of Tongue, they were more than a trifle suspicious. They knew that he had attended some of the Separatist meetings in Assynt and that he had shown clear signs of sympathy with Normanism, as it came to be called in their midst. They wanted none of this in their presbytery, and Alexander was licensed only after declaring his firm attachment to the Church of Scotland and his renunciation of 'the party he had once joined'.

Alexander Macleod was described by Norman C. MacFarlane (author of *The 'Men' of the Lews*) as 'a volume of solid theology bound in stiff boards', but the same Macfarlane tells a story which shows the minister of Uig in a rather different light. After finishing his studies in Aberdeen, Macleod became tutor to the young sons of a farmer in Skye. The boys had a sister and in the best traditions of Daniella Steele she and Macleod fell hopelessly in love. When he broke the news to father, indicating his hope of marrying her, the *bodach* was outraged. Who was he to marry his daughter? He dismissed Macleod on the spot and ordered him out of the house. When the young lady was informed, she said, "Well, if you're going, I'm going, too!" The elopement had all the essentials: a ladder to the bedroom window at midnight, a silent exit and even a boat crewed by some local lads sworn to secrecy (it's interesting that Macleod had won their confidence not only through his occasional preaching but also, probably, because as a fit young former crofter and fisherman he was a handy man to have around). They sailed from Skye to Gairloch, Gairloch to Inverness and Inverness to Edinburgh, the father in hot but vain pursuit. In Edinburgh they married and set up home in the Horse Wynd, only yards from the Free Church College, Macleod surviving even an armed ambush by the maddened brother. It's a shame no dramatist ever reworked the story, but, then, I suppose that if the Scottish stage ignored Edward Irving, it was hardly likely to notice Alexander Macleod.

According to MacFarlane, Skye rang from end to end with the *fama clamosa,* but (if I may retain the antique register for a moment) it made little bruit in Lewis. In case you ever want to chase it up, you'll find it in the chapter on Angus Matheson in *The 'Men' of the Lews*; and the reason you'll find it there is that although Matheson became one of the 'Men' of Lewis (for forty years he was a Gaelic schoolteacher in Callanish), he was a native of Assynt and married to Macleod's sister.

There's no doubt that under Macleod's ministry the parish of Uig was transformed. Nor is there any doubting the stories of the open air Communions attended by huge congregations (as many as 9,000 according to some accounts). But the first stirrings of Lewis evangelicalism were not in Uig but in Ness; and the key figures were not clerics but lay people, male and female.

The first evangelical impact on Lewis came through John Macleod, a schoolmaster appointed to Galson by the Gaelic Schools Society some time around 1820. His story is worth lingering over, not least because it links together Lewis, Skye, Airthrey (in Stirlingshire) and the wider evangelical movement in Scotland and beyond. I don't want to burden you with detail, but perhaps a little will help you get a clearer picture of the background your mother and I shared.

The story begins with the Haldane brothers, James and Robert, heirs to Airthrey estate in Stirlingshire (now the site of Stirling University) and nephews of the Admiral Duncan who sailed with Nelson and commanded the British fleet at the

Battle of Camperdown in October 1797. Both brothers had their own distinguished naval careers but they came from evangelical families and were themselves converted in early manhood. From that point onwards they were linked with almost every stream of British and even European evangelicalism, from Charles Simeon in Cambridge to the French Reformed Church in Geneva to Alexander Stewart of Moulin, one of the principal translators of the Gaelic Bible. They sold the estate at Airthrey, intending to invest the money in a mission to India. The East India Company, then a powerful political force, and terrified of the commercial implications of such a mission, categorically forbade it, and the brothers turned their attention instead to Scotland itself. At the time there was a real dearth of evangelicals in the ministry of the Established Church, and one of the brothers' schemes was to train an army of lay-preachers to take the gospel to every corner of Scotland. These men became known as 'the Haldane Preachers', and among them was a man named John Farquharson, a native of Glen Tilt in Perthshire. Farquharson proved to be an exceedingly effective evangelist and was at the centre of a powerful spiritual revival at Killin around 1802. For some unknown reason, however, he decided to emigrate to Canada. This was around 1805 and en route to Canada his ship put into Uig bay in Skye. Why, we don't know: in all probability because of the weather. The delay seems to have been a long one, and Farquharson used his time to good effect, preaching in Portree, Snizort, Kilmuir, Duirinish and Bracadale. One of his converts was Blind Munro; and one of Munro's converts was John Macleod, a native of Kilmaluag, who came to Galson, in the Ness district, in 1820. This Macleod was the real harbinger of Lewis evangelicalism.

Macleod was employed by the Edinburgh Gaelic Schools Society, which had a rule, very strictly applied, that its teachers must not preach. By all accounts, he was a man of missionary spirit and found it hard to keep silent in a situation where the textbook was the Gaelic Bible and where the natives (to whom it was a complete novelty: it had been published only in 1801) plied him with endless questions about it.

The Niseachs' ignorance of Christianity was almost total. Indeed, when the Reverend Finlay Cook was inducted to the newly erected parish of Cross (which included Galson) in 1829, he described it as worse than darkest Africa. No doubt some allowance must be made for clerical exaggeration, but, compared with the island of Arran where he was born and the county of Caithness from which he had come, Lewis was certainly a shock to Cook's system. It needed missionaries, not pastors, and probably compared unfavourably even with Lanarkshire, where Cook had once worked as an evangelist at Robert Owen's Cotton Mills. In a letter to his brother-in-law, Donald Sage, author of the priceless (and sometimes mischievous) *Memorabilia Domestica*, Cook described his new parish as 'rude in manners, filthy in habits, and lying under the thickest folds of moral and spiritual darkness'. The Lord's Supper was administered, but with outrageous profanity. Tents for the sale of whisky were erected on Communion Mondays and the perfunctory Thanksgiving Service immediately gave way to the rioting and drunkenness of a Highland country fair: very like what happened at the great gatherings at Callanish at the summer solstice last June. Our respite from paganism was to be a brief one.

When John Macleod came to Galson, Ness was part of the parish of Barvas and the only church was twelve miles away in the village which gave the parish its name. It wasn't a huge distance if you had some kind of spiritual hunger (or at least a car). In the circumstances, it might as well have been in Hong Kong. Macleod began to hold some kind of services. I doubt if they amounted to 'preaching'. He probably did little more than hold a Bible Class. Whatever it was, it was too much for the parish minister, Rev William MacRae. He reported Macleod to his superiors in Edinburgh and the report cost the teacher his job. By this time, however, a close bond had developed between Macleod and the local people. Ness was a prosperous community by Hebridean standards, blessed with fertile machair soil highly productive and easily maintained. It also had access to rich fishing grounds. They wanted to keep Macleod and they had the means to do so. They built a house and provided a salary.

There was one final twist to the story. When Macleod died in 1838, he bequeathed what little money he had to the Edinburgh Gaelic Schools Society: the very society which had sacked him.

The Moderate minister who proved such a thorn in Macleod's flesh was something of a conundrum. Unlike most of his class, Rev William MacRae was no flunky of the landlords. Instead he championed the local crofters. On the other hand, Evangelical folklore portrayed him as afflicted by the typical weakness of the clerical time-server. On one occasion (so legend has it) he instructed the local carter to call at the shipping-office in Stornoway to collect a parcel of Bibles. The carter obliged and delivered them to the minister with the words "There's your Bibles, minister, and see you don't break them." In those days, carters did for the reputation of the clergy what tabloid journalists did for our late Royal family.

Of course, for all we know, MacRae's box of whisky may have had to last him the whole winter; and in any case it's perverse to expect clerics who use liquor in the central rite of their liturgy to be teetotallers. As in so many other areas, the clergy are damned if they do and damned if they don't.

The story of MacRae reminds me of what once happened to one of my College professors. While serving as a locum in Lochinver he was prevailed upon by a parishioner to accept 'a refreshment'. Within hours word spread throughout the congregation: "When the Professor visits you, remember to give him a whisky. He likes his dram!" He most emphatically did not, and had yielded to the invitation only to avoid giving offence.

I'm not saying what I would have done myself. No parishioner ever offered.

Yours
DM

9. The boat

Dear Mme Quessaud

Sorry about all the dates in my last letter: habit of a lifetime, I suppose. Just have to know when things happened; otherwise I might put events before their causes.

Oddly enough, never in my entire childhood or adolescence in Lewis did I hear a word about John Macleod and his work in Galson. But maybe it's not so odd. The educational system of the day was totally biased against local (and even Scottish) history and culture. I heard nothing of Alexander MacLeod of Uig either; nor of the Park Deer Raid or the Riot at Aignish. Even Culloden and the Clearances were never mentioned. Instead, I was an expert (for a few years) on the Peace of Westphalia, the Napoleonic Wars and the Balkan Question. No wonder we grew up thinking Gaelic and the Gàidhealtachd were a separate, unimportant world: a backwater without history, heroes or relevance. We were denied access to the story of our people, and by the time we realised it our people were no more. Denied the oxygen of history, they had no memory, and without memory they had no idea who they were, even when they spoke in Gaelic. From the point of view of the British establishment the policy was a brilliant success. It produced a pride in empire and a compliance in exploitation never surpassed in the dark annals of genocide. Without roots, radicalism is impossible.

I can remember only three legendary figures from my own childhood. Even in these instances what came down to us was patchy.

One, the most shadowy of all, was Mac an t-Srònaich, allegedly a fugitive from Wester Ross. He stood out in our imaginations not so much because he was a murderer but because he was a murderer in Lewis (part of the unreality of the whole Gaelic world was that things like murders never happened in it. They happened only in the world covered by the newspapers). I never, absolutely never, heard mention of him in my own home. He was certainly never used as a bogeyman to terrify us into good behaviour. Most of what I knew of him I picked up from an itinerant textiles teacher who used to come occasionally to Laxdale School. That didn't amount to much. The most graphic piece of information was that he was hanged on Gallows Hill (the hill at least was real enough). Besides that, we knew that he lived as an outlaw in the 'mountains' of Uig and that he had once uttered the perceptive words "Ma ghleidheas mise beanntan Ùig, gleidhidh beanntan Ùig mis'." ("If I can keep (to) the mountains of Uig, the mountains of Uig will keep me.") The words were used as an illustration in many a sermon. Beyond that, all that ever reached us was a vague story about his being asked, just before he was hanged, whether he felt remorse for any of his murders and his replying that he regretted just one: the murder of a little boy whom he met on the moor and whom he killed for his 'piece'.

In later life I tried to put some flesh on *Mac an t-Srònaich*, but the result, paradoxically, was to make him more nebulous than ever. Some scholars doubted whether he was ever hanged; others doubted whether he was hanged on Gallows Hill; and some doubted whether he ever existed.

I still find this last position fascinating: the assumption that no-one ever existed and that nothing was ever done unless there are documents to prove it. I have seen the same logic applied to show that Jennie Geddes never threw her famous stool in St Giles. What seems odder still is that it is often the very people who cry up oral tradition who seem most inclined to discount it. We are fast approaching the final paradox where oral tradition has no credibility unless it's written down.

Others took exactly the opposite approach: the story was originally pure myth and fiction, but when evangelicalism came it had no place for the imagination, and so *Mac an t-Srònaich* had to be converted into real history. What can you make of that? I can make something of a historical figure around whom legends grew, but not much of a legendary figure around whom history grew.

The other two legendary figures of my childhood were heroes of the *Iolaire* disaster. It was one of our greatest pleasures, late on a winter's evening, to get my father to talk about the past. These sessions usually began with "Tell us about the War." This seldom got us very far, and even when it did, it was usually someone else's War. A few words explained the wonders of minesweepers and depth charges; a few more described the miserable discomfort of life aboard destroyers; even fewer sufficed to dismiss life aboard the cruiser *Glasgow*.

But it always ended up with the *Iolaire* and the story of two Ness men: the Patch, who had survived by tying himself to the mast and who was picked up accidentally by a small boat circling the wreck in the morning; and John Macleod from Port of Ness, who had swum ashore carrying a rope and had been the means of saving many lives. That was magic. My father had no pretensions to being a hero. The one thing I always remember (and in this he was a marked contrast to myself) is that in anything remotely resembling an emergency he always seemed to have so much time. It's something I always associate with seamen - never rushed.

But the *Iolaire* was everywhere, not simply in the storytelling but in every social occasion. Even in the 1940s and 50s it was impossible to have any kind of conversation without either "He was lost on the *Iolaire*" or "Her father (or husband) was lost on the *Iolaire*" or "He was on the *Iolaire* and never got over it." Ours was one of the few families not directly affected, although the memory of the procession of coffin-laden carts making their way through the parish of Ness remained etched on my father's mind to his dying day. But the indirect effects were everywhere in the widowed women, fatherless children and lonely, lovely women whose fiancés had perished on the Beasts of Holm. Lewis collapsed into unassuaged grief and leaderless, fatalistic villages.

When I was a boy I used occasionally to go to fish for mackerel off the rocks of Holm, a few yards from the very point where the ship foundered. In later years, when I had my own transport, I used to fish there regularly. It was very infra dig. Only boys fished from the rocks. The men had boats. But maybe it was the boyishness that appealed to me. The combination of history and scenery made it a powerful place. On the way, you pass the monument to those who drowned, and once you are there the flashing red beacon seems more of an insistent reminder of the past than a warning for the present. There are two ideal fishing-spots: one at the top of a 20-foot 'cliff', the other right down at sea-level. I always preferred the latter. It brought me into close communion with the sea. But I often wondered how many desperate hands clutched at it in the pounding seas and chaotic darkness of New Year's night, 1919 (we never called it 'Hogmanay'. It was always 'Oidhche na Bliadhn' Ùire').

On a summer afternoon or evening at the rocks of Holm the whole story of Lewis passed before your eyes: fishing-boats on their way to Marvig and Cromore reminding you of the heroism of the seamen of South Lochs in two World Wars and of the deserted villages created by economic change; the austere, functional buildings of Lewis Offshore Limited, an oil fabrication yard which at the height of the North Sea oil boom gave employment to 1,000 men (the ruins of the buildings are there still); the powerboats and other pleasure-boats of Stornoway's playboys, some cavorting like dolphins, others drifting as they put down their darrows, all mocking the poverty of the town's hinterland; and the ferry back and fore from Ullapool twice a day. Even then, before the introduction of the modern hydrofoils, some of the passengers were day-trippers. Most were locals back and fore from holidays. But every day a few were young men and women on the first leg of a journey into permanent exile. I found it hard to watch because that ferry sailing steadily out of sight was my island's story. It impoverished those it left behind. It carried the dreams of the exiles. And it bore many of them into pain, sin and darkness such as they could never have begun to imagine.

Islanders the world over are born for exile. Islands give you a privileged childhood and then, once they've made you what you are, leave you with no place to express it. After the Great War poverty in Lewis forced on the many what had always been the choice of a few. The *Iolaire* had already deprived the island of the cream of its young men. The great emigrant ships of the 1920s, the S.S. *Canada* and the S.S. *Metagama* carried away the rest.

This is not the place for a history of these events. You already know it from your mother, I'm sure. To her (and to me) they were not mere history. They played a part in our lives, as an all-pervading invisible curriculum. The emigrants left, said one of them (Donald Murray, who went on to become a distinguished Presbyterian minister in Boston), for one reason: hunger. At the end of the War they were heroes, their hearts aglow with the promises of government and the prospect of a brave new world. Instead they came home to the stark realisation that half of the boys who had gone off with them would never return. They found themselves in townships with no spare land, except what a brother who owned a croft might give to a newly married man so that he could grow a few potatoes. There was nothing to turn to but the herring, and that, they quickly realised, was a dead loss. After paying for his keep and for the boat and the engine, a man would return home with five pounds in his pocket, or less. If there was any money in fishing, it was for the curers. No wonder the natives fell an easy prey to the blandishments of agents promising Paradise in Canada.

My mother never forgot the night she watched from the croft on Cross Skigersta Road as the *Metagama* sailed past the Butt of

Lewis. She would have been only eleven at the time, saved from exile by her date of birth. But in the culture of Lewis in those days the bond between older children and twenty-somethings was a close one and her heart was broken as she watched the ship carry away the brothers of her friends and the nightly visitors to her home. "Did many of the men go?" I asked. "They all went," she said quietly, "they all went." And the young women went with them.

It was always the *Metagama* that was remembered. It was the kind of name (like Mephiboshet, with the "o" elongated) which a Gaelic-speaker could linger over and pour his soul into. Thirty years later the memory was as fresh as yesterday, though for a child it was all a bit perplexing. The statement 'He went off on the *Metagama*' was hardly self-explanatory, and it took a while before I realised it was a ship; even longer before I realised it had carried all the young men of Ness off to Canada.

It's difficult for us to capture the pain of exile as these people experienced it. By the time I was thirty you could pick up your phone and speak to your sister in Canada. For a couple of weeks' wages you could book a flight to Australia and fly there in twenty-four hours. Today, we have videophones and can speak face to face to anyone, anywhere. If we're prepared to run the gauntlet of security checks, we can even take a supersonic shuttle and fly non-stop to Los Angeles or Sydney. But in the days of the *Metagama*, when you left, you left. One of my mother's uncles left Ness in 1910. His father lived till 1923, his mother till 1931. But neither of them ever saw him again. Worse, they never heard from him. It wasn't that he fell upon hard times or found himself in disgrace. On the contrary, he became a respected blacksmith in Horseshoe Bay, Vancouver. His homesickness, it was said, was such that he couldn't bear to think even of writing a letter. So it was said. I visited Vancouver once in the late 70s of last century and met his daughters. They had an uncanny resemblance to their first cousin, my Auntie Kate, except for one thing. Auntie Kate was a superb person:

one of the salt of the earth, but her lifetime expenditure on cosmetics would probably not have amounted to a couple of dollars. Her Vancouver cousins not only had nail-varnish, they had it on their toes: great big red blotches of it. Their grandfather, Aonghas Alasdair Thomson (Elder), would have summarily disowned them.

Shortly after my return from Vancouver I happened to be preaching in Oban, and I told my host and hostess (both from crofting backgrounds) the story of my Auntie Kate lookalikes and their nail-varnish. The moment I delivered the punch-line I noticed my hostess's toes. They had red nail-varnish.

There seemed to be an infinite number of central story characters who had gone off on the *Metagama*. Some were known to be in Toronto, Detroit, Winnipeg, Montreal, Fort William or Vancouver. Others had come back home, victims of the Great Depression of the Thirties. Many had crossed illegally from Canada to the United States (mainly Boston or Detroit), and when the markets crashed they either got out or were kicked out. Some came back with colourful reputations, deserved or undeserved, as bootleggers during Prohibition. It wasn't greatly frowned on.

But in between was an unspecified number of Disappeared. When they landed on the eastern seaboard of Canada, they were in many cases only halfway to their destination. Many were destined for the prairies, and set out dreaming of their own ranches in sun-drenched sward. Instead, they found themselves, often, working as indentured slaves in a disorientating wilderness of cruel extremes: blazing summers and frozen winters such as they had never known in Scotland. Many were virtually Gaelic monoglots and easily dismissed as second-class citizens. They were at the mercy of their employers, many of whom were themselves only one bad harvest from penury.

How many of these Hebridean survivors of *Iolaire*, trenches and U-boats perished on the way west or died in some barn on the deep-frozen prairies? These are not academic questions, posed a century after the event. They were the urgent, anxious questions of the ceilidh: speculations offered for gaps not even the best genealogist could fill.

Many of these exiles forsook (or 'jumped') their original employment at the first opportunity and went off in search of something closer to their dream. They moved to the granaries, the tanneries and the docks. If they were fortunate, they ended up in General Motors in Detroit.

Only one of these men did I know really well: my predecessor as minister of the Highland Free Church, Glasgow, the Reverend Malcolm Morrison. In the Great War, he had been an outstanding soldier and had been awarded the Miltary Medal for gallantry (he wasn't particularly impressed, regarding such awards as something of a lottery and always suggesting that many a day he had taken greater risks which received no recognition). In the field, he couldn't understand the War. He liked the Germans, disliked the French and hated the Belgians. He recalled the conditions with revulsion and had nothing but contempt for those in charge. A typical British squaddie.

In the 1930s he found himself out of work and in Toronto. He remembered how in their idleness they organised themselves to build a church for the local Free Kirk congregation. He remembered the soup kitchens. And he remembered the Disappeared: the hundreds of Lewismen who, he was sure, had died of starvation in Depression Canada.

Those who survived the Depression, by contrast, eventually did very well. On my first visit to Canada in 1976 I was entertained by many of these people, and my abiding memory is of being introduced to T-bone steaks and being expected to eat them two or three times a day. They (the exiles, not the steaks) lived in gentle, comfortable affluence, the women refined by long years of service in the homes of Toronto's elite and the men refined by long years in the service of their wives. They were noble people in whose presence, for all their courtesy, I felt inadequate. They had been to schools of which I knew nothing.

Yet there was also paradox. In many ways a Highland Presbyterian was an ideal exile. A croft and a boat taught many skills, and the social structures of the islands taught people to be courteous and respectful without being obsequious. They knew the worth of others, but they also knew their own, and this bred a remarkable adaptability as they faced the challenge of coping with the transition from black house to mansion, croft to factory and Highland village to urban sprawl.

But cope they did. They were Canadians and moderns in every sense: masters of urban living, modern technology and pluralist society.

Yet they had their lapses. It is a curious thing how we are defined by our childhood. We spend comparatively few years in our native villages, yet for the rest of our lives that is where we are from. It is (unless we are prodigals deliberately re-designing ourselves in the Far Country) what provides us with our assumptions and our gut reactions. It remains even to old age the world of our imaginations and instincts.

I remember going to the Free Church in Toronto one lovely summer's morning and being greeted at the door by an elder who had left Lewis on the *Metagama*. Full of the joy of life, he told us how he had wakened up in the morning to the sound of a dog barking. He recognised it at once. It was Seonaidh Dhonnchaidh's, his neighbour's, in Leurbost. Even though Seonaidh Mhurchaidh was long since dead and the elder himself had left Leurbost forty years ago, he still slept and dreamed there; and he still woke up there, even in Toronto.

Thanks for listening
D.M.

10. Snow, and sirens

13 November 2022

Dear Mme Quessaud

Once again, a long delay. Sorry! Winter has set in. I suppose you have them in Quebec too, and it's even possible you like them. I used to like them myself, but after you've seen eighty they're not half so exciting.

Mind you, one of my earliest and most cherished memories is of our first winter in Laxdale, 1946. I woke up one morning to a whole new world: a world blanketed in snow. We never saw such things in Stornoway, where I had spent the first five years of my life. I clambered through the snowdrifts up to the road. Below me were square miles of brilliant, shimmering moorland. But the real wonder was the road itself. There were two tracks with the most magical markings: two seemingly endless lines of compacted snow, each line decorated with tiny little dashes, ts and crosses and the road itself dazzling white under a blue, cloudless sky, cold as the Arctic, bright as the Tropics. I followed the lines, mesmerised, for hundreds of yards in the road ('in the road' if you were heading for Stornoway; 'out the road' if you were walking away from it). Somebody must eventually have stopped me, even though in those days and in that world a lone child would have come to no harm. Presumably whoever stopped me also explained what the markings were: a solitary lorry had passed and left its tyre marks in the snow. But lorries were magic too, and so the explanation brought no disappointment.

My love affair with snow has lasted all my life, despite a conflict of interests with clerical decorum some time in my seventies. In fact in these far-off Laxdale days the pleasures of winter matched the joys of summer. We never skated. There was no nearby loch suitable for that. But even a freezing, snowless night brought its own ritual: slides. The roads of those days seemed to have far more surface tar than those of today, and whenever there was black ice these tar-patches became sheets of ice. Ideally they had to be on a brae; and we had an ideal brae nearby, just outside Ailig Hearach's. We would rush out immediately after school, take a short run and then slide. It involved no great skill: left foot just in front of the right foot and arms outstretched for balance. With each slide the strip became glassier and then it became a competition to see who could slide furthest. On a moonlit November night it was magnificent, although it was murder on our boots and shoes. Footwear must have cost our parents a fortune. By the time you had spent a month sliding, playing football and kicking stones and tin cans all the way from home to school (and back), your shoes were knackered. They were the one thing you never outgrew and never passed on. You could only throw them away.

When snow came, a whole new set of options presented itself. You could still slide on the road, once the cars had flattened the snow. But the main thing was that you could sledge. Our houses were set on a steep hillside and in those days there were still several vacant, unfenced lots (allotments). It was ideal for what you, I suppose, would call tobogganing. The first half of the run was very steep, but it flattened out and eventually you came to a halt. Then you had to haul your sledge up the hill again, either for a fresh start or to give the next person his turn. As the day wore on the snow impregnated your trouser-legs till they eventually froze. Then your breeks became stiff as boards. These days and nights were magic: the camaraderie, the thrills and spills and the magnificent environment. It's said that old men are liable to think that the sun always shone when they were young. In my memory it was the moon. Sledging and good conditions went together. You couldn't sledge when it was raining. You could sledge only on bright, crisp days, when the temperature struggled to climb over zero; and on cold, clear nights, when the moon and the stars provided the only illuminations in a world to which electricity was as alien as apple trees and railway stations.

Today there's been soft, wet snow which turned instantly to slush. This afternoon it froze. But I'm afraid I have no intention of sledging. Shortly after I gave up being a theologian my feet stopped doing what my brain told them. I'm not sure whether that's a common withdrawal symptom, but I am sure of this: were I to venture outside, I'd trip on a snowflake. It's hard to convince people I wasn't always old. The trouble is I don't seem to have had anything in between youth and age. For the best years of my life I was a boy minister, too young to be taken seriously. Then, one morning, I was an old minister: too old to be taken seriously. It would have been nice to have had a little time being just the right age.

But as I look out today, on a bleak November afternoon, and think of my own unsteady feet, my mind goes back to my first remembered New Year and a trivial incident which for some absurd reason I've never forgotten. It was our first winter in Laxdale, and the very first time New Year had been anything special. Whether it was the War, or just the town of Stornoway, they never seemed to have the New Year there. But this night in 1945 there was a definite buzz among these old folk. Suddenly, there was a knock at the door and an urgent message: "Thuit Iain Mòr!" ("Big John has fallen!").

This was utterly beyond my comprehension. I knew Iain Mòr well enough. He was the father of Angie MacLennan, owner of the world's greatest sledge, and, as I later learned, had once been a policeman - too benign by far to shine in such a profession. He stayed around in my childhood. At one time, he bought a horse and a very handsome gig which he submitted to the unimaginable indignity of using it to go round the village every morning selling herring. He was also a great benefactor of the human race (and of me in particular). He discovered a well in his own lot, next door to ours, brought it up to commercial standards and allowed us all to use it, saving us the dreaded journey to Roompie's Well, a quarter of a mile 'in' the road.

What I couldn't understand was why it should matter that Iain Mòr, or anyone else for that matter, had fallen. I was falling all the time and I was to become even better at it when I started learning to cycle; better still once I had learnt. In fact, I was so good at it that my grandfather, whose English had been picked up from the Doric of the East Coast, once said to me in exasperation, "You're always felling!" For years my knees had the scars to prove it, but there's some time since I've seen them and I'll just have to trust my memory.

But I've more sympathy with Iain Mòr now. He was big. In fact, he was very big; and although he was no drunkard, he'd been celebrating, and he was in no position to lift himself or even to make a contribution. How the problem was resolved I never knew, but I've never forgotten what a crisis it was to grown-ups nor what a wonder it was to me.

From that night onwards, New Year remained special, and for all the magic of Christmas, we boys were soon discussing in a most adult way, "What do you like best, Christmas or New Year?" The grown-up thing always was to say, "New Year!" and I was saying it long before it was true.

Yet it was a very tame thing by your standards. We had no radio, far less television, to signal the end of the old and the beginning of the new. But we did have what I still think was infinitely better. On the stroke of midnight rockets from the lifeboat station would shoot into the sky and the sound of ships' sirens would suddenly pierce the night air: a kind of timeless, space-defying sound; an annually recurring symbol of both permanence and change; time and eternity. At the same moment the local Harris Tweed mills would sound their sirens (normally these sounded only at five to eight in the morning, presumably as a warning to employees that it was time to report for work). One of us (usually my father) would be delegated to watch and listen, and when the magical moment came, he would shout, "Siud a' chonocag!" ("There's the horn!" - in fact, many horns).

There was nothing extravagant about the ensuing celebrations. The only remarkable thing was that the deacon who lived next door would arrive with his wife shortly after midnight, the men (including us boys) would have a whisky, the women would have port and this would be followed by tea and Christmas cake. The adults would talk, the kids would listen and a couple of hours would pass unnoticed. Sometimes, attracted by the light, a confused reveller would appear; or perhaps the victim of some slight motor accident looking for help. Such people were never turned away. I remember one of then remarking to my mother years later how unusual it seemed. Other folk 'with the *cùram*' would give them a row and shove them out. She took them in and said nothing. That policy never changed. Years later, my younger brother was often turned out of his bed in the small hours of a Saturday morning to give a lift home to some stranded youth who had missed the last bus to Ness or the West Side.

Apart from that, there was little excitement. There was a New Year's Day Service in the church in Stornoway, but it was not part of our routine to go to it (probably because it involved a three mile walk each way). The only thing that could qualify as a major drama would be a fight among the tinkers who lived in their tents a few hundred yards out the road. These were regular Hogmanay occurrences, but by the time we reached they were usually over.

I discovered afterwards that my parents' practices would have been seriously frowned on by some of our co- religionists. We were never under any oath of secrecy and I'm sure that we talked fairly freely about how we brought in the New Year. But long after I had left home my parents ran into the kind of sanctimonious legalism that was later to become the bane of the Church. One night in early January they were visited by a couple from Stornoway, both of them members in the Church.

They spent a while talking and my mother went out to make tea. But first she had to 'give them the New Year'. She came in with a glass of sherry each and a piece of Christmas cake. They were most offended, and most offensively self-righteous. They never took such a thing! And the previous minister had warned them that if he discovered that any of his church members 'had it in the house' they would be taken to the Session.

The mortification cut deep and the risk of giving sherry to any but the closest acquaintances was never taken again. What a load of nonsense! And what gives religious obsessives the power to make other people feel guilty over trifles?

Take care.

Yours
DM

11. Simpletons

15 December 2022

Dear Mme Quessaud

You are very patient; and too kind. What you should really have said was that my letter about oral tradition quickly went off at a tangent and I ended up dreaming of summer days at the rocks of Holm when I should have been answering your urgent questions about the legendary figures of our childhood. But remember, we have an understanding: being old and demented covers a multitude of sins.

There's no doubt that Evangelicalism breeds its own 'Lives of the Saints', even though the process is far less formal and our veneration far more limited than what prevails in Catholicism. The Evangelical counterpart of *Mac an t-Srònaich*, I suppose, was Aonghas nam Beann. His name cropped up often enough, but he always seemed a shadowy figure, and in those days I knew nothing of him except that he was some kind of saint who lived in the mountains of Uig (your mother's district) and that he was a man of great faith but little intellect.

That was a very powerful paradigm in Lewis religion, and it was totally paradoxical. Evangelicalism was highly doctrinal and therefore emphatically cerebral. Yet 'head-knowledge' was always scorned and the mystic invariably more highly esteemed than the intellectual. I was born and bred to such a paradigm and it came as a huge shock to me when I discovered through the American scholar, J G Machen, that disparagement of the intellect was the hallmark of Modernism, not of biblical Christianity. What would the bodaich have thought if I'd told them they were quintessential Modernists! When I read Machen I was well on the way towards a kind of existential escapism, seeking refuge from the intellectual difficulties of Christianity by fleeing into experience and feeling: a world where you didn't need to bother about difficulties in the Bible because what mattered was that it became God's word when it 'spoke' to you. Machen showed me that whatever else Christianity was, it was first and foremost a body of truths.

In later life I had the pain of another revolution. Having spent my strength insisting on the primacy of doctrine and judging other churches and other Christians merely by their creed (or by the lack of it), I learned that the highest orthodoxy could co-exist with undiluted wickedness; and, conversely, that a Christ-like attitude could often be found among all shades of theological opinion. It became my fixed view that humility without orthodoxy was infinitely more biblical than orthodoxy without humility (although lack of orthodoxy is not in itself a guarantee of humility. Heresy has its own orthodoxy and can often be as arrogant and intolerant as the most rigid bigotry).

It certainly never harmed Aonghas nam Beann's reputation that his intellectual grasp was minimal. As I said, the oral tradition by my time was not rich in detail, but I looked him up a few days ago in my old, battered copy of a book by Norman C. Macfarlane called The 'Men' of the Lews. The book itself is something of a puzzle. It is pure anecdote, with no indication of sources or authorities, but in the case of many of these 'Men' it is the only account or even reference that we have. The oral tradition surrounding these men seems to have been very short-lived. They were remembered as personalities, not for what they said or did; for what they were, rather than for what they achieved. But their disappearance also says something about the culture itself. The Lewisman is often fiercely conservative, yet he has no interest in the past. Few buildings, whether church, house or broch, were left standing long enough to become ancient monuments. They would be demolished almost on principle. I knew the mood myself once, when my parents died. I had buried them: what would be the point or the compensation in preserving their house? Bury it, too, out of my sight! It was the same with people. Men would be remembered by those who had known them. Once these had gone, the memory of even the greatest would turn to dust. Without literature and documentation there is no history, and without history there is no people. Is that why the Gael was liquidated so easily: because his greatest music, stories, songs and even sermons were never written down? A whole civilisation fell by the principle 'When we were young, we weren't interested, and by the time we were interested everyone who knew had gone.' My grandfather would certainly have known men who knew Aonghas nam Beann. But I never asked.

Aonghas nam Beann ('Angus of the Hills') is described by MacFarlane as 'a converted simpleton': so simple, in fact, that he himself didn't know whether he was Angus Macleod or Angus Maclennan; and so simple that Alexander Macleod, the minister of Uig, refused to admit him to Communion 'on the ground of intellectual incapacity'. This was beyond being ridiculous. It might make some sense to refuse a man admission to church on the ground that he wouldn't be able to understand the sermon, but the power of the Lord's Supper doesn't depend on intellectual capacity. Indeed, someone whose intellect was unable to grasp propositional truth might well find the sacrament particularly suited to his needs. But Macleod, as Macfarlane points out, was a dictator and the whole Kirk Session supported him. When he first came to the parish, there were upwards of 800 people on the Communion Roll, but in view of their spiritual state Macleod decided to refrain from holding Communion services.

When he eventually did hold one, on 25 June, 1827 (three years after his arrival), only six communicants came forward. Macleod himself wrote, "The whole of the unworthy communicants kept back, and a great many of our young converts did not take upon them to come forward."

With such an attitude to his own role as custodian of the Table, it's not surprising, I suppose, that Macleod refused admission to Aonghas nam Beann. On the other hand, he tried to improve the situation by arranging for someone to teach Angus to read. These efforts were a total failure. Angus was first set to learn the alphabet. He proceeded successfully from a to b, but, Macfarlane says, there was no room in his mind for a third letter and the attempt had to be abandoned. I suspect it was as much lack of motivation as lack of ability. Angus insisted that the whole effort was pointless because he couldn't find Christ in these letters.

Another story circulated, however, which suggests that at a later point Angus may have become a communicant. During one of his visits to a Communion season in a neighbouring congregation, he was found on Sunday morning on his hands and knees on the brow of a peat-bank, scratching and searching frantically. A friend instantly realised what was wrong: Angus had lost his Communion token. The friend asked him in Gaelic, "Have you lost your token?" "No," said Angus, "but I've lost that piece of lead they gave me!"

That needs a bit of explanation. In the old days, when huge crowds used to gather at Communion seasons (as I said in a previous letter, according to one estimate over 9,000 people once attended a Communion service - this was in Uig), the local elders had to have some way (or so they thought) of making sure that only bona fide church members came forward to the Table. This led to an arrangement whereby every congregation had its own little pewter 'tokens', usually rectangular in shape, about one inch long and three-quarters of an inch deep. They would bear the name of the host congregation and perhaps a text ('This do in remembrance of me'). These would be given out to members of the host congregation in a brief ceremony at the close of the Preparatory Service on Saturday. Non-communicants would leave, the doors would be closed, the local minister would offer a short prayer and as the people filed out the minister would shake hands with each one and give him or her a token. There were separate arrangements for visitors. Quantities of tokens were given to elders from neighbouring congregations for distribution to those of their own members who were present. On Sunday morning when people filed to the Table, they handed these tokens to elders who were acting as, virtually, ushers.

It was this token that Aonghas nam Beann had lost. But there was another twist to the story. The Gaelic word for token, *comharradh*, is ambiguous. It can mean a token or it can mean a mark. In Gaelic spirituality it had a technical sense in both meanings. As 'token' it was specifically a Communion token, a kind of ecclesiastical passport or human warrant to come to the Lord's table. As 'mark' it was a mark of grace: a divine warrant to take your place at the Lord's Table. Aonghas nam Beann was deliberately playing on the double meaning of the word. He hadn't lost the warrant God had given him. All he had lost was the piece of lead (pewter) that men had given him.

Such sharp wit belied Aonghas nam Beann's reputation as a simpleton. One day in Stornoway a man introduced to Angus looked at him superciliously and remarked, "Aren't you the Uig fool?" "No," said Angus. "The Bible says the fool is the man who says in his heart there is no God!"

On another occasion he was asked to engage in public prayer but he felt himself completely out of sorts (spiritually) and protested that he couldn't. "Come on," said the minister sharply. "Jonah prayed when he was in the belly of the whale." "Yes, minister," retorted Angus, "but today I've got the whale in my belly!"

There is of course a superficial parallel between the story of Aonghas nam Beann and the story of *Mac An t-Srònaich* in that both were wanderers in the hills of Uig. Some day, I suppose, some scholar will argue that they were both mythical figures, the one a pagan hero, the other an evangelical one. But the parallels won't take us far. Aonghas nam Beann was real enough to Alexander Macleod of Uig.

Yet he raises an interesting question: the relation between intellect and spirituality. Aonghas nam Beann would never have passed an examination in theology. He probably wouldn't even have passed a very basic one in Bible knowledge. Yet all accounts suggest that he was a charismatic figure marked by that holiness which simultaneously intimidates and fascinates. He was neither numerate nor literate and seems even to have lacked basic survival skills. Yet his Christian faith didn't affect him merely at an affective, social or emotional level. It affected him and transformed him in that very area where, by natural endowment, he was hopeless: verbal reasoning. This appears to some extent in the two or three anecdotes I mentioned above. In repartee, he was nobody's fool. But it appears even more in the fact that when engaging in extemporaneous public prayer Angus could carry large congregations with him to the very gates of heaven, setting words to what they felt and wanted and feared in a way that they themselves never could. The Uig fool may well have been closer to God than the Uig minister.

It was this ability of laymen to soar to heights of liturgical eloquence that Donald MacAulay (himself a native of the parish of Uig) had in mind in his poem, 'Soisgeul 1955':

dh'èisd mi ris an ùrnaigh
seirm shaorsainneil, shruthach –
iuchair-dàin mo dhaoine.

I listened to the prayer
a liberating, cascading melody –
my people's access to poetry.

I doubt if Aonghas nam Beann really was devoid of intelligence. Something (dyslexia or the like) had merely choked its normal channels. But certainly there have been many instances of men and women in whom the grace of faith and the life of holiness have existed alongside serious mental incapacity. Not that such things are easily measured, of course. No test can measure potential as distinct from performance. Children (very young children) can have faith long before they have any capacity for propositional knowledge. So, too, can people suffering from Down's Syndrome.

I don't know if you've ever heard of Dr Alexander Stewart of Cromarty. Probably not (and silly to ask!). He was Minister of Cromarty at the time of the Disruption of 1843 and today he is remembered, if at all, only because his congregation included Hugh Miller, the famous geologist and campaining journalist. One of those converted during Stewart's ministry was a young lad called Hector Munro, who had 'the very least intellect consistent with sanity'. Stewart was a man of massive intellect and he kept none of it back when he preached. Indeed, Miller's obituary notice of him contained the remarkable comment, 'Coleridge was not more thoroughly original, nor could he impart to his pictures more vividness of colouring, or more decided strength of outline'. Yet the same flights of intellect which stimulated the faith of Hugh Miller also fed the soul of Hector Munro. What is more remarkable still, Stewart confessed himself indebted to Munro. "I have been edified by his words," he said, "yes, and I have been on occasion instructed by them, and I have often been comforted by them."

I really shouldn't be lingering over this as if there were anything remarkable in it. Faith in our heavenly Father isn't essentially different from faith in our earthly ones. A child who is capable of the one is equally capable of the other, even though she could offer no answer to questions about her parents' dates of birth, marriage, genealogies or academic records. At one level, an employer may know far more about a man than his daughter knows. But the daughter has far more faith. That is the peril of the theologian: confusing propositional with personal knowledge. My hope was that through the former I could lead people to the latter. Yet I always knew that many a fool knew God better than I did.

In my own day there was nobody quite in the category of Aonghas nam Beann. There were, however, men who were prominent in religious circles and yet were illiterate. I still have a clear memory of an evening in 1959 when I was in a company in the village of Back during a Communion season. The conversation was leaden, and when a certain star elder suddenly dropped in there was universal relief. When he rose to leave they pled with him to stay, using the astonishing argument "There's no one here who can read!" (to take the Books). It was facetious, but only half so. It could have been true. There were at least two men in these circles even in my day who certainly could not read. That didn't prevent their being extremely highly regarded. It wasn't, however, that they were highly thought of despite their intellectual limitations. They were both very cerebral men, their memories packed with Scripture, their theological insight keen, their dialectic sharp and their powers of expression far above the average. Their illiteracy was due to circumstances, not to defect. When they became Christians they became students (albeit entirely dependent on oral instruction), and their intellectual rebirth was as remarkable as their spiritual.

One of these was John Murray, of Habost, Ness, known locally as Iain Foilidh (I have no idea what the nickname meant, or even of the proper spelling). He was a contemporary and near neighbour of my mother's and had lost an eye at some point in childhood or adolescence. His background was poor and his education minimal; so minimal in fact that his sister, Seonag, had serious difficulty in distinguishing Gaelic from English. So, at least, legend had it. There was a story that one day she was late for school and was reported to the Headmaster. Asked why she was late, she wasn't allowed like a child anywhere else in Britain to reply in her own native language. She had to reply in English: "Please sir, it was rogie-rogie coming over the moor!" The real reason, probably, was that there was no clock in the house. Instead, she blamed the frost (Gaelic *reothadh*).

Out of that background came John Murray. He was one of two or three men I have known who stood out as living proofs of the divine. In the darkest days of doubt I would think of him and ask, How do you account for Iain Foilidh? The life of God was in his soul and it shone through in a remarkable blend of fun and solemnity, practicality and spirituality, cheerfulness and self-deprecation. In the generation before mine, saints seem to have been objects of terror. Legend has it that if a child saw a minister she would hide behind a peatstack. I certainly remember my dear Auntie Annie telling me that if she ever had to visit her grandfather at the other end of the village, she would choose a circuitous route round the back of the crofts to avoid having to walk past the home of an elder. My generation never had such feelings (except for the policeman and for the school-master). In the case of a man like John Murray they would have been entirely inappropriate. Whatever he may have been feeling inside (and I'm sure he had his own share of private grief and spiritual depression), he always seemed to be beaming, and children loved him.

Many, many years ago, in a seminar on Thomas Hog, the outstanding Highland minister of the 17th century, one of my students remarked how little importance seemed to be attached to Good Works in Highland spirituality. It seems a simple enough observation, but it quite threw me. Not that people were much given to judging other people's spirituality, but they were much given to judging their own: 'taking their spiritual pulse', we used to call it. Someone like Hog would look at his fervour and liberty in prayer, his relish of scripture, his sense of communion with God, his assurance of the divine love, and would then note either the encouragement or the discouragement he derived from such surveys. But the principle 'By their works you shall know them' does seem to have played little or no part in such analysis. Feeding the hungry, clothing the naked, visiting the sick and generally showing concern for the poor were simply taken for granted, rather than as key elements in the spiritual inventory.

There probably were Christians whose whole idea of discipleship was to attend meetings, attend spiritual ceilidhs and observe all the taboos. But John Murray was certainly not one of them. He earned his living as a kind of casual skilled labourer, mainly on such jobs as harling walls and pointing stonework. His evenings he spent visiting the sick. Gaelic spirituality did a very interesting thing with the sick. It called them *na prìosanaich* 'the prisoners', on the basis, of course, that Providence had given them a custodial sentence by confining them to home or to bed and thus making it impossible for them to go to church. This allowed us to argue that all visits to housebound invalids were in fact compliances with Jesus's principle 'I was in prison and you visited me'. Many people did it, of course, but most did it casually, visiting their friends and the homes it was always a pleasure to visit. John did it systematically and indiscriminately, out of conscience.

But he had to be back home every night by 10.30. You might think such a curfew a very odd thing for a grown man, but you mustn't assume that in those days it was dead easy to be a Christian and that such men as John Murray would carry enormous kudos in a community. That wasn't the case. Even then there were some in Ness who were outright atheists, bitterly opposed to the church. There were many others who kept Christians under constant surveillance, noting their every fault and inconsistency and branding their religion as hypocrisy.

In some ways this was a fault of the legalism that was never far away from the spirituality itself. If you laid down rules for church members, every breach would be noticed, and Ness was particularly bad for this. Legend has it that my great-grandfather, Aonghas Alasdair (Thomson), once severely rebuked his minister, Rev Roddy John Macleod, for being so frivolous as to leap over a gate. This was conduct unbecoming a minister. In a way, it served the ministers right. They were sometimes over-given to 'magnifying their office'. A story about one of the most revered of them, Rev Hector Cameron, Back, gives a good illustration of this. Like most ministers, he kept sheep on his glebe and one day he had some men in to shear them. He watched as they worked, showing an obvious interest. "Would you like to have a go yourself, minister?" said one of the men helpfully. Cameron drew himself up to his full height: "I wouldn't stoop to such a degradation of my office!" Can you account for that? How could a spiritual shepherd show such contempt for the model on which his work is based or grandly refuse to identify with a calling of which David himself was proud? I suppose that by the same token a minister would refuse to cut a piece of wood, even though his Saviour was a carpenter. It's hardly surprising that, having given the people such simple tests of clerical decorum and propriety, ministers could cause grave offence by, for example, being seen in their gardens without their dog-collars.

But the censoriousness wasn't directed only against ministers. The people could be equally severe on each other, and once again my great-grandfather seems to have been one of the worst offenders. Like the rest of his contemporaries, he was a crofter-fisherman and, as you probably know, fishing off the Butt of Lewis is a hazardous business, even for large modern vessels. In the days of small, open boats it was close to foolhardy. It wasn't merely that men could fall victim to storms far out to sea. They could often make it safely all the way to the harbour (if it deserved that name), find it impossible to enter and be forced to stand offshore for hours.

One Saturday, my great-grandfather found himself in this position and, strange though it may sound, his main worry was that he wouldn't get home before the Sabbath. Eventually they did, but only just. Indeed, it was so close to midnight that he had no time to shave (it was *de rigeur* that you didn't shave on the Sabbath). Off he went to church in the morning with a few days' stubble, looking pretty dreadful, I suspect, but enjoying the compensations of a warm glow of self-righteousness. What did he find? His crewman and fellow-elder clean shaven! He couldn't possibly have got home before midnight! They had a terrific blowout and went months without speaking.

You can see, then, where my legalism came from. In fact, it was so pronounced in my great-grandfather's case that he was nicknamed 'Seumas' (after the Apostle James, the most Jewish of the apostles, whose epistle Martin Luther dismissed as an epistle of straw, not fit to be counted part of the real canon of the New Testament). At least, so I was told. What I can certainly vouch for is that my grandfather, who was baptised pure and simple 'Angus', was known as 'Seumas' throughout his life. But then, he was never an elder, nor even a church member. He was a tough character physically and mentally, abstemious, frugal, rigorously methodical and self-disciplined, and he could be stern enough. But he never shook off the spiritual shadow of his father.

Sorry for wandering away from Iain Foilidh, but he had to live with this kind of censorious scrutiny within his own home. He had a brother, known locally as the Gaisean, who never went to church or indeed anywhere else. The Gaisean never did a stroke, but he was an expert on how other people should live. He knew all the standards professed by Christians and gleefully informed John of every deviation he found. Hence John's need to be home by 10.30. The Gaisean was of the opinion that in the good old days of real Christians it had been a rule with all the godly men that wherever they were they must be home by 10.30 to take family worship. I've a suspicion he got this idea from my great-grandfather. My own grandfather certainly took a poor view of elders whose families had to go to bed before their fathers returned home from their spiritual ceilidhs. The Gaisean had no relish for family worship, but he had a real relish for spoiling his brother John's pleasure. Every night he would sit up till 10.30 waiting for John to come home. Were he a minute late, he'd be off to bed. The following day the atmosphere would be heavy with a triumphant sense of disapproval and dark mutterings about 'the Christians of today'. John put up with it, perhaps even too meekly, hoping throughout his life (vainly, as it turned out) that his patience would eventually break down his brother's opposition to Christianity.

When John Murray died, my mother wrote an elegy for him. I still have it, and half an hour ago, while having my coffee, I read it through again. It is certainly nothing to be ashamed of, but one of the abiding regrets of my life is that I was ashamed, or at least embarrassed, when it was published in the *Stornoway Gazette* those eighty years ago. It wasn't her only such venture, but I never gave her the encouragement she deserved. Even tonight, almost a century later, the memory of that is almost unbearable. In a way, it was the genre I was embarrased about. These things were usually little more than biblical quotations strung along on lines of doggerel. But had I looked, I would have seen that this one catches its subject to the life.

I mustn't bore you with this, but the opening lines of the poem are, I think, exceedingly interesting (the elegy is in Gaelic, of course). She is heartbroken as she realises that John is no longer in Ness, 'where her spirit used to meet him and come back full'. This meeting wasn't the result of her making a trip to Ness and paying John a visit. It was a meeting of spirits, she in Laxdale and he in Ness; and to them it was somehow deeply refreshing. Can you understand that? It was something often spoken of in Lewis spirituality.

No such mystic gifts were ever passed on to me, though when I disgrace myself by falling asleep (and snoring) in public, I do often console myself with the thought that people think I'm in deep meditation.

Goodnight
D Macleod

22 January 2023

Dear Mme Quessaud

Strange your letter should arrive today, when my head was already full of thoughts of Canada. Somebody phoned up with a question about one of the old Highland ministers, John Kennedy of Redcastle (Killearnan, a parish in Easter Ross), and this led me to think of Rev Norman Macleod, the famous Separatist (I'm sure I told you about him some time ago). It may seem a strange connection, but at one point Kennedy served as Assistant Minister in the parish of Assynt. It was, on the whole, a very enjoyable experience, but there were two problems. One was that his boss, the Senior Minister, was a notorious drunkard whose long absences deprived the parish not only of its minister but also of its piper, who followed the minister wherever he went. The other was that Assynt was the birthplace of Norman Macleod and a natural target for his Separatist forays. Many locals joined his movement and many more would have done so were it not for Kennedy (although, from my own experience, a strong Separatist strain remained even among the people who stayed in the church).

I did once spend some time in Cape Breton, where Macleod and his people settled as uninvited guests among the Mic-Maq Indians. But Cape Breton, of course, is not Quebec, nor even typical of the rest of Canada. You wouldn't believe how frustrating it is to be unable to picture you or your mother in your own 'native' environment.

I'm intrigued that she had tapes of Gaelic psalmody. She always conveyed the impression that she had no interest in such things. Was it pure nostalgia that made her keep the tapes, or do you think it was something deeper? Most Lewis-folk of our generation became fluent English-speakers, but for both your mother and me Gaelic was the first language we heard and the first language we spoke. That meant that it always knew a shortcut to our hearts. This was particularly true of anything which combined Gaelic and music.

I can understand your being enthralled by the psalmody. It needs a large congregation, however (they probably had that when they did the recording you listened to). In a small congregation there are far fewer grace-notes, and because of that they don't blend half so well. Instead of the famous 'waterfall effect' you can get something more like a pack of cats screeching.

I'm not sure I can tell you a great deal about its origin and history. About sixty years ago I did try to do some research on it but there was very little documentation, and those who did have some knowledge (notably the School of Scottish Studies) were jealous for their own intellectual capital (although that particular phrase hadn't been invented then) and desperate to keep whatever they knew to themselves.

The most obvious thing about Gaelic precenting, of course, is the practice of 'putting out the line'. It used to fascinate me as a little child. A man used to stand up in church, in a box below the minister's, and every half-minute or so a peculiar noise came from him. Everybody called him 'White'. I had a vague idea that this was a colour, but wasn't entirely sure whether this particular White was a man or a machine. He held something in front of his face (later I learned that this was a book and later still that it was a Gaelic psalter) and I concluded that it was this book which made the noise. I had no objection to the noise, but the whole thing was most peculiar. You couldn't see anything of White's face and had no reason to believe that his mouth was open or that his lips and tongue were moving and making that noise. You certainly never saw a White or heard that particular noise anywhere else. They were confined to the church.

You know how I love digressions. Would you mind if I went off on another one? Many years later, when I was a relatively experienced minister, I was in the Free Church manse in North Tolsta (probably at a Communion season). One day during the weekend, among those who came for either dinner or tea was a man I recognised instantly: Donnie White. "Hello, Mr White," I said, in my most respectful voice (he was a schoolmaster). "Hello!" he said. A few hours later I learned that he wasn't Mr White at all. He was Mr Macleod, the son of White, the mysterious precentor of my childhood.

In a culture full of nicknames that was something of an occupational hazard. There was a very fine lady in Laxdale, a widow, who was known as Bean Wayne (literally, 'Wayne's wife'). In Gaelic, of course, she would never have been addressed like that. She would have been addressed by her Christian name. But many's the person who addressed her as Mrs Wayne. I probably did it myself. But she was no relation of the famous John (although other Lewis people were). She was Mrs Maclean.

She had relations who caused us even more problems - the Wedgers, a most distinguished Laxdale family. I knew that it was a nickname and that their real name was Mackay, but many did not. The best known of them, Roddy Mackay, was one of my first Sunday School teachers and for many years an elder in Stornoway Free Church. One young father, not local, went to his house once in connection with a baptism, knocked the door and blithely asked, "Is Mr Wedger in?" How could you expect a man from Carlisle to know that the mere fact that a man was known as Roddy Wedger was no proof that he was Mr Wedger, any more than a man's being known as Billy Goat meant that he was Mr Goat? The *faux pas* broke the solemnity of many a prayer-meeting: "Will Mr Wedger please lead us in prayer?"

Anyway, I eventually realised that it wasn't White's book that made the noise. A little further reflection and I even realised it was White himself (although by this time White was probably dead). But this didn't really take me very far. We had singing in school, but precenting seemed a long way from singing. One night I suddenly cried 'Eureka (or I would have cried it if I had known that that's what you were supposed to say when you had made a great scientific breakthrough): "In Gaelic precenting you sing one line of music to four lines of verse."

My parents were extremely impressed by my brilliance in solving such a mystery, and it was, of course, a very plausible theory in view of the fact that it took longer to sing one line of Gaelic than a whole verse of English. But it had the weakness of all my other original theories: it wasn't true.

After that I gave up, and after a few years, as often happens, the truth crept up on me unawares. I am probably the only one in the world to whom it was ever a problem. A precentor like White was simply a pre-chanter. He sang the line first, very quickly; and then the congregation sang it, much more slowly. There is nothing at all intrinsically Gaelic or Celtic about the practice. Nor was it invented for any musical or artistic reason. It was pure practicality. When the Reformation made congregational singing a standard element in public worship, the churches faced a serious problem: few people would know all 150 psalms off by heart, few were able to read and fewer still could afford books. The only solution was for the precentor to 'give out the line' or 'line out the psalm', and the congregation would then sing after him one line at a time.

It used to be said that this was not the practice in the early Reformed church in Scotland: a disclaimer that was usually linked to the boast that the Scots were much better educated than the English, and could read. Anyone who knows anything of the state of parish schools in Scotland in the 16th and 17th centuries will take such claims with a pinch of salt. Knox may have dreamed of a school in every parish, but his dream was thwarted by the greed of Scotland's so-called noble families.

What is certain is that the Directory for the Public Worship of God issued by the Westminster Assembly and adopted by the Church of Scotland in 1645 explicitly endorsed the practice of putting out the line. Admittedly, it wasn't entirely happy about it and made very plain that ideally everyone ought to be able to read and everyone ought to have a psalm-book. "But for the present, where many in the congregation cannot read, it is convenient that the minister, or some other fit person appointed by him and the other ruling officers, do read the psalm, line by line, before the singing thereof."

This, of course, was an English publication intended originally for use by the Church of England (which still has its own kind of precentors. Their primary qualification, apparently, is perfect pitch: not something always deemed essential in the Highlands). Whether it was an innovation in Scotland I am not sure. I certainly never came across any evidence that the very eminent Scottish theologians who attended the Westminster Assembly were upset about it, although it did offend exceedingly those who founded the Scoto-Catholic wing of the Kirk in the 19th century. They blamed it for the very poor standard of Scottish psalmody.

The practice of giving out the line persisted in Lowland Scotland until well into the 18th century, and by all accounts these Goill didn't do it very well. There is one story of a worshipper who entered a church late and heard a psalm being sung to an unfamiliar strain. "What tune are they singing?" he asked his neighbour. "I dinna ken," came the reply, "but I'm at the Auld Hundert!" On another occasion, a Highland minister visiting a Lowland church remarked that when the singing of the psalm ceased he was reminded of a phrase in the Book of Acts (referring to the riot at Ephesus): 'when the uproar was ceased'. Another Lowland worthy objected vehemently to a new tune called *Devizes* because it repeated the last line. In the course of time his objections, so long unheeded, ceased. Then another revolution occurred: *Devizes* without the repeat. The old man protested as vehemently as in his youth. But he went further than mere protest. Whenever the new, truncated upstart was sung, he stuck to the ways of his fathers and sang the repeat as they had done before him. A visiting minister, intrigued by the solo at the end of every verse, sought an explanation. It was duly given and the visitor pronounced himself satisfied. "I see," he said, "you just leave him to his own Devizes."

But a mortal blow against Lowland precenting was struck by the General Assembly of 1746. It recommended 'the ancient practice of singing without reading the line'. Very diplomatic language, as you can see: invoke tradition to bring in the revolution! If the Assembly were expecting trouble, they were right. Change came exceedingly slowly. Twenty years later it was still a matter of comment that a certain Edinburgh church had 'begun to sing every Sunday without reading the line.' All over the country that traditional Scottish virtue, 'resistance to change', asserted itself. In many parts of the country people forsook the parish churches in droves to join the Seceders. In others, people prevented from enjoying their ancient practice in church continued it in their own homes, where no-one could meddle with them.

On one or two occasions in my own distant past I heard the lining-out of the psalms in English. In the parish of Lochcarron, for example, in the 1960s, it was still a standard practice at funerals. The reason, again, was entirely practical: the vast majority of mourners were gathered outside the house of the deceased, without Bibles or psalm-books, and the only way they could join in the singing was if someone gave out the line. The Free Presbyterian Church, even as late as the 1980s, continued the practice of giving out the line (in English), but only in a Communion Service. In both of these contexts, however, the whole mode had been profoundly influenced by the Gaelic style, and it was melodious, harmonious and deeply moving.

But it still mystifies me: how did something so distinctly alien come to be so deeply identified with Gaelic life and culture? At one level it's easy enough to understand. Although a complete Gaelic Psalter was available as early as 1694, very few Highlanders could read; and of those who could, few had the money to buy books. This was the very situation which had made 'giving out the line' necessary in England in the first place, and the early Evangelical preachers in the Highlands simply accommodated to Gaelic a practice already well established in the Lowlands.

We didn't simply adopt it, however. We transformed it and turned it into one of the most distinctive aspects of Gaelic culture. What always puzzled me was that all the raw materials were English. The Gaelic psalms were in ballad stanza: common enough in English, but alien to Gaelic. The tunes (*Kilmarnock, Bangor, Martyrdom, Coleshill* and the like) were English, at least in the sense that they belonged to the Sassenachs of the South Country. A few (*French, London New, Dundee* and *Martyrs*) may have been as old as the Covenanters, and all of them may have had their origins in the Celtic airs of mediaeval Scotland. But none was composed by Gaels.

It wasn't merely the way of putting out the line that the Gaels transformed. They transformed the tunes themselves: so much so that people who are perfectly familiar with the tune as sung in English sometimes cannot recognise it when it is sung in Gaelic. The most obvious difference is that the singing is much slower. This has nothing to do with simply dragging out the notes. It is due to the Celt's talent for embellishment. That talent appears in the ancient Celtic crosses and in such extraordinary works of art as the *Book of Kells.* But it also appears in Gaelic psalmody, where the bare bones of the original tune are fleshed out with an astonishing number and variety of grace-notes. I was told once that in a large congregation there could be as many as sixteen grace-notes on a single beat.

The other side of this is the total spontaneity. Within the limits of the basic notation every singer is doing her own thing, expressing her feelings, improvising and yet listening to all the music around her so that her own note blends in with the rest. In some ways this was the most charismatic or Pentecostal feature of Lewis religion. You would never have found these people clapping their hands or dancing or even shouting, 'Hallelujah!' or 'Praise the Lord!' In fact, the story used to go the rounds of a visitor who punctuated one Highland church service with regular outbursts of 'Hallelujah! Praise the Lord!' and had to be silenced by an elder, who told him, "We don't praise the Lord in this church." But when they sang their psalms, inhibitions vanished and the cares of the world were either forgotten or released. Every time a psalm was sung it was quite literally a new song. She had never sung it exactly that way before; and she would never sing it that way again.

It always seemed to me that that there were remarkable parallels between this kind of spiritual music and the music of America's Deep South. Twenty years ago, some Afro-American scholars who discovered Gaelic psalmody explained these parallels in terms of the contacts between Gaelic exiles and the black population of the American south. I never followed up the theory, but it always seemed to me more likely that the practice of putting out the line made its way to America with the early (English) Puritan settlers. By the 18th century these settlers, even in the northern states of Massachusetts and Connecticut, were certainly singing their psalms in a way that exposed them to exactly the same criticisms as were being levelled at their Scottish counterparts. One irreverent satirist even wrote that a woman had had a miscarriage as a result of the noise.

The spontaneity and improvisation characteristic of both Gaelic and Afro-American psalmody (in, for example, Alabama) probably owed a good deal to the parallel experiences of the two communities. Each had its Holocaust: the bitter experience of repression and violence, enforced emigration and racial hatred. Each endured it with remarkable passivity, partly because they were traumatised and partly because they were deeply schooled in patient endurance. Each went to church and sang: the one group their psalms, the other their spirituals and their blues. And as they sang, they invented, innovated and embellished, weeping into their songs, yearning into their music and assuring themselves that one day there would be deliverance. The result was, in the best sense, soul music.

What I'm not so sure about is whether there is a Gaelic version of Afro-American secular music. Certainly there was nothing like the African passion for instruments. But the song-output of the Gael is astonishing and these songs would have been sung with so many grace-notes as to make Marjory Kennedy-Fraser turn in her grave. Is there a connection between a jazz trombonist in New Orleans and a Highland woman singing her psalms?

As far as the actual precentor is concerned, his main task, obviously, was to give out the line (the first two lines were actually read out by the minister, presumably on the assumption that the congregation could remember two lines long enough to sing them: after that it was up to the precentor). The melody used for the purpose of putting out the line depended on the tune being sung. It could also vary from line to line. Sometimes, each line of the tune would have a precentor's melody all its own. In the case of *Stornoway*, for example, the more or less standard melody for each line was different. In the case of the great precentors, immersed simultaneously in the words, the melody and the responses of the congregation, each line became an utterly unpredictable, unrepeatable and unself-conscious work of art.

There were also regional variations. For example, there was a clear difference between the melodies and styles used in Lewis and those used in Skye, Sutherland and Wester Ross. The latter were much slower and lacked (at least to my ears) the smooth, liquid fluidity and skilful ornamentation which were features of all the best Gaelic singing. On occasion, mind you, the Lewis style could be picked up and imitated. My friend Rev Alasdair Macfarlane, for many years minister of Kilmuir in Skye, was an excellent precentor, and for years afterwards his influence could be clearly detected in the singing of some of the younger precentors in Skye, particularly those from his own congregation. These 'young' men, I have to say, are now long since gone.

But even within Lewis itself there were wide variations between the various precentors, reflecting the influence of some great precentor of the past or the teaching given in the local *sgoil fhonn*. The *sgoil fhonn* was not a singing class. It was a tune class. There might be some instruction in singing (my parents used to say they were taught to sit straight up, with their backs pressed against the seats). There might even be tuition in solfa or staff. But the main purpose was to teach the tunes, including putting out the line. I heard more than once that in these schools the view was taken that the actual words of the psalms were too sacred to be used for practice and that nonsense rhymes in ballad stanza were used instead. But I never came across this. By my time, I think, the reverse philosophy had set in: the tunes themselves were too sacred to be sung to anything but the psalms. Besides, many of the teachers in these tune schools were wise enough to know that one of the best aids to learning a tune was to link it closely and exclusively to a particular part of the Psalter. *Stornoway*, for example, was forever linked in my parents' minds with the words of the eightieth psalm:

> *Oir bheathaich thu do shluagh gu lèir*
> *le aran deur is bròin.*

> Thou tears of sorrow givs't to them
> instead of bread to eat.
> (Ps. 80 :5)

My own closest encounter with the practice of nonsense rhymes being sung to psalm tunes was a story recounted to me over sixty years ago about an Inverness comedian of the 1940s. One of his sketches was an irreverent skit on the area's very worst precentor (probably instantly recognisable to the audience). The sketch avoided the actual words of the Psalter. Instead, the 'precentor' sang, to the tune *Kilmarnock*, some verses of doggerel. Unfortunately, I can remember only two lines, but these alone must have been sufficient, in the context, to bring the house down:

He stole his father's coffin-lid
(first given out by the 'precentor', then sung by
the   audience), followed by
To make a hen-house door
(again, first 'precentor', then audience).

Bad precentors, you must remember, were always around, and they were seldom slow in putting themselves forward. Indeed, there was a proverb in the Highlands 'He's as willing as a bad precentor!'

But outstanding precentors, each with his own individual style, would have many imitators. In Back, for example, there was Donald Maciver (Dòmhnall na Criomaig), who had a very reassuring, no-nonsense, authoritative style which he passed on to men whose voices were sometimes much more melodious than his own (notably, Alasdair Graham). In Ness, there was Murdo MacDonald (Murchadh Darkie), who had a remarkably staccato, rapid and unembellished style. Out of its context, it would scarcely have sounded like music at all. In its context, as the facilitator of the praise of a great congregation, it was profoundly moving: partly because it had a kind of Sinai-like aura and partly because the precentor's stresses captivated exactly the emphases of the line. I think this must have gone back to an earlier generation of Niseachs, because my predecessor in Glasgow, Rev Malcolm Morrison, also had an unadorned but highly effective style. Someone, I suspect, had told them that a line of precenting should not sound like the line of a song, should not draw too much attention to itself and should confine itself to as few notes as possible.

Yet it would be wrong to say that this was the Ness style of precenting. To some extent, possibly, the variations were due to the different qualities and timbres of individual voices. Ness produced the most straightforward, unembellished precenting I ever heard (in the person of Murchadh Darkie). But it also produced the most ornate, liquid and grace-note-laden, in the person of Calum Macleod (Calum an Ùigich). The notes seemed to flow (almost coruscate) out of him. The mystery was that on the first hearing Calum sounded like a tenor. When you tried to sing with him, you realised that this voice with all its trills was in fact a very deep bass: a bass with the timbre of a tenor and utterly unlike anything I've ever heard before or since.

There could not have been two more different styles than those of the two Ness men, Murdo MacDonald and Calum Macleod. You could have said that each was the best; and yet you wouldn't have wanted to add 'in his own way'. But then, the moment you said that, you would have remembered Angus MacDonald, Aonghas Bhràgair or Aonghas Beag. You would have said that he, too, was the best; and not simply for a decade or two, but for the whole period from 1940 to 1990. Angus was one of those who emigrated to your part of the world on the *SS Metagama* in 1923. If memory serves, he worked first as a farmhand on the prairies and latterly in a tannery in Toronto. He returned to Lewis after the War, and by that time he was already, as far as precenting went, the finished article. His style was fluid and effortless, but less embellished and ornate than Calum Macleod's. The voice was a rich baritone, straying sometimes (when he got the pitch wrong) far above the reach of his congregation. Of all the Lewis precentors he had the widest repertoire of tunes. Few others sang *Stroudwater, Stracathro* and *St Paul* in Gaelic; and it was he who introduced *Free Church* and the repeating tune, *New Cambridge*, to Lewis congregations. As far as this last one was concerned, no one could precent it but himself, though many tried, and I often wished, perfervidly, that it had been confined to oblivion (along with *Moravia*, a German melody which no art could Celticise)

There was something very interesting, however, about the way that congregations sang these less familiar tunes. I did a simple experiment once (with a tape-recorder), checking the time it took to sing four verses of Gaelic psalmody to such old favourites as *Kilmarnock* and *Coleshill* against the time it took to sing the same number of verses to a new arrival such as *Free Church.* The new tunes were sung twice as quickly, for the obvious reason, I think, that the process of elaborating the melody by adding grace-notes was still at a very early stage. Gaelic psalm tunes evolve, each generation adding its own ornamentation until, I suppose, we reach the Omega-point.

All the precentors I've mentioned belonged to the Free Church. But the greatest single piece of precenting I ever heard (indeed, the greatest single item of music of any kind) was a recording of a Church of Scotland service from the High Church, Stornoway. I still have the tape. It was taken, I think, some time in the Fifties of last century and the precentor was John Macleod of Cross, in the parish of Ness. For some reason, John was known as 'The Professor'. I never knew him, but this particular recording of the hundredth psalm to the tune *Kilmarnock* is perfection itself. Something about it has often puzzled me. It seems to me to encapsulate the enraptured piety of the Gael at its most reverent and its most assured. Yet it lay on the very edge of the movement, within touching distance of its demise. Had this demise been due to some law of entropy, gradually but remorselessly robbing the movement of its strength, this piece could never have been recorded. It contains not one single sign of a system on the point of collapse. On the contrary, never, I am sure, did congregational praise in the Highlands rise to greater heights. Whenever I listen to the tape (and I still do so frequently), it strikes me as a photograph-in-sound, freezing into a two-minute slot the best of both the religion and the culture. It is a glorious pinnacle, especially in that moment when the precentor hits the high doh in the middle of the second and the third lines with glorious ease and unerring accuracy, and then holds them.

But the culture's descent was sheer. Night came without a twilight and no other generation would ever sing that way. The techniques would remain. Excellent precentors would still arise and there would still be moments which would inscribe themselves indelibly on memory and imagination: Neil Shaw in Back Free Church on a Sunday evening in 1959 leading a huge congregation to the tune *Montrose* and fusing the music to words which perhaps more than any other capture the vision of Judaeo-Christian theism: 'Air ceann do shluaigh tràth dh'imich thu';[1] Donald MacDonald (twenty-seven years of age) singing *Torwood* in Partick Highland Free Church days before he died almost fifty years ago ('They shall not grow old ...'. Beside his *Torwood* I can still hear the phone ringing to tell me he hadn't come round after the operation).

Yes, exceptional individuals remained. But the soul of the community had gone. The language and the religion had both become leisure pursuits: rooms to be visited once or twice a week. They would end up in monographs and under microscopes, not in the hearts of the people. But when our sun was setting another, no doubt, was rising; our ebb-tide, another's flood.

Take care,
D.

1   *O God, what time thou didst go forth*
     Before thy people's face   (Ps. 68:7)

13. Holidays and houses

18 April 2023

Dear Mme Quessaud

Your letter lit up my day. I sometimes wonder how little I know about you while at the same time sharing so many confidences. I have no wish to pry into your dear mother's life. Since she cannot tell me herself, it's maybe best not to be told at all. But your life is private too, and your research has to be kept as objective and impersonal as possible. I console myself with the thought that I am the world's oldest guinea-pig; and that I may be able to answer your queries while still remaining as elusive as Robert Browning. For you, a letter is but one of a hundred things to attend in a day. For me it can be the event of the month.

To take up your question: in adulthood, I never cared much for holidays. Work itself involved as much travel as I wanted and holidays meant that you had to work like mad to clear your desk before you went off and then work like mad to catch up once you got back. Holidays became something you had to recover from, even though they never consisted of anything other than 'going home' (to Lewis).

But in childhood it was different. Others saw to the preparations and others did the catching-up. Besides, you were going to a world of magic: Ness!

It had fireworks' displays, then, and Big Wheels and roller-coasters and illuminated streets and candle-lit processions and the Red Arrows? No! If I ever dreamed of something really exotic, it was a holiday in Glasgow and the chance of seeing Rangers (then the world's greatest soccer club). But you could do that only if you had relations in the city and money for the fare. I had neither.

So, Ness it was, then: only twenty-seven miles, but it was a two hours' drive and a whole world away. The bus had probably begun life in Lanarkshire twenty years previously, and after a few miles on the road, the engine (and the brakes) began to overheat and you continued the journey to the smell of burning rubber. It shoogled along the level bits, struggled up the hilly bits and free-wheeled down the brae bits, looking out anxiously all the while for sheep and oncoming traffic. To meet another bus or lorry was an emergency, which meant that you had to pull hard over to the side of the road, slow down to a crawl and juggle the steering-wheel like mad. A sheep? Well, no-one could anticipate what decision these silly animals would take. They could jump anywhere, and with the brakes that buses had in those days any animal on the road was at risk. Besides, if you killed a sheep, you had to stop and you had to report it the police: an infernal nuisance.

The road took you north-west to Barvas, and the first moment of magic was when you saw the Atlantic ocean. It's not that we never saw the sea. We lived overlooking Broad Bay, but Broad Bay was landlocked and calm; and even the far distance was limited by the mountains of the mainland. But the Atlantic was infinite, stretching as far as you could see, and it had breakers: waves that developed great white crests as they approached the shore and then thundered on to the rocks, sending up white cascades of spray and spume.

In Barvas, the terrain began to change as peaty moorland gave way to machair and grass, and sand took over from the heather. The houses, too, were different. Newmarket, a recent settlement, had only one black house. But Ness was an ancient settlement, densely populated ever since the days of the Norsemen, with an air of stability and timelessness that a suburban shanty-town like ours could never match. People were still being born on the same spot as their great-great-grandfathers, and although the houses themselves were frequently recycled, each generation built or re-built in the style of their ancestors. Even then, the mould was being broken, of course, and more and more proud, mason-built houses were rearing their roofs above the black-houses, but in the early 1940s there was still more thatch than slate. In Newmarket, one was never far from the heather, and the acid soil and the steep hillside made cultivation difficult. From Barvas onwards there were acres and acres of sandy loam and endless *feannagan* of corn, barley and potatoes.

Once past Barvas we began to look out for other landmarks. Today you can bypass London and fly over Chicago without noticing. On a 1940s bus-journey you experienced every bump: the bend and the bridge at Borve; the school at Galson; Sgeir Dhail (Dell Rock), a reef renowned for its ling and conger-eels; the mill in South Dell, and the sharp bend and steep brae as you crossed the bridge; Cross School (actually in North Dell), that my father had gone to; and the little river dividing Dell from Cross.

By this time we had passed 'the loch with the ghost': a shallow, reedy thing, very close to the road. In the old days people always ran past it, terrified lest they see the motor-cyclist with his goggles and greatcoat rise from the water. I met only one man who had ever seen the ghost. That was the Reverend Donald MacDonald, a distinguished Free Church minister who was a contemporary of my father's and a native of the same village, Cross. Then a young man, and walking home from Dell late one night, MacDonald faced the ghost with his usual unflinching courage, asked the ghost his name, and a few other personal questions. The ghost, deeming discretion the better part of valour, kept his mouth shut, and the future minister met with a stony silence. "The least you can do is speak when you're spoken to!" said MacDonald, and resumed his journey.

Cross was followed by Swainbost, the village between Cross and Habost, the birthplaces of my father and mother respectively. The parish of Ness was once dubbed the most densely populated rural area in Europe, and when you came to Swainbost you could see why. The crofts in Ness were almost all in by the shore, and in the old days that's where the houses were as well. But when the road was built from Stornoway to Port of Ness, the houses moved out to the road, far from their crofts. The ruins of the house where my grandfather and my father's oldest siblings were born were still to be seen on the old croft near the shore when I last looked. The new house, built in 1928, was a full mile away, and it stood, by some curious anomaly, on somebody else's croft: presumably a new one, carved out of the Common Grazings after the Great War.

In Cross and Habost the houses were built almost end-to-end, and the same was true in Swainbost, but with one important difference: there were so many houses that they had to build one row behind the other, on the Atlantic side; and when I say houses, I don't mean little cabins but substantial dwellings. It looked as if nobody wanted to leave the village, and once all the roadside building space was taken up they simply began to build two-, or even three-deep. Had you done that in Arnol, there'd have been a war. But Swainbost was as peaceful as Paradise. Siarachs are not like us.

Today, these villages support only a fraction of their old populations. This is no recent thing. Over fifty years ago most of the houses in Habost were either empty or occupied by one single, elderly person. In the 1940s, the village teemed with life, young and old. At No 1 Habost, there was Taigh Dhòmhnaill Sheocain, with three children just slightly older than myself. At No 2, there were the families of two brothers: Calum Alasdair Chaluim and Dòmhnall Alasdair Chaluim. In each of these again there were three children. We were at No 3, where there had been five children. No 4, separated by a drive just wide enough for a cart, was Taigh a' Gheugain (Dòmhnall Aonghais Ruaidh): three girls and a boy. Next down the road was Taigh Thormoid Ruaidh, with my near-contemporaries, Angie, Dòmhnall, John Murdo, Anna and Mina.

This was all within one hundred yards, on just one side of the road. And it wasn't merely that the people were there then:

they'd been there, more or less on the same spot, for generations, give or take some slight adjustments when 'lots' were re-allocated to take account of changes in the sizes of families. No 3 Habost, for example, was home successively to my great-great-grandfather, my grandfather and my mother; and birthplace to myself. Inevitably, too, there was a good deal of intermarriage, but in a parish the size of Ness the consanguinity was diluted by a barrier of two or three generations. Even so, when you put my various bloods (Murrays, Morrisons, Macdonalds, Gunns, Macleods and Thomsons) together, you end up related to most of the people of Ness (and probably Caithness and Moray as well).

The bus to Ness was no express. Not only did it stop repeatedly to allow passengers to alight, it also stopped to deliver newspapers, prescriptions and an endless variety of 'messages'. It could even stop to get news to bring to friends and relatives at the other end of the parish, particularly if someone were seriously ill. But eventually it reached No 3 Habost.

Everything was different from our Laxdale house. The house itself stood at right angles to the road, no more than eight feet from the traffic. It consisted of two buildings, linked, but quite distinct. The end furthest from the road would have been called a black-house, but by this time that meant only that it was thatched. The traditional black house was so called because inside it was, quite literally, black. The fire was in the middle of the floor, there was no chimney and the smoke was left to find its own way out through the thatch. Theoretically, there should have been a point in the roof directly above the fire where the thatch was thinner than it was elsewhere. This was the official exit for the smoke, but it took some finding, and in the meantime the smoke simply filled the house. Two complications exacerbated the problem. One was that the fire never went out: at night it was banked up, ready to be set ablaze again in the morning. The other was that the soot impregnated the thatch and when the rain seeped through in a heavy downpour the soot came down with it. Unless you had the protection of a roofed, boxed bed, you could waken up in the morning with your face streaked with soot; and of course the smell of smoke, stronger even than tobacco, clung to you inescapably, day and night.

Now, I know you think I'm very old, and you're quite right, but by my day there were scarcely any such houses in Lewis. My grandfather's was typical of the so-called black-houses of the period. It had thatch, certainly, but it also had some kind of ceiling. But the main difference was that instead of the fire being in the middle of the floor, there was a huge fireplace, complete with hearth, and a chimney which made its way up through the gable end. Never a wisp or a whiff of smoke escaped into the house.

But I don't suppose you really want to hear about old houses. Would you forgive me if I just stopped here? Sometimes I just feel so weary, but if all is well I'll write again soon.

Take care
Bodach

14. Cows, horses and the good shepherd

18 June 2023

Dear Mme Quessaud

Thanks for being patient with me, and sorry for not writing as I promised. I fear that my days of independence are numbered and that sooner rather than later I shall need to 'go into a home'. The Parkinson's is no better. In fact, I suspect that the medication is having less and less effect, and the sheer exhaustion that goes along with the tremor, plus the effort involved in consciously propelling myself into every movement, takes a heavy toll of what little energy I have.

But no matter. I'm still here, and I'm glad you think old houses are interesting. It's very odd, considering how much else I've lost, how clearly I can still see the old house in Habost, although I'm utterly puzzled that not a single photo of it survives. As I mentioned in my last letter, the days of the fire in the middle of the floor were past and the new style fireplace was a very imposing affair, topped by a mantelpiece five or six feet from the floor (the mantelpiece itself graced with either a brass rod or a simple chain for drying wet socks and such things). It was a good five feet wide, the fire nestling in between two raised pillars large enough to allow the biggest pan to sit there and stay warm while other food was cooking. All the cooking was done on this large open fire, which seemed to us to consume peat as if there were no tomorrow (but then, each summer every family in Ness cut enough peats to fill seven or eight five-ton trucks: three times as much as we cut in Laxdale).

The trick when cooking on such heat was to make sure that no smoke got into the food: especially not into the skillet of tea, which seemed to be a-brewing all day long. But the highlight for us was the *crana*. This was quite literally a crane, forged at the smithy from metal of one inch square. The vertical bar was inserted into a socket at the back and extreme left of the fireplace. The horizontal bar was almost as wide as the fireplace, with a stout chain dangling from it. The whole contrivance turned easily in its socket, allowing you not only to suspend a *prais* (a three-legged cast-iron pot) on a hook inserted into the chain, but also to swing it in or out when you were putting it on or taking it off the fire. The apparatus was obsessively black-leaded, standing out in sharp contrast to the fireplace, which was treated with whitening almost every day.

The floor had linoleum, or at least its remains; the walls were hung with wallpaper, although the paper tended to adhere to the plaster only precariously, and as it flapped freely one could hear the regular fall of masonry dust (or perhaps it was the sound of a mouse?). The shade of the paper depended on the housewife's taste in Distemper, a water-based paint.

Furnishings were scant, with one great virtue: they were the same in every house, which meant that keeping up with the Joneses was never a problem. You had no option. There would be a table and chairs, of course; and a *being*. This was the equivalent of our modern couch or settee, except that it had no upholstery. It was the same size as a park-bench, just long enough to lie on, and made of solid timber, smooth and shining from generations of sitters. There was a dresser, too, probably home-made - certainly made locally - and to our childish eyes this contained a fascinating display of crockery. In fact, what it displayed, often, was the very best china. This would have been brought home by the 'girls' from the fishing at Yarmouth or Lowestoft, and would remain there till the actual purchaser married. Someone would know to whom every piece belonged.

Sitting on the dresser would be two or three enormous earthenware basins, their surfaces a glazed yellow. Each had its own place in the milk-cycle. Today's milk would be in one; yesterday's would be in another, already with a fair head of cream. The milk in the third would be skimmed today, and everything put to good use. The cream would be used for butter, the cuinneag (churn) sitting there at the ready and each of us children waiting for a shot at moving the plunger up and own. The result would be known as ìm ùr (fresh butter), even though one of the pleasures of tasting it was to feel the grains of rough sea-salt mixed into it. It was usually fresh only in the sense that it wasn't shop-bought. Not all the cream was used for butter, however. You have to remember that a good cow produces more milk in a single day than a large modern family could use in a month, but the old crofters wasted not a drop. Some of the cream would be kept for mixing with the crowdie (gruth: hence gruth is bàrr, 'crowdie and cream'). Gruth was made regularly from the thick or sour milk (boinne goirt or boinne tiugh) left over once the cream had been skimmed off. The process was simple enough: you warmed the thick milk till it separated into curds and whey. The gruth consisted of the curds which floated to the surface to be spooned out and squeezed and pressed together in muslin. The whey (meug in Gaelic) would have been drunk by the bodachs, who would also have drunk the thick milk, smacking their lips in appreciation and proclaiming to us youngsters how good it was for you. I doubt it (they also thought warm milk, straight from the cow, was good for us), but they drank it by the mugful and survived nonetheless. Another dairy delicacy was the unns, the colostrum or first milk the cow yielded after calving. I saw this stuff, and heard it talked about in almost hushed tones, but I never tasted it, which is probably just as well. I'm told that when cooked slowly it set like custard and you could cut it with a knife.

Some of the sour milk and whey would also have been used as a raising-agent in baking. Every house had its baking-tray, perhaps 30"x18", with a 2"high frame round three sides to prevent the flour from scattering, leaving the front open for kneading. Baking (*fuinne* in Ness, *deasachadh* in Lochs and on the West Side) had to be done every day: scones (from white flour), oatcakes and barley-bread, all made on the griddle over the open fire.

Can you not taste it still: barley-bread, fresh butter, crowdie-and-cream and (perhaps) a crown of home-made rhubarb jam? But then, Canada never had such delicacies.

From this living-room of the black house a door led directly to the more modern part. The main room here was the bedroom (or 'the room' as it was called), with a large double bed, a fireplace (much smaller than the main one) and some other items of bedroom furniture. There was one window, large enough, but unfortunately facing north, and the general air of gloom was heightened by the photos of various persons, either deceased or unknown or extremely old, which adorned the walls. Several were in naval uniform; one or two were wedding groups; and many had beards (utterly alien to our day).

Juts before you came to the room, there was a closet and, before the closet, a stair. The closet was a dark place with enormous wooden chests, regularly topped up with their boll (144 lbs) of flour, or with oats and barley. Upstairs there was another bedroom, memorable for its two large double beds, end-to-end. In one of these we would sleep (on a straw-filled bolster) with our twice-widowed grandfather and beg him to tell us stories (not to read them). Above the bed, fixed to the wall, was a curious pocket-studded cotton hanging: a piece of old seaman's kit, I think, which on board ship could have been conveniently rolled up and stowed away. The pockets were filled with mysterious letters, papers and old pipes (all the men smoked then, and sailors home on leave were always welcome for their generous cuts from the bogey-roll). The only other object I can remember was an aneroid barometer: brass on a dark-oak plinth. I have it still, my only tangible link with that spot. The bedroom window gave you a view straight down the road through the village. We used to stand there on a Sunday morning watching the long, steady procession, almost as dense as a funeral cortege, as the people made their way to church. Sometimes we didn't bother to look. We could hear the clip-clop of dozens of feet through the thin wall separating us from the road. The distant yet inescapable roar of the sea, the memorabilia of the past, the military and almost ominous precision of the walkers, the silence of the Sabbath and our proximity to the very edge of the world all came together to instil an unforgettable sense of infinitude. We were small, the world was big and beyond it was something even bigger still.

But back to the ground floor. The new part of the house had its own front door, but I never saw this used. All traffic went through the old entrance to the black-house. This included the cow: humans to the left, cow to the right. I'm not going to speculate on how this strikes a posh lady from Quebec, but what it meant in effect was that there was a covered area in between the house and the byre. This area (the *cùlaist* or *cùl a' ghèibheil*), dark and cool, served as a store for potatoes, peats and the water-barrel. The cows' (there was often a heifer as well as a cow) residence was always on a lower level than the humans', to make sure that no drainage seeped back towards the house. The lower end of the byre was always of turf, which could be demolished every spring for the manure to be carted away to the fields.

Besides the house and byre there was also a barn, complete with a hay-loft and a threshing-mill: you took a sheaf, untied the binding, slid it into the machine, turned a large handle and I can't remember what happened after that. We were under the strictest orders not to play with it, which meant that we played with it at every opportunity. But we could never risk putting a sheaf in. You couldn't hide the evidence.

Then there was the sheep-house (*taigh-chaorach*): a fully roofed, sizeable building where around twenty sheep could be kept (for lambing, I suppose). Beyond it was the stable, complete with stall, manger and cobbled floor made of large pebbles from the shore, standing on their ends and closely packed. This was Maggie's, the Highland mare of indeterminate age who was my grandfather's pride and joy (and daily companion and confidante as well). She was a sturdy little thing, purposefully pulling the cart with its enormous steel-rimmed wheels and bright red-and-blue paint behind her. The sides of the cart could be lowered for loading and unloading, and the back door could be removed for tipping.

Besides the cart, the steading was littered with other implements, including a harrow, a driller (to earth-up potatoes or create raised drills for sowing turnips) and a horse-drawn hoe for weeding between rows of potatoes. There was a plough, too: too heavy for Maggie, or even for two Highland ponies. But she could do it well enough if yoked to a larger, shire-type horse. Every village in Ness then had one or more of these, their owners hiring themselves out for the spring ploughing and other heavy-duty work. In the summer, the horses, large and small, roamed freely through the village, foraging on the rich grass by the roadside ditches.

Today, Niseachs have their lawns. They sow grass, cut it and throw it away. That would have been sacrilege in the 1940s, when every blade of grass was precious and all grazing was meticulously managed by an age-old communal policy which brooked no divergence. This was particularly true with regard to the machair. No cattle were allowed near it till the first day of August every year, by which time it was rich in grass and no less rich in its profusion of wild flowers (the only flowers to be had in those days: nobody grew them); and no sheep were allowed till after the potatoes had been lifted in October.

I was about fourteen when Maggie died. The news was broken to me in a letter from my grandfather, probably the saddest letter I ever received. I so much regret not keeping it. "Dear Donnie," it began, "I have very bad news for you. Maggie died." In reality, she hadn't died. She had had to be shot. Working on the machair one winter's day, she had stumbled in a rabbit-hole and broken her leg. The letter spared me the details, but it said enough to extinguish one of the lights of my life. I had ridden her often, bareback, and tried time and time again to make her gallop, or at least to break into a canter. Nothing could induce her to lower herself to such undignified behaviour (I had much more success riding Scottie, the huge sheepdog). She would walk as if she were controlled by a metronome. But that day all was forgiven; and only once since, in Pennsylvania, have I ever ridden a horse.

It wasn't easy for us to break into the circle of local children. In those days, Gaelic was universal in Ness: English was for the classroom (and strangers). Everywhere else, from the school playground to the shop and the church, Gaelic prevailed. Our Gaelic was pretty rusty. We were surrounded by it at home, of course, where every adult and every visitor spoke it, and we understood every word, but in suburban Laxdale we seldom spoke it. In Ness we had no option. Whatever pressure the language might be under, the local boys saw no need to speak in a foreign tongue simply because we were there: strangers indeed, but strangers from their own people, who had no right to be ashamed of the language of their forebears. We struggled manfully, and they sometimes made concessions, but we were only too conscious of our blunders.

The main pastime was football. A game could be organised in some vacant space in no time at all, and when you played you didn't have to talk, Gaelic or anything else. To that extent, things were no different from Laxdale. But they could be very different in the evenings, because the Ness boys had the advantage of huge grassy pitches on the machair, where the teams were much larger and the whole thing much more organised. Besides, in high summer you could play till midnight and when you got home your parents wouldn't even be worried. Social life in Ness began after nine o'clock and by midnight your parents would still be out at their ceilidhs, visiting old friends they could see only once a year.

In between football (when I was completely dwarfed by all these Norsemen bred on porridge, herring and fresh air) you talked. There were, you must remember, no televisions (and few radios), no cinemas, no cafes and no pubs. In fact, at one point the daily papers arrived in Stornoway by the evening mail-steamer, which meant that we had to wait till Tuesday morning for the postman to deliver Monday's papers: only then could we catch up with Saturday's football results. For toys and pastimes you had to rely on very basic resources, with a heavy dash of imagination. You could play with bikes, creating various tests and obstacle-courses. These weren't your modern sophisticated lightweight machines or even the mountain-bikes of the 1990s, but clumsy, heavy-duty things (often army-surplus). They were far too big for children (28" frames). To begin with, we couldn't get our legs over the crossbars; and even if someone else placed us in the saddle, our feet wouldn't reach the pedals. Initially, then, all we could do was ride the bike by positioning ourselves under the crossbar, leaning over to one side, our feet on the pedals, our hands on the handlebars and the whole concern ending up, as often as not, in the ditch. The scars of these early days as a learner cyclist are with me to this day.

We were always struck, too, by the way the Ness boys (we saw little of the girls) engaged in what seemed to us very adult conversations. I remember one discussion on the merits of dungarees trousers (in Laxdale, we were never consulted about our clothes: we wore what we were told); and another on the best way to keep your hair flat (the consensus was 'A cap!'). But the staple talking-point in those parliaments-by-the-side-of-a-peatstack or at the gable-end of a house (depending which way the wind was blowing) was how much people had for their annual trip to Stornoway. As it was twenty-seven miles away, this was a once-a-year event, and the pocket-money involved was mind-blowing to us: £1 at least, sometimes twenty-seven shillings, and this in an age when a joiner was earning £5.10 shillings a week. We, who might have a penny or threepence, or at the most sixpence, to spend on a trip to Stornoway could hardly begin to imagine how many ice-lollies, ice-cream cones, bags of chips and MacGowan's Highland Toffees (known as *tofaidh-bò* because the wrapper had a picture of a Highland cow) you could buy for twenty-seven shillings. I've heard since that the way the posh folk of Stornoway identified the 'lowrags' or the 'maws' from the country was that they carried an ice-cream cone in the one hand and a bag of chips in the other. But I knew no such wisdom then, and don't particularly want to know it now.

The day after the Big Day the conversation would shift from how much money they had to "Dè cheannaich thu ann an Steòrnabhagh?" ("What did you buy in Stornoway?"). Not all of it, and probably not much of it, went on gluttony. They bought what boys would buy all over the world (pocket-knives, rubber balls and such things) and then began to save for next year.

It wasn't only the boys who went to town only once a year. Many adults were in the same position (hence, no doubt, the Gaelic song that begins 'Bha mi latha samhraidh an Steòrnabhagh' ['One summer's day I went to Stornoway']). My own granny, who lived till 1960, was in Stornoway only once in her life. Tradition has it, however, that the men of Ness used to make an annual pilgrimage to the town to buy new boots. It was this that bred the story of the Niseach who was seen hopping, breathless, across the moor. He had bought new boots, but the laces were tied together and he had no option but to hop all the way home. The slander was spawned on the West Side and the Niseach response was the story of the crofter from Shawbost who, after a lifetime of outside toilets (something of a euphemism), had at last had an indoor loo installed. "How are you getting on with the new bathroom?" he was asked. "All right," he said. "The only thing is that every time I flush it I lose the soap."

The precocious adulthood of children, both boys and girls, from the crofting areas of Lewis probably stemmed from the fact that from the earliest age they were mixing with grown-ups, doing the same work, sharing in the same conversations and unconsciously picking up the wisdom of the ages. They lived with sheep, horses, cows, boats, peats, ploughing and harvesting, and the resulting maturity could sometimes dig pits for unwary professionals. In those days, ministers still went to the schools once every year to examine the children on their religious knowledge. One clerical gentleman, knowing that the youngsters knew a good deal about sheep, decided to build his approach around the theme of the Good Shepherd, and opened up the subject by soliciting answers to the question, "What does a shepherd do to sheep?" Things went edifyingly enough for a while, till the minister spotted one young fellow desperately trying to catch his attention. "Well, Iain, what does the shepherd do with sheep?" "He castrates them!" In Gaelic, the words would be spat out, appropriate enough since the original implement of castration was often the shepherd's own teeth: "Bidh e gan spoth!" Since this admitted of no obvious spiritual application, the examination came to an untimely end. But to these boys such an answer was entirely natural. That was what shepherds did. And when, at the age of fourteen, these boys left home to sail the oceans of the world, they needed all the maturity at their command. If you'd never been further than Stornoway, and even that but occasionally, it was a long way to Portsmouth; and that was only the end of the beginning.

But that's quite enough for you for the moment, and more than enough for a bodach like me.

Write soon.
DM

8 August 2023

Dear Mme Quessaud

Sometimes I think it's not fair, how much you know about Lewis and how little I know about Quebec. School taught us all about General Wolfe and the Heights of Abraham, of course, but I can no longer view such things through the rosy spectacles of empire. A few weeks ago I was reading a new biography of Jonathan Edwards, once famed as a great 18th century preacher and theologian, but now much more in vogue as America's greatest home-bred philosopher. Edwards lived in New England, not far from Boston, and one of the intriguing features of the story is the way that he and his compatriots regarded themselves as provincial Englishmen. Edwards was eventually driven out of his congregation and worked for a while as a missionary to the Mohawk Indians. The mission was supported by the wealthy English residents, but it was all too clear that underlying the evangelistic programme was the much more sinister desire to acquire as much real estate as possible. To begin with, English and Indians lived together very much as equals, but there was obviously no equality in purchasing power and all the property soon ended up in English hands. That's the property, I suppose, which now defines American aristocracy and funds Presidential elections.

But, then, we can't be too hard on the Yanks. Our own Highland people did the same to the Indians of Nova Scotia, usually without even the fig-leaf of commercial propriety. They didn't bother buying them out. They simply shot them.

Back to Ness, then, with the proviso that I was never anything but an outsider there. Nor, as far as crofting goes, was I ever more than an observer, and some of my comments would probably bring an amused smile to the face of my grandfather. Of course, research would clarify many things, but it would be dishonest to have research masquerading as memories, and at my time of life that's what I'm trading in: impressions recollected in tranquillity (as Wordsworth almost said).

Anyway, I think I'm on solid ground when I say that a crofting home, and indeed a crofting village, was dominated by the cow. First thing every morning she had to be milked and then, immediately afterwards, she had to be led to the machar. To begin with, we were allowed only to accompany the adult in charge, but eventually, at least occasionally, we took her solo. It wasn't quite the equivalent of reaching for the sky, but neither was it as simple as it sounds. Each pair of crofts had its own route to the machar: a *rathad mor* (right of way) between the two lots. You put a halter round the cow's horns and off you went, she leading and business-like, knowing the journey was about food. The problem was that on either side of the rathad mor, literally within inches of the cow's mouth, there was a field of either lush green corn or even lusher green barley. On a bad day the cow would insist on helping herself to huge mouthfuls, not only delaying the journey, but threatening to set off an international incident. It was bad enough when she gobbled your own barley. If she gobbled Dòmhnall Alasdair Chaluim's there would be real trouble.

One you reached the machar you opened the gate (again, each pair of crofts had its own), loosened the halter and released the cow. In the old days children used to have to tend the cattle all day long. This had little to do with cattle and even less with the romance of childhood. It was a matter of crofting politics. Each township had its own grazings, separated from others by boundary-markers which were themselves a matter of oral tradition. The children's job was to make sure that the Habost cattle didn't stray on to the Swainbost grazings. By the 1940s there was a sturdy fence and no further need for child-labour. You could applaud it as a blow for children's rights; or you could deplore it as a piece of unwelcome technology which would eventually lead to fully automated car-parks and banks that speak to you via machines with serious learning difficulties: "Sorry to keep you waiting" (not enough emotion for an exclamation-mark).

In the evening, around seven o'clock, you had to repeat the process. Only once, to the best of my knowledge, was I given this responsibility. I was accompanied by my friend, John Murdo Dhòmhnaill Sheocainn (at least, I wanted him to be my friend, but he was three years older than me and probably not very happy about my pretensions). On the way in, I regaled John Murdo with a eulogy on our cow, drawing on all the resources of my Gaealic to extol her virtues, particularly how 'solt' (quiet and biddable) she was. This was no exaggeration: the creature, a large Friesian, was very docile, and there she was, waiting at the gate as usual. I approached her, as nonchalantly as I knew how, holding the halter and talking to her nicely. She wasn't impressed. What gave this creature, a total stranger, the right to chat her up in that familiar way? And what right had they, back home, to send this little neaff to escort her home at the end of a hard day's work making milk on the machar. She stood off, sullenly. I approached. She twisted and turned. I reached for her. She scurried away.

I have no idea how long the stand-off lasted. All I know is that it ended only when she decided it should end; and that was only when a real man, John Murdo, intervened and got the halter round her neck. "Isn't it her that is quiet," he murmured (more than once) on the way home: "Nach i tha solt!"

I wouldn't want you to get the wrong impression. It's not that I was taken off the job. I simply didn't volunteer any more. But it wasn't only me that cows could twist round their little fingers. Between them, the cows controlled the village: when you got up in the morning, what you did first, what you planted, whether you could have a day off, the times of church services and even when you could hold your mid-week prayer-meeting.

In our part of Ness it had to be at 12 noon on Thursday: in between taking her to the machar in the morning and going back again for her in the evening. She was a demanding cow.

Beyond the machar was the shore: the cladach in Gaelic. Years and years have passed since I last saw it and it would be best not to take my description as the basis for a map. But I recall it as three separate beaches, covering about three miles of coast: Tràigh Chrois, Tràigh Shanndaidh and Tràigh Eòropaidh (*Cunndal*). To reach it, we had to pass the cemetery, something else which had no parallel in Laxdale. People didn't die in Laxdale in those days. Newmarket was made up almost entirely of young families and there was scarcely a breach in their ranks till the 1960s, when almost all the men died together. Few of them reached the allotted span.

But judging by the cemetery, lots of people had been dying in Ness: so many, indeed, that there were two cemeteries, one in Swainbost (the Old Cemetery) and one in Habost (the New Cemetery). The Swainbost one was almost completely neglected, although there were still occasional burials there. It had been taken over by *gallanan*: wild rhubarb, we called it, sometimes waist-high, through which you walked at your peril because it covered all sorts of hidden holes and sharp, pointed objects. It looked more like a landscape from science-fiction than a piece of machar. My grandfather almost always went in when taking us to the shore. His first wife, our grandmother, was buried there; and so were his parents, who followed him, like a super-ego, all his life. Hidden among the *gallanan* were ancient headstones, many of them erected to the memory of merchants, builders and other men of substance, long since forgotten. We had little interest in these. Far more poignant were the small, marble headstones erected by the Admiralty in memory of the dozens of Ness seamen who had lost their lives in one or other of the Great Wars. They were identical, except, of course for the names. Young as we were, we could enter into some of the pain. We had a neighbour in Laxdale whose teenage son had been buried at sea, and for long months afterwards she used to slip out of the house in the middle of the night and go down to the shore to look for his body. How many mothers in Ness must have cursed the sea!

The new cemetery was a complete contrast: neat as a war cemetery in Flanders. Now and again we had seen a funeral cortege leaving one of the neighbouring houses in Habost: a crowd gathering as if for church on Sunday, some going inside the house, but most remaining outside. After a while, men would come out carrying chairs and arrange them in front of the house. Then the eileatram, (bier) made of long pieces of black timber, would be brought out and placed on the chairs; and on the eileatram the coffin. The men would gather round and for some moments the coffin would be hidden from our view. Just as the men began walking, the women would emerge from the house and stand at the door watching the cortege wind its way slowly along the road, men dropping off every now and again and standing by the side of the road till the end of the procession reached them. Then they fell in again. We knew nothing of the ritual then, but it was an exercise carried out with military precision. Every man took a grip of the bier in turn. Checking with his partner on the opposite side of the cortege, he would move over and take hold of the bier by handle number one (at the front), the man at the front moving back to number two. After a few steps, each moved a position further back until he eventually relinquished position number four. Then he stepped away, let the cortege pass and joined it again at the end.

In these days there was no presiding undertaker and no hearse. The coffin would be carried manually from the house to the grave, and we would eventually see the cortege snaking its way across the machair and up the slight slope to the cemetery, before disappearing from view again. All outside work had stopped the day of the death and you could almost slice the sense of solemnity as the whole community united in grief, taking farewell of someone whose whole existence from cradle to grave (apart from war service or some such thing) had been spent in this one village, and probably on this one croft. Those who had accompanied him to school accompanied him on his last journey.

There was an undertaker in Stornoway, but his only involvement would have been to provide the coffin. Relations would have hired a local van and gone over to collect the *ceann-crìoch* (the last bed, I suppose: a euphemism for the coffin. Once the body was in it, it would be simply a *cist*, or chest) - well, they would have gone over to collect it (and probably pay for it in cash) shortly after the death, and, by the time they returned, the neighbouring women would already have prepared and dressed the body. Somehow or other they had worked out an arrangement whereby the deceased was dressed in the clothes which had come with the last coffin; the clothes in the new coffin would be kept for the next funeral.

To us the cemetery meant chiefly all those curious headstones and obelisks which stood out on the skyline. Some (usually those commemorating ministers) were enormous. One of these was our landmark for navigating the cemetery. It was a memorial to the Reverend Donald MacDonald, minister of Ness at the time of the Church Union of 1900. Few of his people followed him into the United Free Church, and even fewer would have followed him had it not been for the influence of the local doctor, Dr Ross of Borve, whose daughter, Lab, was the mother of Iain MacLeod, one of the few truly great politicians of post-war Britain. But Mr MacDonald was still remembered with awe even by the people of the Free Church.

The reason that MacDonald's obelisk was a navigational aid was that beside it were the graves of two infants. One was the daughter of another minister, the Reverend Roddy John MacLeod, Free Church minister of Ness from 1920 to 1927. Adjacent to it was the grave of my little sister, Annie Murray Macleod, who died a few months before I was born. My stricken father had devoted endless hours to carving a headstone out of mahogany: an exercise as much therapeutic as anything else. Unfortunately, in carving out the block capitals of her name he mistakenly carved 'E' instead of 'L' (MacEeod instead of MacLeod), and for the whole of my childhood the symbol of that awful anguish lay semi-hidden in the cellar. After his own death, we did what we could to cover up the error and placed it on the little girl's grave beside his own. It was still there the last time I looked: a piece of timber rescued from some Admiralty junkyard in the 1940s and now standing on the edge of the Atlantic eighty years later as a fragile memorial to a life which burned brightly for fifteeen months and was then in the space of four awful hours extinguished by meningitis.

That mistaken 'L' would have cut my father to the quick: the anguish, guilt and frustration of that simple lapse of concentration, and the work now useless. How did he explain it to my mother? And did she say, "It doesn't matter"?

Anyway, we skipped past the cemetery and rushed headlong to the shore, scampering down the dunes, racing along the sand, jumping from rock to rock further and further out towards the breakers. On the horizon, almost always, would be the silhouette of some steamer, too large by far for Stornoway harbour. Where had it come from? Where was it going to? Had it been in the War? How vulnerable it seemed out there, how easily the Germans could have got her and how far it would have been for the sailors to swim! Bits of metal and bits of wood lay here and there. Shipwrecks? Mines? At school we had to know the difference between flotsam and jetsam. Were these bits and pieces flotsam or jetsam? You could paddle at the edge of the sea, but strictly no swimming. The local boys did swim, but not in the sea as such: they swam in the larger rock pools and we had often heard the story of the one who refused to jump in, protesting, "If I drown, my father will kill me."

But we weren't here just for the fun: at least, gran'pa wasn't. We were here to pick shells and he was here to pick them not for his own sake but for ours. We loved them because they were a novelty (and because sweets were rationed). We picked *maorach* (limpets), mostly, we knocking them off the rock with a sharp stone, he flicking them off with a knife (he would no sooner go out of the house without his knife than he would go out without his cap). *Faochagan*, (winkles) too, went into the pail: once we'd briefly boiled them, we'd pick out the flesh with a needle. So far as I can recall, such eating was never regarded as a meal. Afterwards, you'd have dinner as usual.

For some reason we never ate mussels, though they were there in abundance and offered by far the tastiest food on the shore. Aren't dietary quirks intriguing? The people of Lochs loved mussels, but wouldn't eat limpets, conger-eels or dogfish. The people of Ness ate limpets, loved conger-eels and dogfish, but used mussels only for bait. This happened mainly when they were fishing with the *taigh-thàbhaidh*. This consisted of a stout pole, about two inches in diameter and twelve to fifteen feet in length, with a bag-net some five feet in diameter at the end of it. My grandfather's was of legendary size: so large that wise men said no man should have used it single-handed. Such feats were quite beyond me and I never even saw it being used, but so far as I can gather, the operation was theoretically simple enough. The *taigh-thàbhaidh* (pronounced 'tai-havee', with a soft 't') was generally used in the late autumn when the shoals of *cudaigean* (cuddies: young coleys, the size of large sardines) came in close to the shore. You threw the mussels (crushed, I think) into the sea as a ground-bait to attract the fish, then put out your *taigh-thàbhaidh*, turned it over, scooped up the fish and half-lifted, half-pulled your catch ashore. When you had a sackful, you headed home. You usually had a good deal more than you could eat, but you also had widows and other neighbours who could use them. Besides, dried, they were a kind of insurance. The people of Ness would never starve so long as there were fish in the sea, but you couldn't always be sure that you'd be able to go out and get them.

From the shore there was a splendid view of the Ness skyline stretching from Knockaird to Cross, the lighthouse away to your left, the two Cross churches on the right. In between, it seemed as if every inch of land was occupied. Centuries of skilled husbandry had turned the land into superb potato and turnip country (nowhere else in Lewis, to my knowledge, was the harvesting of turnips a specific event in the agricultural calendar; nowhere else in Lewis did crofters use basic slag; and nowhere else in Lewis did men grow such enormous swedes). The result was a landscape more like Buchan than the rocky, peaty terrain usually associated with crofting. I doubt if it's like that today. Cultivation has ceased long since and even the most fertile soil, once neglected, quickly reverts to wilderness.

It's a curious thing, the power of landscape to evoke a sense of infinitude. In Ness, there was an almost numinous sense of space. If you stand on Tràigh Shanndaidh the next landfall is Newfoundland. In between, there is nothing but three thousand miles of tempestuous ocean. Landward, by contrast, all is tranquillity. Nothing seems to move, or even to have moved in a thousand years. The houses stand solid and immobile. The fields are empty. Even the dead are still with us, in the ordered silence of the cemetery. In old age it's not really places you miss and would love to go back to but times, and I think that's much more of a problem for mobile generations like yours and mine than it was for our forebears. For them, place preserved time, perpetuating its culture and traditions. For us, place betrays time. Or is it time that betrays place: same latitude and longitude, different place.

Yet that world of infinitudes, where land met sea, sky met ocean and the living were surrounded by the dead, was also a world of miniscules, where children found their pleasure at the end of a peatstack, playing with little 'lorries' made of a 12" plank, a block nailed to its front for a cabin, but nothing for wheels. They could go forwards and backwards, you could load them up and you could crash them. Come to think of it, they could even have done vertical take-offs and landings, because they were lorries only of the unbounded imagination.

But reaching out to this world was another represented by the *ceàrdach* (the smithy). It was virtually next door to our house in Habost, and to us it was a world of wonder. We grew up surrounded by wood and we knew what you could do with it. You could cut it and nail it and glue it and plane it and chisel it and even burn it. But no tool we possessed could do anything with iron. In the *ceàrdach* all was different. Here was a man who could bend iron and shape it and twist it and even join bits of it together. And there was the fire. In Laxdale, if the fire went low, it took you ages to get it going again. Very often, in fact, you had to take a big sheet of newspaper and hold it up against the front of the fire to create a draught (we didn't know how it worked. We just knew it did work. We also knew it was dangerous, because if you didn't pull the paper away in time it caught fire). There were no such problems in the *ceàrdach*. Here there was a large tin box with a pile of ashes, just like the fire in Laxdale on a bad day. Every so often the blacksmith would step up to it, turn a wheel, and in no time the ashes turned into a brilliant red-hot glow. He would put a piece of metal in, pull it out glowing red a few moments later, take it to the anvil and give it a few mighty blows with his hammer. The drama ended when, without interrupting his conversation, he plunged the red-hot metal into a tub of cold water and clouds of hissing steam erupted into the air.

The other piece of magic was the welding. This was used mainly in repair jobs: fixing the towbars on tractor trailers and the like. But how could you join bits of iron? Two huge cylinders; long, red, rubber hoses; and a kind of torch thing with a narrow blue flame roaring out at its end. How did it work? Melting the iron and fusing it together? Was that all?

But the greater miracle was that we were allowed in there at all. Today, Health and Safety officials would ban us, parents would be aghast and the smith would have to have disclosure. But in that world children were totally secure. Every adult in the village was their parent, and they didn't mind you watching them as they worked or even your listening as they gossiped. You just stood there, particularly on a rainy day, and observed. No one took any particular notice of you because (and this, too, was remarkable) the *ceàrdach* was a kind of drop-in centre, where those waiting for a job to be done would be joined by others who simply happened to be passing by: a news-and-views bazaar.

It's odd what sticks in your memory. One day the parish minister happened to be there, probably to get some repair to the bodywork of his car. He was regarded as something of a Moderate, perhaps even a Modernist, and he didn't help himself by going about without a hat (a sure sign of serious frivolity). In accordance with this non-evangelical image, his sermons were noted for their preoccupation with astronomy: an interest that left him slightly vulnerable. One Sunday night while he was waxing eloquent on the moon, an aggrieved voice came from the body of the kirk: "Nach tu gheibheadh Call' innte!" ("I wish you'd get a Call there!") Eventually the wish was granted, though the Call came from Uist, not from the moon. But that, in turn, bred its own story. The Free Church minister at the time wasn't universally popular either, and as he approached the age of retirement hopes were rising that they would soon be quit of him. But just as the parish minister was about to leave, news broke that the Free Church one had taken out a lair in the local cemetery, whereupon one exasperated Free Church *cailleach* congratulated her neighbour from the other church on their good fortune: "Aren't you the lucky ones! We can't get rid of ours, dead or alive!" So much for ministers being on pedestals.

But the link between the minister and the *ceàrdach*? Just that while all the work was going on around him, he was earnestly pressing on the locals who crowded the smithy the importance of reading the *National Geographic Magazine*.

Bye (if you're still with me)
Bodach

19 December 2023

Dear Mme Quessaud

I had convinced myself you were fed-up with my maudlin meanderings. Your letter appears to have gone off on some kind of world tour: a victim, I suspect, of the Christmas rush. At least, that's the Letter Force's excuse.

I remember being very surprised when a visiting Japanese scholar told me away back in the Nineteen-Nineties that, yes, they did celebrate Christmas in Japan. "Not in Christian way," he said, "but we have holidays and parties and gifts."

That's very much the way it is here now. The world begins to go crazy some time around the twelfth of December. It's not so much the parties and the shoppings that are so disruptive but the holidays. In the old days, things closed for Christmas Day, reopened on Boxing Day and then closed for three days over the New Year. Now everything closes on Christmas Eve and remains closed till around the fifth of January; and even then it takes days for normal service to be resumed. To make matters worse, many of those you depend on (particularly at my age) take what they call 'extended holidays' which seem to last from mid-December to mid-January. All the doctors, lawyers, dentists, slaters, plumbers and heating engineers are off to the Caribbean or the Mediterranean. It's a nightmare for us noble neurotic geriatrics. Every year, come November, I have to begin to worry about my ears. Will they be waxed up by Christmas? I have to know by 20th December. After that it's useless: I just couldn't get a doctor and I'd have to live inside my head with all its ominous noises for an interminable couple of weeks.

There are still lots of Christmas cards, but without the Christian symbols. There are trees, crackers, Santas, robins, holly, wreaths, snow, geese, candles, ice-skating, parcels, ribbons and baubles, but the Wise Men, the Star, the Manger, the Angels and the Holy Family have all but disappeared. My old Puritan friends would be pleased, I'm sure. They never had much time for such Popish symbols. But I'm afraid that the demise of the old-style Christmas has little to do with a growing concern for liturgical purity. The card-makers, whether in Lewis or Japan, are dancing on the grave of Christianity. In any case, the trouble with Puritanism (an essentially English phenomenon) is that it never reckoned with human nature. It's all very well to try to turn us into disembodied religious monomaniacs, as if nothing mattered but the things of the spirit and the concerns of eternity. But it will never work, because we're on earth, not in heaven; and we have bodies as well as souls. Our nature rebels against the life of the solitary. It also rebels against a religion without art or symbolism and against a Christian Year without high days and holy days.

That's why Scottish Protestantism had no sooner expelled Christmas and Easter than it introduced Communion seasons and filled the year with special monthly and quarterly meetings. Sermon twice on Sunday was all very well, but people had to have special times when they could come together and light up their lives (and rekindle their faith) with festivals. When Communion seasons fell out of fashion, their place was taken by conferences, for the same reason. Even in the matter of symbolism, our old Presbyterian churches were by no means as devoid of it as first appeared. Of course, it was possible to miss it, just as I used to miss the Masonic symbols in many Australian churches. But it's there nonetheless. Apart from all else, the Highlanders cherished their church buildings. Towards the end of last century the more rigorous English Puritans used to make a big thing of not calling a building a church. The church, they insisted, was the people: the people of God. We even used to see the most tortuous adverts in the religious press as people strove to publicise their meetings while at the same time avoiding referring to the venue as a church: 'The church of Jesus Christ which meets at 17 Old Ferry Road will conduct worship there each Lord's Day at 11 a.m. All welcome.'

Lewis religion had no such misgivings. Rightly or wrongly, the church was the church which stood there in the middle of the parish as it had in the days of their fathers and grandfathers before them. They knew that simply going there didn't necessarily do you any spiritual good. But it was the house of God: the equivalent, for them, of Solomon's temple. If unable to attend it for reasons of age or health, they would speak of their predicament precisely in the words of an Old Testament psalmist: 'My thirsty soul longs vehemently, yea faints thy courts to see.' It was linked in their minds and imaginations with the Tabernacle in the wilderness; hallowed in their memories by the highlights of their spiritual experience; and hallowed in anticipation by the hope that some day some even greater blessing might come their way there.

The result was that these church buildings were lovingly tended. We took that for granted then, but in retrospect it seems quite astonishing. Most Lewis parishes were erected only in the 19th century and had nothing of the mainland tradition of heritors or landlords maintaining their buildings. It was up to the people. Several of the Free Churches in Lewis were among the largest public buildings in the Highlands. In fact, the only larger buildings were the Free North Church in Inverness and possibly the Free Church in Dingwall. It used to be a constant topic of conversation which of the churches could hold the most. Those in Point, Stornoway, Ness and Back could seat well over a thousand. The biggest of them, I was led to understand, was the one in Point. Stornoway and Ness were just about equal. And the one in Back (said my father) would just fit nicely inside the one in Ness. Crossbost had the most interesting story of all. The man who built it promised that it would seat a certain number (probably about 800). He made his calculations carefully and concluded that he would need a certain floor-area and dug the foundation accordingly. Unfortunately, he forgot the space that would be lost to the thickness of the walls. "No matter," he said, "I'll get them in." Which he did, but for generations the poor people of Lochs had to sit with their knees up to their chins. Maybe that explains something.

Such statistics mattered, and would be discussed in the ceilidhs the way modern football supporters argue about the capacities of various football grounds. It's fascinating, too, that these churches were built in the last fifty years of the 19th century: a time when conditions in Lewis were pretty grim. We had the Potato Famine, evictions, emigrations, insecure tenancies and land riots. Apart from the minister, the doctor and (latterly) the schoolmaster, the whole population lived in black-houses. There was no old age pension, no National Health Service and no social provision for the able-bodied unemployed. Wages of any kind were comparatively rare. Even the weavers were paid on the barter system, receiving groceries in lieu of payment from merchants who also happened to be the Harris Tweed producers.

Yet they managed to erect magnificent churches. The one in Ness, in particular, is a triumph of the mason's art. Admittedly, they don't have the grandeur of Gothic cathedrals. But then they were built for a different purpose. I was never quite able to work out the raison d'etre of Cathedrals. In essence they are monuments to themselves. I preached in one or two of them in my previous life and they certainly weren't built for preaching. But that's precisely what the old Lewis churches were built for, and even in the days before public address systems, preachers like Kenneth Macrae (Stornoway) and John Morrison (Ness) could easily be heard by congregations of over a thousand.

The pulpits, of course, were high and dominant. This was partly functional: a preacher had to be seen as well as heard. But it was also symbolic. Protestant worship is primarily a liturgy of listening. The word, especially the word preached, is central. This is why the pulpit is dominant. In the old days this was further underlined by the beadle's carrying in the Bible before the minister. This practice was still in place in the Free Churches of Edinburgh in my youth, but I never saw it in Lewis.

But I mustn't weary you with further details about church architecture and Presbyterian liturgy. It's just that the time of year set me thinking about such things. Traditionally, of course, the Highland churches didn't celebrate Christmas. I doubt if they always knew why. The decision had been taken many centuries previously and few knew the reasons behind it. Partly it was simply a reaction to the constant disruption caused by the rash of mediaeval holy days. Partly it was the core Puritan argument that there was no biblical warrant for such a festival. Partly it was an argument about the date being wrong in any case: Christ couldn't have been born on 25th December because that was the dead of winter and the shepherds wouldn't have been watching their flocks 'in Bethlehem's fields by night'. And partly it was the claim that 25th December was simply the pagan festival of Mithras, with a late Christian veneer.

Everyone knew these arguments, more or less, but I doubt if any of them, or all of them together, constituted the real reason for the non-ecclesiastical Christmas. It had more to do, I suspect, with fear and inertia; and with the fact that, since the only hymns allowed in church were the Metrical Psalms, you couldn't have a real Christmas service anyway. As late as the end of last century holding a carol service could get even a mainland Free Church minister into serious trouble.

I don't know if I ever had any sympathy with such arguments. I might say, "No, never!" and find that my memory was simply playing tricks. But I certainly have no sympathy with them now. The only one that ever seemed to have any theological force was the claim that there was no biblical directive to celebrate the birth of Jesus. However, that could mean, at most, only that the church could never make Christmas compulsory: that is, it could never 'discipline' someone for not observing it, the way Presbyterians might discipline someone for breach of the Sabbath or Roman Catholics might frown on someone who failed to attend Mass at Easter. At that level the issue is one simply of liberty of conscience. Christians are free not to celebrate Christmas.

On closer examination, of course, the argument that there is no precedent for celebrating the birth of Christ falls to the ground. The Shepherds celebrated it. Even the angels celebrated it. But in any case we had many other things for which we certainly had no clear biblical warrant: Question Meetings, Quarterly Meetings, Private Meetings and Monthly Meetings to name but a few. The older I became, the clearer it seemed that the apostles had a very pragmatic attitude to such things. They weren't sticklers for ecclesiastical and liturgical minutiae. They did whatever seemed best for the Kingdom.

Whatever the Church said (and I didn't really know till I was much older), it never spoiled our Christmases. Certainly my parents never spared any effort. I can still remember the time, around 1947, when 'decorations' appeared in Laxdale for the first time: coloured paper streamers and bells and stars hanging on walls and suspended from ceilings. For a year or two, my parents said, No! But it didn't last and soon we had a fine collection, kept in a special box and taken out every year. Part of the magic, I suppose, was seeing old favourites hung up again. There'd be a day for Christmas shopping when we would go down town with our half-crown and buy something for our parents: mostly something useless, I suspect. The purchasing would be preceded by many hours' window-shopping. I don't suppose the displays would have seemed much compared to those in great city stores, but we had never seen great city stores. Stornoway was our metropolis, and these glittering, tempting windows with their Christmas lights, Santas and gift-wrapped ties, socks, chocolates and toiletries were Wonderland. We could only look, of course. Everything was far beyond our price-range, but I can't recall that it ever provoked any envy. We were lucky to be able to look. And when we'd finished looking at every window on Cromwell Street (Woolies, Murdo Maclean's, James MacKenzie's, Kenny Froggan's, Peter Squeak's, Tolmies, DG's, the Saddler's and the like), we'd go round the butchers. There you would see unplucked hens (we never called them chickens) hanging outside; and even turkeys. You saw such displays only at Christmas and you thought about those who would eat turkey. We had never done that. It wouldn't even occur to us. I doubt if it was just the price. Few ordinary houses in those days had ovens; and (always a hugely important consideration) it would have been deemed pretentious. Turkeys were for such and for such as such.

The Christmas build-up began in school. I have no clear memory of decorations or of special Christmas events. There was certainly no Christmas tree. But (as befitted a school where singing was an obsession) by the time we were twelve our repertoire of carols was complete, and when the time came for the school to close for the Christmas holidays (two weeks and a day during all my years in primary school), excitement was at fever-pitch: partly because of expectations of Santa and partly because of the dream of a white Christmas and endless sliding and sledging in frosty moonlight.

Christmas Eve was often fraught: sometimes extremely fraught. Excited, sleepless children sharing bedrooms doesn't make for domestic bliss. Every year, the lady next door would come in, some time after 8 o'clock. If we had ever had to mention her name to a teacher or headmaster or other representative of the Sassenach establishment (which always confused patronymics with nicknames), we would have had to call her Mrs Campbell. But we knew her either as Seonag Ailein (Seonag, the daughter of Allan) or as Bean Bhaila (Bhaila's wife: Bhaila pronounced as Vala, with the first vowel heavily aspirated); and she was our hero. At Hallowe'en, she always gave us half-a-crown (the most anyone ever gave). Whenever you called at her door with a message, you always got cakes and pastries. We didn't know at first why she always came to visit on Christmas Eve. The truth, when it came out, was simple enough: Santa never came down her own chimney (she had no children) and she made up for it by sending him down ours.

On the morning of Christmas Day, our pleas for permission to get up began some time around 4.00 a.m. It normally took about three hours' pleading before any concessions were made. Then we bounded down. Presbyterians or no Presbyterians, our stockings were full: an apple, an orange, a chocolate, pens, pencils, crayons, whistles and (always) some little model cars, normally wooden. A larger object or two might lie in a parcel on the table or on the couch: items of clothing usually. And always there would be a *bodach*: a life-size cloth dummy made by my father, sitting on a chair and smiling benignly. He'd be in Presbyterian black, never in St Nicolas red. We'd eat the chocolate and the fruit and wait for Christmas dinner: chicken (a hen, boiled, not roast), Christmas pudding (lots of coins hidden in the mixture) and Christmas cake. For many years I thought my mother was the only person in the world who could make icing. She was certainly the only mother in the village who could be bothered with such nonsense. But then my mother had a lot of brilliant nonsense in her head: ideas she couldn't execute and dreams she dared not express.

When all that was over, you started looking forward to New Year. After that there was nothing till Hallowee'en (except the summer holidays).

But summer seems very far away tonight: impossibly far away, in fact. It's hard to imagine the sun shining or even anyone going outside the house. The wind is absolutely howling, the sleet lashing, and I shudder to think what it's like for poor souls at sea. It's only four o'clock in the afternoon, but already it's pitch-dark; and I won't see anyone till the home-help comes for half an hour tomorrow morning. I suppose it's colder in Canada, but I think I could stand the cold. It's the wet and the darkness that weigh your spirit down.

Take care
DM

14 February 2024

Dear Mme Quessaud

You've been on my conscience these last few days. There's a full month now since your last letter arrived, a speedy reply to mine, but the weather's rendered me utterly paralytic: one of those spells in the Hebrides when it seems to rain non-stop for weeks on end. In the old days we'd have said it was very hard for the lambs, but there are few lambs now. The slump in prices towards the end of the last century put paid to them. Not that I'm particularly sorry. I never liked the creatures. It's difficult to forgive them for what they did to places like South Lochs, where, in the early 19th century, more than twenty villages were cleared to make way for a sheep-farm. They wrought even greater havoc in places like Sutherland: "improving" it as Hugh Miller said, "into a desert". Cattle eat anything from barley to clothes-pegs. Sheep eat nothing but the best (maybe that's why they taste so good), picking at the fine grasses till there's nothing left but the coarsest, and at the same time trampling once arable soil until it's as hard as concrete. Today, the vast county of Sutherland has a population less than that of Lewis: most of it concentrated in a few towns (Dornoch, Golspie, Brora, Helmsdale, Bonar Bridge and Lochinver). The interior is empty. The crofting communities which once supported a rich spiritual, intellectual, poetic and musical culture are all gone. But gone, too, are the great sheep farms themselves. It's terrifying to think that they were once seen as representing progressive thinking. Almost enough to put you off thinking.

It's not always the forces of reaction that are dangerous. Sometimes the forces of progress bring only poverty, misery and degradation, except, of course, to the tiny minority with the capital to exploit the weakness and misfortune of their fellow-men. To this day, despite the land reforms of twenty years ago, the injustice remains in the shape of the huge sporting estates which provide a few hereditary indolents with their own private fiefdoms and take vast tracts of the Highlands out of the economy altogether.

For some odd reason Lewismen have loved sheep ever since they were first introduced. The infatuation begins at an early age. My mother once told me that the only time she saw my uncle cry was when he staggered into the house at the age of three or four, sobbing, "Bhàsaich Daisy!" ("Daisy died!"). I was so dumb I had to ask for clarification. Daisy was the name of a sheep. I had no comprehension of this. The discovery that you could tell one sheep from another, and even give them separate names and identities, was one of the great revelatory moments of my life. I could understand "a sheep" and I could understand "sheep", but a sheep called Daisy? No!

The discovery did nothing to endear me to them. As you probably know, the Western Isles have one of the worst records of coronary disease in the world. I blame the sheep and I can claim medical science in my support. A wise doctor once remarked, "Half the men in this island die chasing sheep and the other half die eating them!" The Lord was exceedingly perceptive when he chose sheep as a symbol of His people: always going astray, utterly beyond discipline and utterly incapable of learning from their mistakes.

We had our full share of them in Laxdale - indeed, more than our full share. As if we didn't have enough of our own, we had to give hospitality to thousands of woolly pests from Point. This was a great puzzle to me as a child. I had never seen Point. It was extremely far away (a good six miles), and since I had no relations there, I had no occasion to visit it. I had to work out *a priori* that there was no grass there and not even heather (since the sheep lived on the moor and since the moor had nothing but heather, I assumed that sheep lived on heather). Empirical verification of this theory had to wait a few years. The Rubhachs (which is what we called the Point people) were something like the 19th century Jews: a lot of history, but little geography.

But they made up for it with industry and enterprise, and one sign of that enterprise was that they sent their sheep to the Laxdale and Barvas moors every summer. Indeed, the event, along with the cuckoo and the May Holiday, was one of the signs of summer. For a few days, lorry after lorry would transport these creatures from the Eye Peninsula to Laxdale for their holidays. But there was a slightly more romantic dimension to the practice. Not all the sheep came by lorry. Some hoofed it all the way from Point round the back of Stornoway and out the Barvas Road to Laxdale. It was quite a splendid sight early of a summer's morning: a couple of hundred sheep, a shepherd and three or four dogs. The first hint we'd have would be the chorus of 'Mehs ...' as the flock bleated its way out the road, and we'd hotfoot it to the gate to watch. It would be in late May or early June, after the lambing. The lupins and other perennials would be maturing in the garden and the sun would be climbing steadily in the east, behind Point and over Broad Bay. It was no easy task to keep the sheep on the straight and narrow. In those days the roads were not lined with fences and the sheep were desperate to make a dash for it and bolt down the moor. It was the dogs that enthralled us. We weren't crofters, or even cottars. We were mere allotment-holders, and we had no experience of dogs who would do what they were told. Every dog we knew simply went berserk when it saw a sheep. But these? A whistle, and off they went to head off or confront a sheep. Another, and they sat. It was magic; and it was part of the inevitable, gentle rhythm of life: the way it had always been and the way it would always be.

But it wasn't sheep you were asking about. Sorry! What were they like, these religious people? I don't want to paint too rosy a picture. There is a good deal of human nature in every man and woman, even in the religious. There were bitchy women, for example, whose main pleasure in life was hurting others, and they were quite capable of standing their theology on its head. Once, during a very long prayer (about thirty-five minutes, I think; and you had to stand all the time), I suddenly saw the world turning very white and then very black and the next thing I knew I was lying on my back in the vestibule with lots of strange faces looking down at me. My mother got a rollicking from one of her "friends", who told her categorically that teenage boys like me should be left sleeping in their beds on Sunday morning. The same lady would have been quite capable of categorically announcing the opposite: that all teenage boys should be in church on Sunday morning. It depended what best suited her malice. There was another Christian in our village with whom my brother once had some kind of altercation. "You'd better shut up," he was told, "air neo gearraidh mi 'n gàillean agad!" Unfortunately, the force of this was completely lost on us because we had no earthly idea of the meaning of 'gàillean'. We soon found out. The worthy man had warned us that he would cut our throats. Such thoughts came from a world we didn't understand.

But in my part of childhood-history-and-geography such people were wholly exceptional. I cannot recall anyone from my childhood remotely resembling Holy Willie, tippling and fornicating under the cloak of predestination. Converted and unconverted mixed freely in a daily common round where many of the tasks were communal and everything depended on teamwork: in the sheep-fank, for example, or unloading the boats in the docks. One of the most highly respected of the elders worked as a drayman, transporting barrels of beer to the pubs by horse and cart. No-one questioned it; and none questioned either his Christianity or his humanity. Wherever he went, laughter followed, and when he left respect remained. He is still an almost living presence with me after more than sixty years. I suspect that the day he left school he could scarcely write his name, but he was a man of outstanding intelligence and considerable powers of debate and argument. Like many of his class, he also had the charming habit of adopting some utterly indefensible position or one that was exactly counter to his real opinion simply for the purpose of starting an argument. The more heated it became, the better he liked it. The fun lay in the fact that the other man didn't twig that he was being led on.

There was nothing cloistered about these men. They couldn't have survived if there had been. Later, towards the end of the century, the demography of the Church changed dramatically. We suddenly woke up and discovered that most church members were middle-class professionals. In such jobs (teaching, medicine and accountancy, for example) it's easy to hide behind your work. A civil servant cannot work against the background of a *luadh* or to a chorus of banter. But manual work is different. It goes on amidst incessant chatter. In my own childhood the day for taking home the peats was one of the highlights of the year. The tractor had not yet taken over and peats had first to be carried from the banks to the road by creel or barrow (or, in our case, by sack. No barrow would work in the boggy ground where we cut our peats). The lorries themselves were five-tonners and it took a crew of about ten people a full hour to fill them, throwing peat after peat from the heap by the roadside. This meant, of course, that families had to help one another: normally one from each home in the neighbourhood. You went to theirs and they came to you. We youngsters could be thrown in as a bonus, but we wouldn't count as repayment of the debt: certainly not in my case, because my father was the best stacker-of-peats-on-top-of-a-lorry in the neighbourhood (it became something of a game to see if you could hit him, but he always managed to see the peat and catch it first).

Even while the work was going on, there would be incessant banter. But it was when the lorry was full and set off for home that it became serious. It would be forty-five minutes at least before it returned for the next load, and in the meantime the exchange of reminiscences, gossip, yarns and teases proceeded apace. There was no place for either the godly or the young to hide, although their presence inevitably moderated the exchanges. I remember one vivid exchange about one of the would-be toffs of the village. He wasn't noted for his Calvinist work-ethic, but unknown to me he was noted for other activities. The debate as to his merits concluded with a brief summary: "There's one thing we cannot deny," said the man who knew him best. "He was good at making children!" I don't think I was meant to hear.

On another occasion, a godly woman was becoming more and more alarmed at the rapidly plummeting level of the conversation. She decided that something must be done. The occasion needed a dose of solemnity, and what better than to remind her companions of the brevity of life and the imminence of eternity. She cleared her throat and announced in most solemn tones, "Tha feadhainn an seo am-bliadhna a bha san t-sìorraidheachd an-uiridh!" ("Well, well, friends, there's some here this year who were in eternity last year!") A fatally easy confusion of word-order, but no handmaid to solemnity.

And, of course, there were eccentrics: Iain Dilidh, for example, a bachelor who throughout my young days was the most regular of all the Communion-goers. For most folk, by my time, Communions meant from Friday evening to Sunday evening. But for Iain they started on Thursday and lasted till Monday. It's difficult to believe nowadays that someone could get on a bus, set off for a town thirty miles away without making any arrangements whatever, and be perfectly certain that once he appeared at church he was sure to be offered hospitality for the night. Every night of the Communion he would sleep in a different bed and every day he would be somewhere different for dinner. The economics of it still amaze me. How could people with absolutely nothing to spare offer a lavish supper, comfortable bed and lavish breakfast to as many as ten people for four nights? But they did.

Even the sleeping accommodation puzzles me. To begin with, of course, visitors slept in barns and other outhouses, possibly because the sheer weight of numbers made it impossible to provide beds for everyone. But as far back as my memory goes, everyone slept inside. This meant sharing, of course: often three and sometimes four to a bed. It wasn't so bad if you were on the outside, but in the middle it was grim, and many's the man who got up and slept on the floor. It never seemed to occur to anyone that there was anything unhealthy or morally dubious about men sharing beds. In any case, the amount of undressing, I suspect, was minimal; and people were used to the conditions. There wasn't much space or privacy in the old black-houses.

But Iain didn't like sharing and he became adept at avoiding it. He knew the houses where few others were likely to go. He also knew houses which were large enough to be able to offer him a bed to himself. And he knew that with just a little effort on his own part he could make himself unpopular enough to ensure that folk might want to avoid him.

Iain had a caustic tongue, the servant usually of his anti-clericalism. Once, he and some other deacons were counting the collection in the vestibule of the church on a Sunday morning. The minister had something of a penchant for lambasting the congregation for their poor givings, and particularly for waxing eloquent on the contrast between what the community spent on beer for the *bothan* and what they gave to the Sustentation Fund (a central church fund which paid the ministers' stipends). The Collection Plate in those days was full of pennies and suddenly one of them fell on to the tiled floor. It spun and spun interminably, and in the silence (the minister was praying at the time) it sounded like the last trump. "What a noise that penny made!" said Iain's companion. "Hoch!" said Iain, "what a noise if it hadn't been there!"

Another time Iain was standing outside a house at a funeral. In those days hundreds of people used to gather for such events. The service (a simple act of family worship) was held in the home of the deceased and accommodation was obviously limited. The practice was that close relatives along with elders and others who might be called on to pray would gather inside while the rest would wait outside. Iain's place, obviously, was inside, but he chose instead to stand at the peatstack with the young men of the village: many of them men with little time for the church. The minister was late. He had a shieling on the moors and he spent much of the summer there. Suddenly the minister's bright yellow car appeared. "Oh!" said Iain, quoting a Gaelic proverb, "it's a bad omen when the moorhen comes to the village!"

Incidentally, that car itself, the minister's pride and joy, was something of a mistake. Funeral practices in Lewis followed a strictly Puritan burial code. This code had a particular horror of the practice of praying for the dead, and in order to make sure there was no possible misunderstanding there was no prayer at the grave. To make assurance doubly sure, the minister stayed away from the cemetery altogether, returning to his manse immediately after the cortege left the house of the deceased. This meant that there was no graveside ceremony at all. When the men reached the graveside (in those days women were never present at the actual burial), they immediately lowered the coffin and filled in the grave.

As the years went by, this caused more and more resentment. I well remember at my grandmother's funeral one of my uncles (not a churchman) commenting how terrible it was that there was no minister there to pray. "But the Free Church doesn't have prayer at the grave," said my father, defensively. "Huh!" snorted my uncle, "there's no Free Church away from here anyway!"

Anyway, the minister of Ness never countenanced the cemetery. Shortly after he had purchased his bright yellow car, he asked the local doctor, "How do you like my new car?" "Very much," said the doctor, "but it's not much use for going to the cemetery."

Religious men of that generation always wore hats and, as I mentioned before, to be bare-headed was a mark of frivolity. In fact, one of my own more bizarre memories goes back to the first night I attended the prayer meeting in Partick Highland Free Church in Glasgow (sometime in 1958). There was a considerable number of young men there, all of them in their early twenties. Afterwards they stood in a huddle outside the church and I watched them from a distance. They were all hatted. The practice was even more de rigeur for ministers: so much so that when I was licensed as a minister, the very first thing I did was buy a hat. After all, I had never seen a man with a dog-collar without a hat. The one demanded the other. My eventual purchase was grey, enormous and ridiculous, and I spent a few very embarrassed days going about in it. Its first official appearance was at the funeral of Rev Kenneth Macrae in May 1964. Even in that most solemn context (and it was extremely solemn: a massive concourse of thousands of mourners), people were reduced to giggles as they came to congratulate me on my new status. "Not only a collar but a hat!" said that most irrepressible of elders, Murdo Mackinnon (Murchadh Alasdair Ruairidh), "and what a hat!"

For men of Iain Dìlidh's vintage a hat was not only a religious statement but a practical necessity. Butt of Lewis hurricanes had no pity for scalps. Once when he was on his way to the Lionel meeting-house (where the midweek meeting defied all economic revolutions and continued to be held at noon), a sudden gust blew Iain's hat right off his head. It eventually ended up in the grounds of the neighbouring Free Presbyterian Church. "Your hat must be very light!" quipped one of the brethren. "It's how light it was that left it ending up where it did," said Iain. The remark had special point in the circumstances. One of Iain's fellow-elders had suddenly decided in his eighties that he could no longer stay in the Free Church and had thrown in his lot with the Free Presbyterians.

In his later years, two things happened to Iain: he became less and less concerned about his appearance; and he discovered that there were Communions beyond the shores of Lewis. His excursions extended first to Uist, then to Skye and eventually to Wester Ross. When you added these to Lewis, Iain had a full programme for the year. He was no believer in infrequent Communion.

One of his favourite venues became Gairloch, where he found excellent and very patient hospitality. One year, when Iain looked even more than usually unkempt, his hostess, more than a little mortified, made him a gift of one of her husband's suits. Iain received it gratefully and took it home. Next year he appeared in the same old suit, looking even worse for wear. "But where's the suit I gave you last year?" said Cathie. "Och!" said Iain, "that's for special occasions." Gairloch was clearly not one of them.

Again, sorry for taking so long to get back to you. As they used to say in the NHS, I must try to reduce your waiting-times.

Yours
Bodach

18. Patricians

Dear Mme Quessaud

It wasn't my intention in my last letter to bring even a wee smile to your face, but I trust you came to no harm. Sometimes Presbyterians laugh too.

But maybe I shouldn't have given you so much encouragement to ask whether there were many 'characters' in the church in those days. There were certainly eccentrics, like Iain Dìlidh and a few others. Just before my time there was an almost legendary character known as Tormod Sona. His name is almost always translated as 'Happy Norman', though I could never understand why. In Gaelic a happy man would have been *duine dòigheil* or *duine toilichte. Sona* had quite different overtones. It meant someone who was easy-going and didn't believe in pushing himself too hard. Translated into a theological virtue, it was pretty close to contentment, but always with the suggestion that the bearer of it wasn't afflicted with the Calvinist work-ethic. This certainly seems to have been the case with Tormod. He seems to have been a classic case of being too heavenly-minded to be of any earthly use, though there were extenuating circumstances: he had been seriously injured on board a fishing-boat as a young man. Whatever allowances we must make for that, true it is that, come the Communion season, everything else took second place, and in a crofting economy that was a pretty serious problem. The season began in August with the Stornoway Communion and didn't end till November (Point): the very time of year when peats had to be taken home, corn and barley harvested and potatoes lifted. In Norman's case, by all accounts, these tasks were devolved to his wife; as was the earlier Spring work, which clashed with other Communions from February to April.

I always had some difficulty with this, not only as a detail but also as a symptom of a wider problem. There was a danger of divorcing piety from ethics; a danger of neglecting family and other responsibilities; and, perhaps above all, a danger of reducing Christian discipleship to a constant round of meetings. *Eud* (zeal) was reduced to an insatiable desire for religious services. This demand created its own supply, and a Protestantism which had denounced Catholic Holy Days soon made up for them with more than enough of its own. There were the two Sunday services, of course, and at least one midweek prayer meeting (which all who were serious about religion were expected to attend). In addition, there was a monthly meeting (on the first Monday of every month). Most interesting of all was the *coinneamh uaigneach.* This was literally the Private Meeting. It was for church members only, it was held once a month and it was still in existence in some parts of Lewis at the end of the 20th century. Its value lay in the fact that what happened there was strictly confidential and would be kept within the Christian family. Here a nervous, tongue-tied young man would be asked to pray in public for the first time. Here faults would be confessed, differences ironed out and admonition given. From these points of view the *coinneamh uaigneach* was similar to one of the older institutions of Scottish Presbyterianism, the Privy Censure: an arrangement which allowed ministers to give their colleagues a friendly warning without the formality of due process.

It's the sub-text here that's fascinating. So long as Lewis Evangelicalism retained its original flavour, Christians were genuinely protective about one another and extremely careful to ensure that 'the world' wasn't given ammunition against the church. If they knew something about a fellow believer or had something against him, it wasn't broadcast. It was kept for the *coinneamh uaigneach.* Within that framework, of course, the censuring of gossips was itself an important element. In the long term, sadly, this whole protective framework fell victim to denominationalism, where the stock of one group rose as that of another fell.

Anyway, back to the number of meetings. Apart from the local ones, there were also, of course, the more distant ones. The two major Communion seasons would have taken people like Tormod Sona away from home almost every week-end from the end of August to the middle of November; and again from mid-February to mid-April. In addition to these there were what came to be known as the *Òrduighean Beaga*: the 'Little Communions'. These were introduced to Lewis only in the1920s by Rev Roddy Macleod, of Ness. At the time they were innovations, and Macleod came under heavy fire. By the 1960s these meetings were proving a time-consuming burden and some ministers tried to have them discontinued. These ministers then came under fire as reckless innovators, changing the ancient landmarks. Such is ecclesiastical life.

The designation *Òrduighean Beaga* always fascinated me. These meetings involved no Communion, at least in the sense of the Sacrament. They were evangelistic meetings, conducted for one week throughout the winter in every congregation throughout the island. Their specific target was unconverted people; their specific aim, conversion. But committed meeting-goers soon got the message and in no time at all people were flocking to them from all over the island. This is why they came to be known as the 'Little Communions': a worrying reminder that what constituted Communion was not the sacrament but the visiting preachers and the visiting hearers. This itself changed the whole character of these services. The preachers began to aim at the godly and to preach the same kind of sermons as they would preach at Communion. In the case of some preachers, the discourses became stratospheric, and young folk found themselves subjected to sermons on the order of the divine decrees and the distinction between nature and person. That killed off the *Òrduighean Beaga*, so far as their original purpose was concerned. Yet they lived on for another fifty years : dead.

As I said, I never knew Tormod Sona, but the Gaelic singer, Kitty Macleod, once told me of a moment when she herself met Norman. Kitty's parents were both members in the Free Church and Kitty herself in her younger days (she left Lewis for Edinburgh University early in the 1930s and spent little time in her native island thereafter) sometimes accompanied them to the various Communions. On one such occasion she was in Gravir. Her father was standing talking to Tormod Sona, whose eye suddenly caught a glimpse of Kitty. "Is that your Kitty over there?" he asked (in Gaelic, of course). "Yes," said her father. "Have her bones been broken?" Norman asked.

It seems a strange question. In fact, it was an allusion to Psalm 51, verse 8: 'that so the bones which thou hast broken may rejoice.' In the Psalm, David was expressing his contrition. His bones were broken with grief for his sin. What Norman was asking would have been instantly intelligible in that particular setting: "Has she undergone conviction of sin?" The question would have been prompted by her presence at the Communion. On the face of things, no young girl would have been there unless she was under some kind of spiritual concern (there's nothing particularly Highland or Presbyterian about that. Remember what someone said about General Booth, founder of the Salvation Army: "He was the only man who ever convinced me I had a soul.")

The use of such coded language was common among these older Christians. In earlier generations it would have been even more impenetrable, when the Men spoke in what was known as *dubh-chainnt* (black or obscure language). I never had any experience of this: it seems to have been a device to allow them to speak to each other in company without 'outsiders' under-standing what they were saying. On a less esoteric level, however, the use of an insider language did continue until near the end of last century. For example, it was very common to refer to the Communion season as the *Fèill* (the Feast). Kitty Macleod (again! Sorry for the name-dropping!) once drew my attention to the fact that this usage can be found in such a well known Gaelic song as 'An t-Eilean mu Thuath', where one of the lines reads, 'Rachainn don fhèill mar iolair air sgèith'. The song was composed on an emigrant ship bound for Canada by a lay-preacher, John Macleod (Iain Thormoid Mhòir, from North Tolsta), and as Lewis faded into the distance one of his most poignant memories was of these Communion seasons.

I have seen it suggested that this use of the word *fèill* represented (and proved) the Christianisation of pagan words and practices: the Evangelicals took over the old feast-days and market-days and gave them a veneer of new content. This is too clever by half. Like my earlier allusion to broken bones, this usage goes back to the Bible itself: more precisely, to the passage in John's Gospel where the people ask (referring to Jesus), "What think ye? Will he come to the feast?" The reference here is to the Feast of the Passover. Granted that the first Lord's Supper arose out of a Passover Meal it was perfectly natural to apply Passover language to the sacrament and in the build-up to Communion seasons the hope that the Lord would be present "at the Feast" would be built into every prayer.

What I remember most, I suppose, is the patrician character of these men and women, many of them from the most humble origins. Individuality and spontaneity there certainly was, but it was reined in to avoid drawing attention to oneself. One whose memory survived down to my day was John Smith from Shawbost, known locally as 'Ain Sheoc. 'Ain Sheoc had some relation who was a minister and who used to send him his cast-offs, but it must have taken a fair measure of unself-consciousness to walk into a prayer meeting in Shawbost dressed in pin-stripes and frock-coat! 'Ain Sheoc wasn't a communicant (maybe because he suffered from chronic spiritual depression), but his standing was such that the rule that only men who were 'professing' should be called on to pray in public was overlooked in his case. John's spirituality was temperamental, however, and sometimes he was completely out of sorts. On one such occasion, he refused to get up when called on. This wasn't all that uncommon, but it always created moments of awkwardness, and those around 'Ain Sheoc began to whisper, "Siuthad, Iain! Siuthad, Iain!" ("Come on, John! Come on, John!"). At last the prompters prevailed and John rose, but he was completely tongue-tied. Not two words could he string together. He sat down, disconsolate, muttering loudly, "Siuthad, Iain! Siuthad! Siuthad! 'S nuair a shiuthad thu, shiuthad thu!" ("Come on, John! Come on, John!' they said, and when you came on you sure did come on!")

But such tongue-tied occasions were rare, and 'Ain Sheoc's prayers were often marked by such epigrammatic profundity that they lived on in local evangelical tradition. Once, for example, he addressed the Lord as follows, "Bu tu fhèin an lighiche coibhneil, uasal, sgileil, faisg air làimh dhuinn" ('Thou art the kind, noble, skilful physician, always near at hand'). On another occasion, he observed, "Nuair as gile neul, agus as fhaide air falbh an cunnart, bi thusa, Dhè, faisg air làimh oirnn" ('When the sky is brightest and danger farthest from us, do thou, Lord, stay close to us'). On yet another occasion he strung together, quite spontaneously, a remarkable string of alliterative adjectives, all affixed to the single noun 'instruction': "Gum biodh do theagaisg bhrìoghmhor, bhuadhach, bheannaichte, bharraichte, bhuannachdail, bhuan-mhaireannach oirnn" ('May your instruction, so weighty, so powerful, so blessed, so well-founded, so profitable and so everlasting, be upon us').

Another worthy of the same vintage was Angus Mackay, 'Bodach Lìniseadair' (Linshader is in Uig, where your own roots are). Apparently he had an endearing habit of addressing little girls as 'A lasag bhochd!': my wife was one of those so addressed. It is odd, considering the impression he made, how little of his time Angus actually spent in Lewis. For most of his life he lived in Bury in Lancashire, working for a clothing firm. This may account for some of his exotic tastes. He was a skilled caligrapher and book-binder and kept a large volume into which he had transcribed, in copperplate, all his favourite passages from the Bible. He seems, too, to have been something of a natty dresser, particularly noted for his sealskin waistcoat, the result of a holiday in Norway.

It was only in 1946, seven years before his death, that Angus returned to Lewis. He took with him his housekeeper. She had rendered faithful service in Lancashire, but her powers were clearly failing and Angus employed a local girl, Ciorstag, (mother of Mòr Bhrù, later famous in her own right as a depository of local history and tradition), to be her colleague and later (Angus hoped) her successor. The arrangement worked spendidly, but unfortunately Ciorstag's older sister decided to get married, which meant that Ciorstag herself now had to give up her work and go home to look after her mother. Reeling from the shock, Angus found his woes were compounded by a culinary disaster which occurred at exactly the wrong moment. He had ordered some fish and some venison and the old lady, having taken delivery, decided to cook them at once: in the same pan.

Crestfallen and frustrated (there's nothing worse than to be all psyched-up for a sumptuous meal, only to see it ruined), Angus sat at the table and delivered himself of the following effusion (aimed at the departing Ciorstag):

Cò dheasaicheas ar biadh 's tu 'g iarraidh dhachaigh?
Chan fhiach a' chailleach, tha crùib oirr'.
Chan aithnich i fiadh bho cliathaich langa -
A chiall, bidh mise gad ionndrainn!

Which, roughly translated, reads:

Who'll cook our food, and you wanting home?
The cailleach 's no use, she's old and crooked.
She can't tell deer from the side of a ling -
Goodness, am I going to miss you!

I doubt if I would have reacted so graciously, but it seems to have come naturally to Bodach Lìniseadair. He once had to sit through a sermon which was riddled with gamhlas 'hate', (probably aimed at some other denomination). It was to some people's taste, but not to Angus's, and when someone approached him commenting what a great sermon they had just heard, Angus replied that he hadn't been able to understand it, because he had never harboured ill-feeling against anyone in his life.

His poetical flights weren't confined to the low points of domestic politics. At least one other weightier composition survives, composed, in her old age, as a tribute to Catherine MacAulay, one of the last surviving converts of the revival in Uig under Rev Alexander Macleod. This Catherine was Angus Mackay's aunt, and great-grandmother to Duncan Maclean, for many years the highly respected Surgeon at the Western Isles Hospital. At the time of her conversion she was a young girl of twelve. Angus's poem has some of the style of an elegy, but the poem envisages her as still alive, though on her deathbed. I have only two verses of it, but since I suspect you'll have difficulty finding it elsewhere, I'll give it to you as I have it.

A Chatrìona, b' òg' a dhùisgeadh tu
Bho dhùsal is bho shuain:
Chaidh feadan òir nam pìoban ud
A shìneadh thro do chluas.
Nuair shaothraich gràs Fear-saoraidh ort,
Gun do strìochd do chridhe cruaidh,
Is stamp an Rìgh air t' aodann -
Leam as prìseil bhith ga luaidh.

Ged tha thu nis air fàilligeadh
Is do thàmh ann an Àird Ùig,
A chaoidh gu bràth chan fhàg E thu
Mar chrìch don bhàs 's don ùir;
Bhon thug E 'n gath mu thràth às dhut
Tha d' àirc a-nis fo shùil,
'S cha stad i nis air Ararat leat -
Air Pàrras tha a cùrs.

I hesitate, after that, to give you my one remaining Bodach Lìniseadair story, but it is, again, part of the larger picture. Besides, I can vouch for it unconditionally, since I had the benefit of a first-hand account. Once at a Communion on the West Side he was asked to dinner after the Sunday morning service by one of the first Free Church women in Lewis to own a car. Unfortunately, as the Bodach struggled into it, she slammed the door on his hand. She got him home, administered such first-aid as she could, and gave him a large whisky - very large. When the time came for the evening service, she was very much of the opinion that the effects of the whisky had not worn off and that he would be much wiser to stay in the house. He would have none of it and insisted on going. It was a short service, followed by a prayer meeting. The Bodach was the first to be called to pray, and the lady's heart sank. But up he got and prayed with such fluency, liberty and fervour as she had never heard before.

Sometimes the apparent eccentricities of these men were not so much traits of character as the results of the asymmetrical bilingualism (Gaelic strong, English weak) which was common in the islands in the first half of the 20th century. Lewis people would be instinctive, fluent and even eloquent speakers of Gaelic, but with just enough English to get them by in business and in dealing with officials. With few exceptions, they shrank from public prayer in English. In fact, this was still the case during my ministry in Glasgow in the 1970s, although by that time the problem could work both ways. One of the elders had been thoroughly Anglicised (or at least Glaswegianised) by forty years in the Clyde shipyards, and during his pre-conversion years he had lost touch with the vocabulary of the Gaelic Bible and Gaelic worship. But he wasn't a man to be daunted by such handicaps and he unhesitatingly accepted his responsibility to pray in Gaelic, often teetering on the brink of verbal disaster before invariably staging a remarkable recovery. But there was one confusion he never overcame: he regularly thanked the Almighty for giving him personally 'talents He hadn't given to many'. The reason was simple enough: he really wanted to thank the Lord for his spiritual privileges, but there was no way he could lay hold of the relevant Gaelic word, *sochairean.* Week after week his mind alighted, instead, on *tàlantan.*

In the islands, it was praying in English that caused panic and few of the elders would venture. There was however one admirable character, Aonghnas Caoidh (Angus Mackay from Kershader), who was never frightened to be a fool for Christ. On his first venture into English prayer, Angus found himself in serious difficulty: he didn't know how to conclude a prayer in that language. Round and round he went, like a distressed aircraft circling an airfield, until he had a sudden flash of inspiration: 'Yours faithfully, Angus Mackay. Amen!' It owed more to the J. D. Williams mail-order service than to the Prayer Book, but at least it got him down.

Angus was also a regular speaker to the Question and all the regular Communion-goers were familiar with the story of his conversion. He was in the Royal Navy at the time, serving on a cruiser, and after a few years the cruiser was almost as well known in Lewis as Angus himself. Angus was particularly anxious to let it be known what an ungodly place the ship was, and how difficult life on board was for a young Christian. His punch-line was a description of the crew, which went something like: "The ship was full of Blacks, Catholics and about a dozen Hearachs ('Harrismen'). Almost as bad as Sodom.

On one occasion, he happened to be at a Communion where his own minister, Rev. Murdo Macrae, was the senior visiting preacher. The practice was that the local minister called on those he wanted to speak to the Question, but just as he was about to call Angus, Macrae turned to him and said, in a loud whisper, "Cuir torpedo dhan a' chruiser an toiseach!" ('Put a torpedo in the cruiser first!')

It seems odd, but amid all the solemnity of such liturgy there was sometimes an undercurrent of solemn banter, as elders sought to trip up ministers and ministers sought to get their own back on the elders. One weapon at the disposal of the elders was the text given out for the Question. They had the whole Bible to choose from, but normally chose a well-known text on which it was easy for the presiding minister to offer a few illuminating comments. It was also easy enough, however, to hand the minister a hand-grenade instead. Such bad habits never made it across the Minch to Lewis, but on one occasion in Inverness an elder with no love for the presiding minister proposed the text "Saddle me the ass" (1 Kings 13.13). Even the most inveterate allegoriser would have found it hard to spiritualise that one. The minister, however, was equal to the occasion and in no mood to take prisoners. "If you find the saddle," he said, looking at the elder ominously, "I'll soon find the ass." A similar incident occurred in the neighbouring parish of Kiltarlity, where an elder proposed the text "I beheld Satan as lightning fall from heaven" (Luke 10.18). "I think," said the minister, "he has just fallen into this church."

Another man I recall was renowned less for his eccentricities than for his waspish anti-clericalism. He was an elder in Ness, was probably related to myself, was regularly entertained in my grandfather's house and went by the name of Dòmhnall 'Ain Thangaidh. Probably the reason he was never in our house in Laxdale (where most Ness folk appeared at some time or other) was that he was so antagonistic to his own minister that my parents refused to countenance him. I did hear him speak once, in the church in Stornoway, but I remember nothing of it except this: "When we were young," he said, "and people were taking farewell of each other, they used to say, 'God bless you!' Now they say, 'Cheerie!'" Not much to edify in that.

This gentlemen was a regular Communion-goer, but in between Communions he stayed at home. Nothing would induce him to sit under the ministry of the Free Church minister at Cross, Rev John Morrison. In that respect, Domhnall 'Ain Thangaidh was an authentic representative of the long tradition of Highland Separatism. Lewis is often portrayed as a clerically-dominated community, but nothing could be further from the truth. There was an endemic anti-clericalism. This probably owed something to the genesis of Lewis evangelicalism, particularly at the north end of the island. You will remember that John Macleod, the schoolmaster in Galson, was forced out of his job by the parish minister for daring to preach (in contravention of the rules of the Gaelic Schools Society). Another great lay-preacher, Finlay Munro (a folk-hero to my parents' generation), faced unrelenting clerical opposition. Such attitudes inevitably created polarisation between clergy and people. This appeared at its most dramatic in 1900, when virtually all the Free Church ministers in Lewis (Hector Cameron, Back, was the one exception) joined the United Free Church. The people disowned them and stayed in the Free Church, reduced by the Union to a rump of twenty-six ministers.

Some ministers did, of course, command respect. A few were even revered. But that owed little to their office. Domhnall 'Ain Thangaidh could even say to one minister daft enough to fish for a compliment, "We never heard your like. And we hope we never will!" And Iain Dìlidh could tell his minister at a Congregational Meeting, "You're not the only one here who can speak English." If such things could be said to their faces, you can imagine what was said behind their backs. They lived in glasshouses, their every move under scrutiny, their every proposal obstructed, their every comfort grudged and their every sermon liable to instant dissection and damnation.

You can understand, too, my mother's absolute horror when she realised I was going in for the ministry: "Caithidh tu do bheatha ann am beul dhaoine!" ("You'll spend your life in people's mouths!"), by which she meant that I would always be the subject of controversy. That was her view of the minister's lot. In my case, she spoke truer than she knew. But by the time it was at its worst, she was beyond knowing.

The other side of this is that ministers figured only minimally in our lives as children. We heard (or, more accurately, saw) them in the pulpit every Sunday, and if we judged them at all it was on their voices. Most of us never saw them in our homes; and we would certainly never have dreamed of being asked to theirs. Great store was certainly set by 'attendance on the public means of grace' but most of the real religion took place away from church buildings, in the homes of the people.

Yours
Donald

19. A woman in the house

1 May 2024

Dear Mme Quessaud

Thanks for the photos. I don't see much of your mother in yourself, but Chirsty, your eldest daughter, strongly resembles her. That may be because she is about the same age as your mother was the last time I saw her that day on the *Loch Seaforth*. She has the same chestnut-coloured hair, the laughing, mischievous eyes and the unself-conscious poise I remember so well.

The MacLennan genes have moved a long way from Mangersta: you an ethnographer and Chirsty a physicist, and both of you so enthusiastic about Quebec. It's ironic that while your mother and I, along with our whole generation, acquiesced so meekly in the extirpation of our own Gaelic culture, her descendants should be struggling so manfully (if you'll pardon the expression) for the survival of the historic language and traditions of the country she adopted.

Sorry I came across as such a male chauvinist, but I was simply trying to describe things as they were. Besides, I hadn't progressed far beyond the 19th century, and at that time not only the church but the whole world, including Canada, was patriarchal. Women seldom had the opportunity to be pioneers, innovators or foundation-layers.

Just to put things in perspective: my theology of gender is similar to that of the little boy who said to his mother, "Mammy, God made women, but who made ladies?" The original human pair were created equals in the image of God. Gender is a later social construct, putting girl babies in pink and boy babies in blue, giving dolls to the one and toy tractors to the other, grooming the girls for submission and training the boys for domination. That's how we arrived where we were by the 1940s; and that roughly is where we are still, despite the heroic efforts of feminism. The meek shall inherit the earth, but not in this life. There are too many power-hungry men and too few power-hungry women.

Yet I'm not convinced that Lewis Evangelicalism presents a picture of unrelieved patriarchalism. Some of its most fascinating characters are women.

Forgive me if I take you back again to the beginning. In 1800, Christians in Lewis were as rare as snakes in Iceland (I think the comparison is borrowed from someone else, but I can't remember who). There was certainly no Protestantism of the kind to be found in Easter Ross. Not that the Reformation didn't touch Lewis. It did, but only in a nominal way. The first Protestant minister was settled there some time around 1566, a mere six years after the Reformation was ratified by the Scottish Parliament. To begin with, there were two parishes, Stornoway and Barvas. A third, Lochs and Uig, was erected in 1722. But there was little power in the religion, and the island remained riven by feuding, partly between Protestants and Catholics, but mainly between rival families. The ministers appear to have owed their charges more to heredity than to zeal or piety and to have joined in the feuding with relish. One of these was Kenneth Morrison, who succeeded his father as minister of Stornoway (and was himself succeeded by his cousin) some time around 1689 and appears to have been known as Coinneach Dubh. By all accounts he was more suited to the ministry than most of the succession, but still found it necessary to have a drawn sword by his side when walking from the manse to the church on a Sunday morning; and to have the added precaution of having the church door guarded by two men with drawn swords during the service.

Only at the beginning of the 19th century did things begin to change, and, as often happens at the beginning of a movement, the early converts were remarkable figures. One of the very first was John Mackay of Barvas. Unfortunately, our information about him is exceedingly scanty and the reason for that is that not long after his conversion he emigrated to your part of the world. Today, we on this side of the water instinctively associate Quebec with the French, anti-Britishness and Roman Catholicism. But, as you know from reading Margaret Bennett's book, in the 19th century it was a haven for Lewis emigrants, many of whom settled in the area known as 'The Eastern Townships'. They took the love of the mother country with them, called their settlements Tolsta, Dell, Gisla, Bosta, Ness, Galson, Stornoway and Balallan, set up Gaelic church services and commemorated their dead with Gaelic epitaphs. When they hit Canada, they were Gaelic monoglots. Within a generation, they were fluently bilingual in Gaelic and English. In the next, they were fluent in English and French. Today, they tell me (but maybe in jest), you, the descendants of Quebec's Gaels, are almost all French monoglots.

The fate of Gaelic in Quebec simply parallels its fate in the home country. Emigrants didn't have to face the persecution of the language experienced by those who remained at home, where the educational establishment was determined to suppress what it saw as a barbaric tongue. But the social and economic pressures were, if anything, stronger in Canada, even though in the 19th century the country was only a pale shadow of the confident giant it has now become. A Gaelic monoglot was certainly a second-class citizen, with no chance of economic progress, and the learning of English was an urgent priority. But there were also issues of status. The young, the posh and the progressive quickly reached the point so common in my own early days, when people felt inferior if they spoke Gaelic and where there was strong social pressure to deny it. It may seem a bold comparison, but this attitude always reminded me of Peter's denial of Christ. "Chan eil Gaelic agam!" parallels Peter's, "I don't know the man!"

Women, if you'll forgive me, were at least as likely as men to fall into this trap, 'forgetting' their Gaelic and affecting some of the airs and graces of the mistresses they served as housemaids. But it was a risky business to come back to Lewis and parade such vanity. One woman, refined by some years as a housemaid in Glasgow, grandly minced her way onto the bus after her voyage across the Minch and asked with the superior air of a stranger, "Where shall I sit?" A voice came from the back: "Suidhidh tu far an suidh an còrr de chloinn nan daoine - air do mhàs!" ("You'll sit where the rest of the human race sit - on your buttocks!") She then knew she was home. But isn't it odd that anyone should be ashamed of being able to speak a language, let alone a mother tongue?

One of the most fascinating things about the emigration to Quebec was that some of the outstanding figures in early Lewis Evangelicalism joined the migrants. I always found this hard to understand. There they were in the middle of a memorable religious awakening, yet they turned their backs on it and set off for a world where they could never expect to enjoy their familiar cycle of monthly meetings, quarterly meetings, prayer meetings, fellowship meetings and Communions. It's not as if, like the Pilgrim Fathers, they emigrated in search of religious freedom. They had freedom enough at home. Nor were they driven by the disillusionment with Scottish Christianity which drove the Separatist, Norman MacLeod of Assynt, to sail off with his followers to Cape Breton. Separatism had no hold in Lewis: at least, not till the 1990s.

These emigrants may have believed, quite sincerely, that their religious culture would emigrate with them: they would establish Gaelic congregations and perpetuate their own unique brand of Peasant Presbyterianism (not a term I use in any derogatory sense) in their new world. But the ultimate and cruel truth, I fear, is that they were driven by the same primal need as filled the *Metagama* a century later: hunger.

Among those who emigrated was John Mackay of Barvas, converted some time around 1805-07. All our knowledge of this period depends on oral tradition, and this itself deserves some comment, because Evangelicalism is often accused of destroying oral tradition. The real truth, in my own view, is that mega-changes in the culture set oral tradition off in completely new directions.

Two things happened. First, the two World Wars. I hardly need to tell you how deeply affected Lewis was by these conflicts. Throughout the wars, the taigh-cèilidh persisted, but its character inevitably changed. It became the place where people caught up with news of the war, particularly as it affected local boys. The advent of radio gave the occasion yet another twist. To begin with, very few houses could afford a 'wireless', and those which had one inevitably served as a magnet. In these, throughout the War (the second War), people would gather at nine o'clock every night to hear John Snagg announce, "This is the BBC Home Service. Here is the news." News of any sinking immediately generated fevered discussion: "That's the ship Calum Murdo was on!" or "Were there any boys from the island on her?" Later, memories of the conflict itself became the stuff of legend. I may have heard nothing of *Mac an t-Srònaich*, but I certainly heard about the *Iolaire*. Then there was the night the *Royal Oak* was sunk in Scapa Flow; and the *Hood*; and the *Bismarck*; and El Alamein; and the blitz on Clydebank. Later came the stories of the exploits of island seamen such as Malcolm Morrison from Calbost and Angus Murray from Shawbost.

These stories eclipsed whatever traditions had survived about Goraidh Cròbhan, Cuchulain and the fairies. You will probably argue that it is a pity that such prosaic, factual memories should have silenced the imaginative traditions of the past; even that the obsession with fact at the expense of fiction is itself a symptom of the tragic blindness of Calvinism. But oral tradition survives only so long as it serves its community, creating the mythical or living history which gives it its pride and its sense of identity. Men who had fought at El Alamein didn't need legends of Culloden; and villages which could boast of war heroes didn't need myths about the Fingalians. Oral tradition can no more be static than can history itself.

The other thing that happened was that Lewis Evangelicalism developed its own oral traditions. They've been lost long since, but mercifully they were gathered together early last century in several different publications produced independently. When I was younger, some of my historian friends used to rail against these books because they provided no documentation. But I thought then, and think still, that that criticism is entirely inappropriate. There were no documents, only traditions; and the men who collected them were all within striking distance of their roots. For example, Principal John Macleod, whose *By-Paths of Highland Church History* gives us our best account of Finlay Munro, taught in Stornoway as a young man in the 1890s and became a close friend of Angus Morrison, who in his own youth had been Finlay Munro's precentor. Norman Macfarlane (author of *The 'Men' of the Lews*) had his roots in the parish of Ness, where he was born in 1870, a time when the memories of the early days of Evangelicalism were still strong. Murdo Campbell (*Gleanings of a Highland Harvest*) was born in the same parish a generation later, and had the added advantage that his own father was a Catechist. John Macleod, whose Gaelic biography of Tormod Sona, *Am Measg nan Lili*, is probably the best-earthed (and best written) of all these written summaries of oral tradition, was Free Church minister of Barvas (the first parish where Evangelicalism took hold) from 1922 to 1956.

All these men were familiar with Christians whose contacts took them right back to the early 19th century and whose memories were stored with evangelical lore. In some cases, indeed, their contacts would themselves have been outstanding figures in the movement. Such people would never have seen it as their main responsibility to pass on the stories: after all, the business of Evangelicalism was to produce saints, not seanachies. But it produced seanachies nonetheless, and when their stories passed into the pulpit and the taigh-cèilidh they survived till they died with Evanglicalism itself. It could even be said that Evangelicalism died when it lost its own oral tradition.

It is to this oral tradition that we owe the story of the conversion of John Mackay. The story begins with the discovery of a leaf of the newly translated Gaelic Bible by a young girl in Barvas. She passed it around, and its contents (I have no idea what chapter of the Bible it was) seem to have struck a chord among her friends. Among those affected was John Mackay; and among those who were led to the Lord by John was Catherine Mackay, known as 'Catrìona Thangaidh' from the district in Barvas where she resided.

A remarkable bond developed between John and Catherine: a bond which survived not only his marriage but his emigration to Canada. Mackay was by all accounts an extremely lovable man, who bonded with men as well as with women, and he and Catherine corresponded regularly to the end of his life. The tradition called it *ceangal-anama* or soul-bonding and we have no reason to think it was anything other than that. Later it would be known as *gràdh spioradail* (spiritual love), to distance it from the erotic.

In his last letter to Catriona John wrote, "Before you get this letter, I will be in glory and you won't be long after me." While the letter was in the post Catriona rose one morning and announced, "My beloved doesn't need my prayers today." By the time the letter arrived news had come that John had passed away that very day. Catriona herself died shortly afterwards. I have no reason to doubt the factuality of any of this.

Catriona's life was full of remarkable providences. On one occasion she went off to the Communion in North Tolsta, fortified not only by the hope of spiritual blessing but by a 'promise' that she would receive a pair of shoes. The weekend passed and on Monday afternoon Catriona headed back to Barvas with the promise still unfulfilled. When she reached Mùirneag, she sat down to rest. At that very moment a

Sassenach (probably from Gress Lodge) was out shooting. Seeing a movement, the man mistook Catriona for a deer, took aim and fired. The gun jammed and in that instant the hunter saw Catriona and realised what he had done. She, of course, knew nothing of what had happened, but he approached her and told her. "It's all right," said Catriona, totally unmoved, "my heavenly Father won't let you or anyone else hurt me." The man then saw that she was barefoot, and gave her the money to buy a pair of shoes.

Catriona, oddly enough, was very loyal to Rev William MacRae, the Moderate minister of Barvas. MacRae was something of a conundrum. For all that he was regarded as a Moderate, and for all that he was so heavy-handed in his dealings with John Macleod of Galson, there must have been something in his preaching to stimulate an interest in spiritual things. Otherwise it's very hard to explain how the discovery of a mere leaf of the Gaelic Bible could have had such dramatic effect. There must have been some previous point of contact. Besides, MacRae was a champion of the crofters, he was good to the poor and he was good to Catriona. Her father had been his shepherd and after he died MacRae allowed Catriona to continue living in his bothy. MacRae's successor was equally generous, but his grieve appears to have been of a different kidney. He couldn't throw Catriona out, but he could make life difficult. He forbade her to plant potatoes and moved his own three grey horses in to graze on the shepherd's plot. With no means of support Catriona was in dire circumstances, and one day she went out and started pulling up the shaws which had sprouted from the previous year's potatoes. The grieve spotted her, lost his temper and gave her a merciless going-over.

Catriona, bruised and battered, turned for support and comfort to her friend, Fionnghal (Fiona) Bheag, who lived in Park, Barvas. "Od! Od!" said Fionnghal, "it couldn't have been as bad as you're saying!" "Ge-tà," said an aggrieved Catriona, "it wasn't your head he was banging on the ground. But the

Lord will take him away, and the three grey horses will carry him out." And of course

Barvas illustrates very well just how useless labels such as 'Moderate' and 'Evangelical' can be. There was one woman in Barvas who was very much given to visions but had a very dim view of her minister. MacRae had a much-loved white horse, and in one of her visions the lady saw the minister and the horse going headfirst into Hell. There's not much point in having visions if you can't get some kudos from them, and she quickly put the story into circulation. Eventually it reached even the minister's ears. "Well," he said, "Whatever happens to Mr MacRae, there's one thing sure: the white horse will never go to Hell."

Catriona had a completely different estimation of MacRae: so much so that when he died she composed a fulsome elegy, praising him not only for his wisdom and for his prayerful attention to the sick, but for the fact that the word of truth was habitually before his mind. She certainly didn't see him as a hell-bound false prophet (Catriona's *Laoidhean agus Òrain* (Songs and Hymns) were published in a 38-page booklet in 1917, edited by Rev Alasdair MacRae).

Apart from possessing considerable personal charm and a happy, optimistic personality, Catriona cut a tall, handsome figure and was instantly recognisable far outside her own peasant-evangelical circle. On one occasion, Sir James Matheson saw her in Stornoway, approached her and invited her to the Castle. There she was shown round the magnificent rooms and halls by Lady Matheson's mother, Mrs Perceval. "Isn't this a lovely house my daughter has!" said Mrs Perceval proudly. "Yes, indeed," said Catriona, "but it wouldn't make a kitchen in my Father's house." Mrs Perceval knew her Bible well enough to get Catriona's point. Catriona, for her part, left the castle with a good length of Matheson tartan, which graced many a Communion for years afterwards.

Sometimes she comes across as a blend of incorrigible joker and spiritual flirt. On one of her journeys across the Barvas

Moor she met a young boy. On asking who he was, she discovered it was the son of her friend, John Mackay. "Then," said Catriona, "you go home and tell your father that you are the son of a right thief." The boy, disconcerted at having made such a discovery about his revered parent, delivered the message as instructed. John knew at once that the 'stranger' was Catriona, and the next time he met her he asked, "Why did you tell my boy I was a thief?" "You know very well," said Catriona, "that you stole my heart from me long ago." It looks very much as if in these circles of evangelical *agape* there were many brethren besides John Mackay who had been guilty of the same felony.

Catriona's friend, Fionnghal Bheag, was almost equally eminent in the oral tradition. She too had her visions, one of which meshed with a story which was still vividly recalled and recounted by my father's generation. Around 1890, some of the elders in Ness became disaffected with the minister, Rev Duncan Macbeath. I'll not bore you with the reasons: on the face of things, the problem was about a roof (roofs are the key to many a problem: a College Principal in England once told me he spent his whole period in office trying to get the roof repaired). Macbeath appears to have been fairly limited academically, but he had a powerful personal hold over most of the congregation: a hold which owed something to the fact that he represented that type of Highland piety which claimed to have 'the secret of the Lord'. Many certainly saw him as a prophet, and one of his prophecies was that none of those who were causing the disunity would die in his bed. There were four elders involved, I think: one rose from his sick-bed to go for a walk, and died of a heart attack; another left his house one morning and not a trace of him was ever seen again; and two went to live in North Rona to make sure, in the words of John Macleod, that they wouldn't have to hear Macbeath preach.

One night Fionnghal began to have a very powerful impression that one of the men on Rona (probably well-known to her from the Communion circuit) was in desperate need, and she began to pray for him. At the same time she was gripped by words from Psalm 73, peculiarly appropriate to men clinging tenaciously to clifftops in the North Atlantic: 'my steps near slipped, my feet were almost gone.' She came to be convinced that the man was dead: so convinced, in fact, that she had word sent to Dr Ross, the local doctor, informing him that there had been a death on Rona and that he should send people to investigate. They found the two men dead, one inside the bothy, the other outside.

The revelation received by Fionnghal also assured her that the man who had been on her mind was, for all his short-comings, a true heir of salvation. But the limitations of the vision are also fascinating, as John Macleod pointed out. It gave few details, only the fact of his death. The cause of the deaths was never established either by revelation or by official investigation.

The lives of Fionnghal Bheag and Catrìona Thangaidh cover almost the whole of the 19th century: a period, as you know, of great hardship in the Highlands. Yet they present a very different picture of a woman's lot from the one drawn in Sorley MacLean's searing poem, 'Ban-ghàidheal'. In the poem, the Highland Woman is slaving away at the kelp-cutting, the toil destroying the golden summer of her youth, ploughing deep furrows on her forehead and driving her to the black peace of an early grave as she struggles to earn enough to keep her children and pay the landlord; and when she goes to church on Sunday she hears of nothing but the lost state of her miserable soul.

This is a brilliant snapshot, but it is not a picture Catrìona Thangaidh would have recognised. In terms of cash-flow, she was certainly in straitened circumstances, but her own temperament, the compassion of the minister (Moderate though he might have been) and, above all, the support of the community gave her a lifestyle removed as far as possible from that of the pauper. Even if we leave the spiritual dimension aside, she and Fionnghal had a full social life, an extensive and lively circle of friends and endless opportunity to share stories and discuss the deepest theological and metaphysical questions associated with Christianity.

This fully accords with my own recollections of Lewis religion. I hate the phrase 'the role of women'. They were not playing a role, any more than the men were playing a role. Nor were they marginalised. Catrìona Thangaidh was 'an eminent person' in the circles in which she moved, revered by young and old, male and female. Women took no part, of course, in church services, but these represented only a fraction of the religious life of the island. Much of the reality happened after church and outside the church, where the apparent Pauline prohibitions on women speaking weren't deemed to apply. In these fellowships, women could recount, debate and discuss with the best of them. Women like Catrìona Thangaidh could even hold court.

Our oral traditions weren't limited to Lewis, of course, and we were also aware of other spiritual giants like Ceit Mhòr ('Muckle Kate') of Lochcarron and *Bean a' Chreideimh Mhòir* ('The Woman of Great Faith'), one of the most attractive characters in the history of Highland Evangelicalism. Born Margaret Macdiarmid, she left her native Argyll as a young woman, settled in Sutherland and became (as was inevitable in *Dùthaich MhicAoidh*) a Mrs Mackay. She's worth a book in her own right. Even the formidable Dr Kennedy praised her in language as fulsome as any of his eulogies of the Men: "Her brilliant wit, her exuberant spirits, her intense originality of thought and speech and manner, her great faith and her fervent love, formed a combination but rarely found." And just to confirm that the Highland worthies weren't just a bunch of dour misogynists, it's interesting that when a brief biography of Macdiarmid was published in 1929, the profits were to go to a Fund for the erection of a memorial. I can't recall any elder to whom such an honour was extended.

One story about Margaret MacDiarmid will have to suffice. On one occasion, she was invited to the manse of Dr Ross of

Lochbroom after the usual Thanksgiving Service on the Monday morning of a Communion. Such occasions are often very jolly affairs. The ministers are exhausted after conducting so many services, but the strain is over, and they often collapse into a state of banter and frivolity, as nature takes its toll of taut nerves after a stressful weekend. The conversation at Dr Ross's table wasn't very edifying and Margaret made an effort to raise the tone. Dr Ross, a Jupiter-like figure, wasn't at all impressed with this and pointed out that the Apostle Paul didn't allow women to speak in public. "Indeed, sir," said Margaret, "if the Apostle Paul were here, no woman would need to speak."

Frivolity in Highland churches? Just one more story. When I was young, one of the characters was Anna a' Bhillioin, the life and soul of many a gathering and the mother of my first girlfriend, Chrismar Mackay, whose tricycle I requisitioned shortly before my fourth birthday (Chrismar later became a distinguished journalist). Anna's own mother, Bean a' Bhillioin, was an even more charismatic character, but when she left the Free Church in 1900 and entered the United Free Church, there was some little tension between herself and her friends, including her clerical ones. Among these was the Reverend Roderick Macleod of Knock, and Mr Macleod was once unwise enough to cold-shoulder Bean a' Bhillioin in public, probably outside a church, after some service. She was having none of it. She put her arm under the Reverend's and propelled him into a jig while she chanted, "Ged a tha mi dhen an Aonadh, bidh mi còmhla riut an Glòir" ("Though I've joined the UF, I'll still be with you in Glory").

Now that must be that. I'm beginning to see double, and it's not just because I'm wearing my father's black-rimmed glasses.

Yours
Bodach

2 June 2024

Dear Mme Quessaud

I was wondering when you would discover Alexander Carmichael and his *Carmina Gadelica*. I hadn't read him for many years, but your letter sent me back to him, just to check. The picture he draws is still, to me, utterly incredible. According to him, the ministers had completely extirpated all music and song by the beginning of last century. No-one danced at weddings. No one composed songs any more. No-one sang. All these things had been pronounced vanity by the godly ministers and the people had meekly submitted to them. There was nothing but church and whisky.

I wasn't around, believe it or not, at the beginning of last century, but my parents were, and they spoke often enough of their own experiences as children and adults. Neither of their homes was musical. In fact, both were probably uncommonly strict and puritanical. But one of their clear memories of life in Ness in the 1920s was of *danns an rathaid* (literally, the road-dance). My father was from Cross, my mother from Habost, and the venue for these dances seems to have been the bridge at Swainbost, the village which lay between. That was where they first met (they lived only a mile apart, but a mile was a long way in those days). The music came from melodeons, not from mouth-music (puirt-à-beul). No ecclesiastical ban seems to have cast a shadow over the entertainment.

Kitty Macleod was a contemporary of my parents. Her father and mother, as I mentioned before, were both members of the Free Church, but her home, unlike my parents', was intensely musical. By Carmichael's account that was impossible. But Kitty was clear about it. She didn't speak of it as something she had to prove. Music and song were as much part of her childhood as the machair and the skylark. Indeed, she once said that she spent her early years swimming in music (*a' snàmh ann an ceòl*). This explains why she was so hurt, once, when one of the insufferable snobs of Stornoway said to her after a performance, "It's a pity you can't sing to accompaniment!" The memory never left her. I remember her relating it to me on her deathbed and I can still see her throwing back her head, catching her hair in a pony-tail and running off a list of all the musical instruments in her house: a piano, a violin, bagpipes and a Jewish harp (and a few more). Not only was this in Ness: it was in the home of church members.

Kitty Macleod herself had an incomparable repertoire of Gaelic song, and almost all of it was in the strict sense traditional. She hadn't learned it from books or garnered it from the songs prescribed for the Mod by the Comunn Gàidhealach. She had imbibed it from the people around her. Some she had picked up in the taighean-cèilidh: places where, in those days, a child would have seen no evil and heard no evil and where she'd been welcome from her earliest years. Others (indeed, many) she had picked up, as she would have said, "on the bus". In the 1930s and 40s Lewis buses were an institution, particularly the Ness ones. They carried all kinds of cargo from bundles of Harris Tweed to barrels of paraffin and bags of Ness Bakery's 'Famous Biscuits'; stopped at almost every house with newspapers or messages or medical prescriptions; and invariably carried at least one or two inebriated passengers. Some would be men from the Merchant Navy coming home on leave. Others would be men who went to Stornoway but once a year and made the most of it. Kitty, as a pupil in the Nicolson Institute, was on the bus frequently. The one thing she always mentioned about it was the singing. Men who would never sing when sober lost all their inhibitions when drunk. That's where she learned all her songs, she would say mischievously. It was certainly where she learned many of them. The efforts of the godly ministers had clearly been unavailing.

The other contributor to Kitty Macleod's repertoire was the *luadh*. The *luadh* was a working-party of women called together for the specific task of 'waulking' tweed. I never saw this in real life, but the object of the exercise was to improve the texture of the cloth by beating it roughly against a wooden table. As they did this, the women sang, working to the rhythm of the song. By the time I arrived on the planet, the practice survived only in the contrived setting of Mod performances and concert platforms. But in Ness in the 1920s and 30s it was still very much alive.

I was rather incredulous about this, and pressed Kitty about it. "No," she said, "they didn't waulk the tweed, because they were no longer producing tweed locally in Ness. But they were still waulking the blankets (*cuibhrigean*), which were woven locally."

I never much cared for these songs (*òrain luaidh*). They always seemed to me superficial in both music and sentiment and not even nostalgia can make me change my mind. But Kitty cherished them, because for her they were part of a living and precious past, rich with the memories of laughter and friendship. She had a huge repertoire of them and she conveyed the clear impression that when the *luadh* was in its heyday these songs had little fixity, at least as far as the words were concerned. Each time they were sung new verses were added, often reflecting local romances and other gossip.

Another interesting point made by Kitty Macleod was that there were two kinds of *luadh*: the *luadh làimh* (waulking by hand) and the *luadh chas* (waulking by foot). I have the impression that the latter (which obviously gave the blankets the more thorough battering) was the first stage in the process. The men were put out, the skirts were tied just above the knee, the women sat on the floor and the thumping began. It's hard to envisage anyone singing while engaged in this process. On the other hand, if you could do it, it was probably excellent training in breath-control and the use of the diaphragm.

As I said, by the 1940s the *luadh* survived only in the highly stylised forms of the concert platform, although anecdotal evidence suggested that traditional waulking of cloth was still practised on the West Side of Lewis into the 1950s. It's fair to say that in the Mod and concert forum my old school, Laxdale, enjoyed splendid success, and many's the day the cry went round the playground: "We won the *luadh!*" It was, of course, an exclusively female preserve, and one of the reasons for the success was that Laxdale had a splendid *cailleach.* I doubt if a *cailleach* was *de rigeur* in the real-life *luadh,* but on stage every *luadh* had to have one: a girl dressed in a shawl, wearing spectacles, carrying a creel and providing the focal point for the whole routine. In their glory years the *cailleach* (and star) of the Laxdale *luadh* was Margaret Mackenzie. Laxdale also introduced an innovation: the *luadh* team came on to the stage singing. The headmaster, Mr Kenneth Smith, attributed much of their success to the dramatic impact of this entry. But it did, of course, carry the whole routine ever further away from its historical roots.

Not that it ever occurred to us at any point in our childhood that anybody had ever performed a *luadh* in real life. I was born into a world fifty years further into the dissolution of Gaelic civilisation than Carmichael's *Carmina Gadelica* and by his criterion, Gaelic song, well-nigh extinct in Lewis by 1890, should have been utterly extinct by 1940. But that was very far from being the case. By the time I became aware of such things (around 1945), Kitty Macleod was a pop star; buses (especially buses carrying football teams and their supporters) rang to the melodies of 'Fill-oro', 'Fàilte Rubha Bhatairnis' and 'Brochan Lom, Tana, Lom'; and our schooldays were saturated with Gaelic song.

I've thought long and hard about the reasons for this. Laxdale was not a Gaelic community. Indeed, in some senses it wasn't a community at all. Old Laxdale, south of the river and Benside (not Ben-side, but *Beinn na Saighde,* hill of the arrow), was almost entirely English-speaking and had a reputation as a tough area noted for its hard men. Indeed, old Murdo Macleod, minister of Park Free Church from 1914 to 1960, once told me that in his days as a schoolboy in the Nicolson Institute they would never dare to walk out to Laxdale. The north end of the village was populated only after the First World War; and at the extreme north, where we were, everyone was new. Houses were being built every year from the Forties onwards, and this continued long after I left in 1958. These families were from the landward areas of Lewis. As, first, the West Side and, then, South Lochs were depopulated, Laxdale grew, due, of course, to its proximity to Stornoway. These new arrivals were Gaelic-speaking, but we, their children, weren't. Spoken to in Gaelic, we replied in English. Asked "'Eil Gàidhlig agad?" we replied, "Chan eil!" and it took us years to understand why this made grown-ups laugh.

Yet this school, serving an essentially non-Gaelic community, where the adults were firmly of the view that Gaelic gave you no advantage in life, was more committed to the musical heritage of the Gàidhealtachd than any other school in Scotland. This was due to successive headmasters, culminating in the head of my own day, Kenneth Smith (whom we always called 'The Master'); to the conductor of the school choir, John MacDonald (Iain Beag nan Òran); and to the Infant Mistress (no one then spoke of 'Early Ed'), Maggie MacArthur.

Miss MacArthur was fierce. Indeed, she was a terror; and that was before she lost her temper. But she made us sing, from day one to the year's end. And not only sing, but voice exercises and deep breathing. 'Oh-Ah-Aay' she would say, and off we would go up and down the scale, singing doh-me-soh-doh to every vowel and diphthong she could think of, first up the scale and then down. Sometimes the songs were English, although pure Kennedy Fraser. In fact, the first thing I ever learned in school, my memory assures me, was

> Westering home and a song in the air,
> Light in the eye and it's goodbye to care,
> Laughter o' love and a lilt in the air,
> Isle o' my heart, my own one.

The words have stuck there ever since, even though they tormented me as a five-year-old child. Bear in mind, we couldn't read the words. We simply heard them, run together to music. What was "islomyhart"? What was a "lightintheeye"? What was "goodbye" (a word we never used)? And what on earth was "westering home"? School was certainly a funny place, but the whole experience might have been different had someone either tried to explain the words to us or chosen songs a little bit more child-friendly.

But most of the songs we learned were Gaelic, although not a Gaelic that made any sense to us. The first, I think, was 'Buain an rainich taobh Loch Èitibh'. It's a beautiful melody which for long enough seemed to have no currency beyond the Infants' Class in Laxdale Public School. If you hum it to yourself, you will hear at once that its rhythm is ideally suited to a group of children. I can almost feel us now, swaying in our desks, half-terrified, half-mesmerised:

Fire, faire, ho ro gheallaidh,
Fire, faire, ho ro èile,
Fire, faire, ho ro gheallaidh,
Buain an rainich taobh Loch Èitibh.

The words conveyed nothing to us. There was no 'raineach' (bracken) in Lewis - at least, not in our part of it. And as for Loch Èitibh, we had never heard of it. Indeed, I'm not even sure that we understood the words to refer to a loch at all. The whole concept of a loch, especially a named loch, was quite foreign to us. At the most, you might pass some on the bus on the way to your annual holiday in Ness, but they had no names. My father knew the names of the lochs in Ness, but not the names of the lochs in Laxdale. In any case, knowing about Loch Èitibh wasn't important. The important thing was to keep your eye on the teacher and make sure your mouth was wide open.

In later years, life was dominated by the Mod: the local Mod in June and the National Mod in October. Other things were important, too. The school had a football team, but it never achieved greatness (largely because it lost its best players to the Nicolson at the age of twelve). Every year, too, there were 'The Sports': inter-school athletics at Goathill Park. I think I was once a reserve for the sack-race. And the awesome, life-defining Qualifying, 'the most important exam you will ever sit in your life' (at the age of twelve!). This determined whether you went to the Nicolson (and University) or stayed in Laxdale (and went on to become a van-boy in Lipton's).

But none of these was as important as the Mod. The whole village was gripped with a kind of Mod Fever, past generations wishing the new ones well, listening anxiously for news, and thrilled when the results were good. When the choir went to Stirling, Edinburgh or Perth, there were months of frantic fund-raising (raffles, sales of work, concerts), and during the days of the children's competitions everyone was glued to the radio. On at least one occasion, Mod Week was a school holiday; and when in 1949 Iain Murdo Macleod won the Silver Medal and Donnie Murray was runner-up, the whole school basked in the glory.

For those directly involved, these Mods meant a huge amount of practice. Every song had to be learned by heart. I was often amazed in later years to see choirs with song-sheets in their hands on the stage. We would have been thrown out if we didn't learn the words; and savaged if we took our eyes off the conductor. Many hours of the school day were devoted to practice, both choir and solo; in the weeks before competitions you had to go to choir practice every Monday evening; and you were inevitably involved in many other ceilidhs and concerts, some for fund-raising, some for pure entertainment and some because the event's organiser was having difficulty filling out his programme.

The educational benefit of all this affected the whole school, and by the time we left we had an extensive repertoire of Gaelic songs. At this distance, of course, it's easy to assume that what we know now we knew then, but I think I am still capable of making the distinction. I know, for example, that I didn't know 'An Ciaora' when I left Laxdale. Indeed, I can still remember vividly the first time I heard it on a Gaelic radio programme because it reduced my mother to floods of tears (it was composed by one of her contemporaries, Murchadh Beag from Habost, who died in 1932). I also know that I didn't know 'A Pheigi, a Ghràidh'; I did, however, know the tune of this latter song. The choir had used it in a special arrangement composed by Duncan Morison ('Major'). He had added significant embellishments and I've always been at a loss why it's been so completely forgotten. I still remember the challenge of rising to the dramatic high-doh he had put in the middle of the third line of the chorus (*Rìgh!*) and the magical beauty of the 'Scotch-snap' on the last syllable of the second. Unfortunately, I have little memory of the actual song, but I think the first verse (and chorus) was as follows:

Mo chridhe fo leòn ochòin nach fhaod mi bhith ann;
Mo chridhe fo leòn ochòin nach fhaod mi bhith thall;
Mo chridhe fo dhìobhail, Rìgh nach robh mise thall
An eilean mo chrìdh' fo thaobh ghil leitir nam beann.

I 'm not going to bore you with a list of what we did know. I'll send it to you separately if you wish. In many cases the words have long since gone from my memory, but a glance at *A' Chòisir-Chiùil* quickly brings them back. Sometimes, I suppose, we learned only the choruses. The melodies, however, remained, and there are some which I have probably sung to myself every single day for the last eighty years.

How (and whether) we learned anything else is a mystery. But did it arouse concern or attract criticism? Did the church try to suppress it? Not for a single moment! In those days the local ministers came to the schools every year to inspect the teaching of Religious Education. They seem to have been completely satisfied, and not a whisper ever came to our ears that they were unhappy about the time devoted to music (they could hardly have been ignorant of it: the choir's achievements, particularly before my time, were the stuff of legend). In any case, even if they had disapproved, it would have made no difference. The Church was ethnic: education was controlled from Dingwall.

Unlike me, Kitty Macleod did cherish some bitter memories of her own experience. These are not easy to evaluate. They were certainly not on the same scale as her resentment towards those who controlled An Comunn Gàidhealach in the 1930s and 40s; or even her extreme negativism towards the town of Stornoway ever since her days in the Nicolson and her early experience of its pretentious snobbery. She was adamant, too, that from her parents she never received anything but encouragement and support, even though they were both Free Church members (and her Tong grandfather was an elder). Her memory, looking back, was that it must have been almost risqué for them to have a daughter 'on the stage', and she certainly felt that they had suffered some gossip and ostracism as a result. She particularly recalled that her mother had once been scheduled to address the local Literary Society (in Ness, in the early Thirties!) and the minister and an elder had come to dissuade her. She had yielded for the sake of peace, but the prevailing attitude of her parents towards her musical career remained firm and supportive. They had a deep commitment to their native language, culture and music, and they said simply and repeatedly, "Lean gu dlùth ri cliù do shinnsir!" The only caution they would add was "Fhad 's nach toir thu nàire air an teaghlach!" (As long as you don't bring shame on the family). That warning had nothing to do with singing.

I was never involved, of course, the way that Kitty was, but my parents' attitude was exactly the same. They accepted the school's policy as perfectly natural, took pride in our success and realised that the experience we were gaining (particularly in standing before large audiences) would stand us in good stead in the future. They had to suffer as we filled the house with our songs, and they took it as perfectly natural that whenever there was Gaelic music on the wireless we would be listening (if it wasn't too late at night). In my father's case, he also accepted that he had to accompany me to the various concerts and ceilidhs at which we would be performing: partly, I suppose, for moral support; partly because he enjoyed it; and partly because I couldn't be let out on my own (my 'career', I have to say, came to an abrupt end at the age of twelve).

Which doesn't necessarily mean that it was the same everywhere. Later in life I knew a worthy deacon who would sit up all night to hear a commentary on a boxing match in America (especially if it was Joe Louis), but would leap from his chair and silence the radio in an instant if a Gaelic song came on air. I was vaguely aware, too, that in the background there were voices that spoke of *òrain dhìomhain* (vain songs), and no doubt my parents heard many more such comments than I did. But if they were got at for being so permissive, we heard nothing of it.

It may have been different with the previous generation. My grandfather certainly had little patience with fiction and would chide us for reading 'lies'. In this respect, he closely resembled Thomas Carlyle's father, a worthy Seceder and so fiercely opposed to imaginative literature that Carlyle never heard of Shakespeare till he arrived at University. In our case, the old man's disapproval made little difference; and for some strange reason, some of the most engrossing fiction was in his own house. His personal passion was for stories about the martyrs, and every time I took farewell of him, he made the same request: "Feuch am faigh thu leabhar dhomh mu dheidhinn nam martarach." (Try and get me a book about the martyrs). The odd thing (and it now strikes me as very odd indeed) was that I had little idea what he meant. Even by the age of twenty

I had never heard of Howie's *Scots Worthies* (translated as *Eachdraidh nan Urramach ann an Alba*) or any others of the genre (such as Smellie's *Men of the Covenant*). But he revelled in these harrowing stories of men being hounded on the moor, shot in cold blood and hanged, drawn and quartered in the Grassmarket. If the stories were in Gaelic, so much the better.

I've often wondered where the appeal of such narratives lay. My grandfather was never a member of the church and was notorious for being critical of many who were. He inherited a strong strain of legalism (and probably a spiritual inferiority complex) from his own father, and I think that in the depths of his psyche these stories of martyrdom met a spiritual need. Reading them was 'a good work', compensating for the ways he fell short (particularly of his father's standards). It was also a kind of vicarious atonement, enduring the pain of the almost unbearable accounts and transferring to himself the sufferings of the heroes of the Covenant.

Against such a background Gaelic lyrics must indeed have seemed very frivolous. But church or no church, Calvinism or no Calvinism, by the time I was twelve I knew far more of the songs of the Gael than I knew of the sufferings of the martyrs.

There was, of course, other music besides song, although song had the distinct advantage that you didn't have to buy the instrument (a major advantage in our house). Our next door neighbour played the pipes, stepping out of doors to do so; and further out the road the tinkers played them regularly. We thought they were magic. Every Monday night in the summer, the Lewis Pipe Band paraded the streets of Stornoway, stirring both eye and ear and appealing to the primal military instincts of our young hearts. And at the ceilidhs and concerts we attended (often when we'd have preferred to be somewhere else), the tedium of endless solo singers and choirs was broken by the virtuosos of the accordion (Waddel, John Crichton or Angie MacIver); or, more rarely, by the violin of Nommie

'Clean. With age, my priorities changed. Today I could listen to Gaelic songs for ever, while the Celtic instrumentalists have been relegated to resented intrusions.

But I'd better stop. These letters are becoming more like treatises by the minute.

Enjoy your summer.
Bodach

30 July 2024

Dear Mme Quessaud

Thanks once again for your letter, written, I suppose, from sunny Quebec. We're having the worst summer on record, or at least the worst summer in my memory (these two things are now just about synonymous). It's hard to believe that between May and June we used to walk to school barefoot; or that we sometimes used to pull great big divots out of the melting tarmacadam simply by walking on it. It was such a pest getting it off your shoes. It's hard to believe, too, that our "pitch" used to be hard-baked for the whole of our seven weeks' summer holidays, with only occasional downpours (which allowed us to have great fun building dams in the ditches and trying to create underground-drains. I should really have been a plumber).

Anyway, it's a different world, at least in my head: incessant summer rain and the new phenomenon of July storms. I should have listened to the lady who gave me splendid advice some forty years ago. After a working life in Detroit she had returned, briefly, to Lewis in her retirement. "I don't mind the winters," she said, "but I can't stand the summers."

I think the idea of Evangelical converts regularly burning their bagpipes and breaking their fiddles is pure myth. Its origin lies, I think, in the experience of Donald Munro, the Blind Fiddler of Skye. Munro, in his pre-conversion days, doubled as the residential catechist and local dance musician and, not surprisingly, was more proficient in the latter capacity than in the former. On his conversion, he was faced with a stark choice. He had to be one thing or the other. The fiddle went in the fire. Bear in mind that this was the action of a man in the first flush of conversion, repudiating his past life and guilt-ridden over his neglect and abuse of a spiritual office which he had milked for all it was worth. We have no idea what he thought of his action on more mature reflection. He probably saw it as an unnecessary outburst of zeal.

I know few parallels to this. I have heard it said of the late Alex MacRae, a colourful Free Church elder from Lochcarron, that he threw his pipes into the Minch (he was a fisherman) shortly after his conversion. Something similar happened in the case of Rev Angus Finlayson, who was minister of North Tolsta in the early days of my career. Of all the older ministers, he was the one I knew best: a man with a dour exterior who had the heart of a lamb; a severe preacher whose totally unembellished sermons gave no hint of the vast compass of his reading. Finlayson enlisted in the Army at the outbreak of the Great War (is that really over 100 years ago?) and remained there until 1927, seeing many years' service in India, where he was captivated by the beauty of the Himalayan foothills. He was an award-winning member of the regimental pipe band and, if my memory is correct, once held the Army record for the longest continuous march playing the pipes. Finlayson didn't break his pipes at his conversion, but he did turn his back on them and never played them again. Yet whenever he heard them every muscle in his body twitched.

There is no denying that this kind of world-renunciation became the norm among Lewis Christians, but it was by no means confined to them. The same underlying attitude is found in many - indeed, most - religious traditions. For example, two outstanding Anglican evangelicals, J. C. Ryle and C. T. Studd, were both brilliant cricketers. Each felt bound to renounce the game. In Studd's case it was linked to a specific incident. After one particularly fine stroke his partner at the other end shouted, "Well hit, parson!" and the words went through Studd like a knife. Other converts went even further: Origen, one of the early church fathers, had himself castrated in order to ensure immunity to sexual temptation (I've no idea whether or not it works).

It's also slightly annoying that while the form of world-renunciation typical of the Highlands is constantly ridiculed, the form typical of Roman Catholicism is admired and lauded. In Catholicism, the spiritual elite abandon the world altogether and withdraw into monasteries. No-one ever thinks of mocking them for not going to ceilidhs and dances. Protestantism, of course, had no patience with such elitism. It expected all Christians to be saints and to practise the priesthood of all believers. But it expected them to do so, not in some rarefied spiritual atmosphere, but "in the world".

This is certainly what happened in Lewis as I knew it. There was no segregation between saint and sinner in daily life. The village elder and the village drunkard lived and worked side by side, often engaged in the same communal occupation. The dockers and stevedores in Stornoway included some of the most revered elders and some of the most notorious drunkards in the town.

It was when it came to leisure activities that the divide appeared. Christians did not go to the pub or the *bothan*, to the concert, the dance, the theatre or even the football match. We shouldn't be altogether negative about this. It might sometimes have been misguided and sometimes carried to extremes, but it seems to me to have arisen out of some clear New Testament concerns. For one thing, it is a matter of priorities. Jesus made very plain that for his disciples self-fulfilment and self-indulgence can never be uppermost. They seek first the kingdom of God; and they do so, according to St Paul, with all the intensity and dedication of an Olympic athlete. You may not think much of such an agenda. But try to see it from their point of view.

It's also a matter of taste. It may seem hard to believe, but there are people who actually love going to church, attending prayer meetings and reading the Bible. I'm sure it's not a taste people are born with, but it's real nonetheless, and it's probably the greatest single sign of what's often cheaply dismissed as a born-again Christian. Not that it's a peculiarly New Testament virtue.

It was already cultivated in the Old Testament. If you look at the first psalm (or even better, the 119th, but who has that much time nowadays?), you'll see that King David absolutely loved the Torah (the Jewish Bible). Such tastes bred a spiritual appetite, often voracious, sometimes insatiable. This is probably what we today find most difficult to understand. My parents looked forward to "the Communions" with all the eagerness of a child longing for Christmas or a football supporter with a ticket to the Cup Final.

Another side of this religion was the social. These Highland evangelicals weren't hermits. On the contrary, they were intensely gregarious. Indeed, one of the instant effects of conversion was that you were received into (or sucked into, depending on your point of view) a whole new social network extending over the whole island. In its own way, of course, it was distinctly hierarchical, but it was a hierarchy not of class or wealth, or even office, but of age. You joined it as a junior, expected only to be silent. I always thought that was fair enough, not least because it was intensely egalitarian. You might be the local doctor or the only person in the village who could read, but the day you were born again you entered the kingdom of heaven as a little child, and in that particular spiritual society there was little hope of rapid promotion. There was certainly no fast-track.

Ministers, curiously enough, were no part of this social structure. They were often products of it, of course, but once they were ordained they lived in manses and were seen only in pulpits (and latterly in cars). It was the elders (by definition, old men) who were revered, particularly those who spoke on the Question. Alongside them were the "mothers in Israel". Such women tended to say little in company, and many, of course, were confined by infirmity in any case. But every village had its *cailleach dhiadhaidh* ('saintly old lady'), and it was to them, oddly enough, that young converts, both men and women, would go for spiritual counsel. Even a city like Glasgow numbered such women among its expatriate Gaels. They functioned as Mother Confessors. Not any old woman would do, of course. There were, inevitably, caustic, judgemental and sometimes even embittered old women in the Christian community. These would be avoided, becoming, as a result, even more unpleasant. But there was no shortage of good listeners and great encouragers, and their homes often became the natural *taigh-cèilidh*.

These opportunities for socialising formed a large part of the attraction of Communions. People not only worshipped together and took the sacrament together, they walked together, talked together and ate together. They also loved each other and talked about such love openly, sometimes in almost erotic terms. The social fulfilment afforded by such a lifestyle was both so demanding and so fulfilling that people saw little need for alternatives or supplements.

This partly explains why, by the time I came on the scene a millennium ago, the word 'ceilidh' had little of the specialised connotation it seemed to have had latterly. There were, of course, formal events known as ceilidhs. In that context, the word was synonymous with 'concert'. Ceilidhs took place, for the most part, in Stornoway Town Hall. But if you said, "Tha mi dol a chèilidh air ... " you meant simply "I am going to visit so-and-so." It didn't need to be a gathering of multiples. It could be one-to-one. In the same way, if you said, "Sin an taigh-cèilidh againn", you didn't mean some purpose-built place. You meant simply a local house where people gathered frequently. It might have been occupied by only one person, and she the poorest in the village, but all were welcome.

The arrival of Evangelicalism did nothing to displace this. The old habits continued and people went to different *taighean-cèilidh* according to their individual interests. In some, the evening might have been spent largely singing; in others, reminiscing. Even the *bothain*, often dismissed as mere drinking-dens, were to an extent *taighean-cèilidh*: exclusive male preserves where men could discuss the War or their recent voyages or the great village fights of the past. But in many other ceilidhs the evening would have been spent in what Evangelicalism worldwide would have called Christian fellowship. People talked, discussed points of theology, shared spiritual experiences, related news of such things as conversions or revivals elsewhere, recounted spiritual anecdotes, went over sermons they had heard and repeated the sayings of the great preachers and "Men" of the past.

You're probably thinking that all this amounts to no more than exchanging one kind of social life for another. To an extent that's true. Conversion immediately gave these people a whole new set of social preferences. They genuinely preferred the prayer meeting to the pub and the Communions to the *bothan*. And they themselves were fully aware that the whole thing could have been merely natural: they enjoyed the company of "the Lord's people" simply because they were a great set to be with (which in those days they were). This is why one of the perennial questions among them was, How can you tell spiritual love from natural love? That's a bit too esoteric, and I'll leave it, at least for the moment. But I do remember one particular evening in a house in Laxdale when that question was raised and received a memorable answer. "I know," said one man, "that my love is spiritual because the person here I love most is the ugliest woman in the whole room." That produced instant merriment. But it was also making a serious point.

If challenged why they lived such quasi-monastic lives, these folk would have instinctivly responded that immersion in secular entertainment would have taken the edge off their spiritual lives. For some, however, the problem was more serious. In that background many of the church members had had dramatic conversions from destructive lifestyles. Many had been seamen and tasted all the sins on offer from San Francisco to Hamburg. Many others had had serious drink problems. They wanted (and probably needed) a complete break with the past and weren't always able to distinguish between what was harmless and what was dangerous. Songs, dancing, accordions, drinking, fighting and womanising were all linked together in their minds. At bottom, you had a choice between two different social circles: one which would enmesh you in the mindless hedonism of drink, dance and fight; the other which enmeshed you in an elaborate spiritual support-system.

I don't want you to think that everyone followed either the one road or the other. It wasn't as if all the non-church people frequented pub and *bothan*. They certainly didn't; and the Comunn Gaidhealach scene as I knew it in Lewis during my schooldays was not awash with alcohol. It was the domain, for the most part, of the island's headmasters and a group of sober, decent coadjutors who mucked in for all kinds of reasons, from snobbery to love of Gaelic to the sheer pleasure of being involved in running something. For the most part, these folk came from a kind of elite, and they included at least a few church people, especially at the level of children's mods. For example, Bella Morrison, a teacher in the Nicolson who later married Rev Angus Finlayson, regularly acted as a Gaelic adjudicator at the local Mods. In fact, on one such occasion I sent her into uncontrollable laughter. She was adjudicating one of the poetry recitals, and it was the rule that after you had done your bit you were asked a few simple questions to ascertain whether you had any clue what you had been reciting. My piece must have been a love poem. I haven't the remotest memory of its actual contents, but she asked me whom the poet was writing about. Digging deep into my Ness Gaelic, I answered, "A chlig!" It was the only word I could think of that lay in the same general area as "his girlfriend", but it was totally colloquial Ness slang, probably with connotations a ten-year-old boy was supposed to know nothing about: the equivalent, I suppose, of "His bird!" in 1970s Merseyside. Whatever chord it struck, it was too much for her. On the other hand, what is the the Gaelic word for a girlfriend? But I shouldn't be asking a Canadian that.

Thanks for listening
DM

3 September 2024

Dear Mme Quessaud

Our summer is over. Not that there is much difference nowadays, and, of course, we lost our spring and autumn long ago. No-one ploughs, plants or sows; and no-one lifts, cuts or reaps. Yet despite it all, the landscape constantly changes. Plants and vegetation aren't like us: they seem to depend on light, not temperature, and I suppose that's why, however cold it may be in spring or warm in winter, they still obey their natural cycle. It's easy to sit by the window for hours, looking north-east to Mùirneag over the miles of unbroken moorland, fascinated by the ever-changing light and the subtle varieties of brown, green, blue and purple blanketing the ground. For some curious reason, the overall effect seems to be a reassuring orange.

But landscape is treacherous. It may be OK to speak of the "everlasting hills". You certainly cannot speak of the everlasting moor. The greens we played on as children have been swallowed up by bog and heather. There's no sign of the burns where we used to draw water and where women once washed the blankets. The sandbank on the face of the river (once our landmark as we headed across the moor) has all but disappeared, as have the salmon that young locals used to hunt with their gaffs in the 1940s. But the oddest thing of all is the complete absence of animals. Maybe "odd" is the wrong word. It's actually almost eerie. Not a cow or a horse in sight, nor (I am told) a grouse or a rabbit in the heather. Eeriest of all, even the sheep have been liquidated.

But to more important things. You asked whether everybody in the village was religious.

In Laxdale? I can't resist quoting the inimitable (fortunately) John McEnroe (is he still alive?): "You cannot be serious!" The church was probably at the zenith of its influence there during my student years and I remember noting with elation one night that there were 21 men regularly attending the local prayer meeting (the main church in Stornoway had several satellite churches in the surrounding villages and each had its own prayer meeting: Laxdale was one of them). That is more than most entire Free Church congregations could have boasted last century, but to see it in perspective you have to remember that this was in a village of 1,500 people. If one assumes that there were twice as many women as men in church membership, that gives a total of 63 Free Church members: less than 5% of the population. Of course, many attended church, particularly on Sunday evenings, who were not members, but even then, as I recall, the numbers were comparatively small.

When we first came to Laxdale, in 1945, the only way you could get to church was by walking. For us, that meant forty-five minutes each way every Sunday morning, our little legs working like pistons and, more than once, our need for the toilet getting the better of us. That's one reason why I think the weather must have changed. Now it rains every day, especially on Sundays, yet I can't associate childhood church-goings with soakings. What I do remember is that we always felt we were late. The *clagan* (the church bells) started ringing at quarter to eleven, and if you hadn't reached Dan Dougal's Brae (just beside the present Western Isles Hospital), you would never make it to Kenneth Street in time.

I also remember that we were greatly fussed over, because very few children went to church. In Ness, where we went for holidays, no children went except ourselves, and this was the pattern throughout rural Lewis. In the generation before mine, boys never went to church until they had earned enough money to buy themselves their first suit. It was a kind of coming-out: one of life's rites of passage.

As you can imagine, it needed a good deal of motivation to go to church under such conditions, and my recollection of the years immediately after the War is that scarcely any of our neighbours bothered. Within roughly a mile of our house there were seven church members, six of them women. In the whole of Laxdale at that time there were only seven male communicants. A few others might make it to church on Sunday evening, especially if the weather was fine, but on the whole the place was pretty pagan.

Then something happened which I've never quite been able to understand: the bus. On the face of things the last thing you'd expect to see running in Stornoway on the Sabbath was public transport. But that's exactly what happened. One of the local magnates was John Mitchell, the bus-operator. Some time around 1950 he was converted, and I can only assume that in the wake of that he began to cast around in his mind for some way of helping the work of the Kingdom. In the event, he decided to run a church bus service to Laxdale every Sunday morning and evening. There was no way he would have done this without the Reverend Kenneth MacRae's prior consent, and the remarkable thing is that the operation was run on totally commercial lines. Passengers paid the same fare as on weekdays. There was, I think, a compelling reason for this: the driver and conductress could hardly be expected to do it for nothing. In fact, they were paid double-time (I know this because my aunt was a conductress, as we called them then. We thought this was magic because we could sometimes get free tours on the bus, seeing areas around Stornoway we could never reach on foot).

Anyone who expected such desecration of the Sabbath to bring condign judgement was sorely disappointed. The Lord of the Sabbath, far from disapproving, blessed the entire operation. People began to attend church, particularly on Sunday evening, who had never been seen there before, and the congregation in Laxdale blossomed as more and more folk were converted. In a short space of time the bus was packed to the gun'les, and soon it was having to make two trips.

Yet the situation produced its own paradoxes. We youngsters loved the bus, vying with each other to be last on so that we could stand on the step and prove our virility. But my mother strongly disapproved of such profanation of the Lord's Day and refused to countenance it. She kept walking; and I've no doubt that at one level the bus represented a loss: particularly the loss of the talking and socialising that used to go on as groups of worshippers merged with each other on the road. Eventually, however, she conformed, either because her scruples were overcome or because ill-health made the long walk impossible.

But then, perversely, we youngsters stopped taking the bus and started walking. It was partly rebellion, partly the sheer pleasure of the walk and partly that it was the only time in the week you could enjoy the leisurely company of older boys and have a civilised conversation. We used to leave home inordinately early. The evening service began at seven o'clock, the walk took forty-five minutes and we set off at half past five. This gave us time to take a stroll round the Quay before taking our seats in church half an hour before the service. Yes, half an hour! By quarter to seven you had to sit near the front; and from there you couldn't watch the people coming in. Later, when I went to the mainland, one of the things that struck me was how late people were for church. When I attended Buccleuch Free Church in Edinburgh in the 1990s, the place would be empty till a minute before the service. In Lewis everyone was in place half an hour before.

But (in case you've forgotten) what I was talking about was the comparatively low level of church attendance in such a community as Laxdale in the Forties and Fifties. Even allowing for the fact that the bus was full, that it made two trips and that some made their way to church on foot, the total turnout from Laxdale on a Sunday evening wouldn't have reached a hundred.

How, then, did the church have such power? The short answer is that it didn't and that the whole idea is built on a misconception. A vibrant secular life went on unmolested. The choir flourished. A village hall was built by local fund-raising. There were sales of work almost every week, dances (often accompanied by serious disorder) every Friday, regular concerts and frequent ceilidhs.

Why did the church allow it? Because the church was not in the business of allowing, the church couldn't have prevented it, and, above all, because the church never thought it was any of its business. People seem to have real difficulty grasping this. The church did indeed have strict rules, but they were for its own members. If an elder went to a ceilidh, he might face some censure. If his teenage, unconverted daughter went to a ceilidh, the elders would not only turn a blind eye but regard it as perfectly natural. If she preferred going to the prayer meeting, they would regard that as a miracle of grace. In fact, far from placing the community in a straitjacket, the elders often gave their own families astonishing latitude. Many's the elder who regularly went to bed without having a clue where his children were (or being pretty certain that they were lying drunk somewhere).

Behind this, as I've probably said already, there was a kind of hyper-Calvinism that saw no link between nurture and conversion. Those who were strictly brought up might never "get grace"; those who were debauched libertines might easily be "snatched as brands from the burning". In any case, it wasn't deemed healthy if the young weren't young. You expected them to sow their wild oats and it was no part of your responsibility to make that difficult for them.

Every Friday evening, then, the seven o'clock bus would be packed with those going for a night on the town; and every Friday night there would be fights at the Hall. That's the way the world was, and if the sons and daughters of church members were among the leading revellers, that cast no reflection on their godly parents. Real censure was reserved for the *trocan* (scum), and that classification was reserved for the thief, the wife-beater, the draft-dodger and the son who put his mother and sister out of the house after his father died. Even the young man sent to prison commanded a kind of grudging admiration, especially if his sentence was as the result of a fight.

Such a culture inevitably bred a community full of characters, totally unchurched, utterly pagan and quite unforgettable. In our immediate vicinity these far outnumbered the godly.

There were the Krujers, for example. I have no idea as to the origin of the nick-name. It looks Germanic (linked to Kruger?), but I doubt it. The father was John Fraser, a native of Stornoway, which means the nickname probably wasn't Gaelic. Krujer himself was an utterly harmless man, the hard-working handler of one of MacBrayne's horse-drawn lorries and totally unremarkable except for his swearing, his family and his wife. The wife was formidable. She was Peggy O'Hara, a native of the Gorbals, and she was a mixture of harridan, duchess and Mafia godmother. There were five children (another had died of TB as a teenager), she ruled them with a rod of iron and they doted on her. So long as she lived they never stepped out of line: no smoking, no drinking, no falling foul of the law. When they worked, their unopened pay-packets fell straight into her lap. She never cooked. Instead, they lived on bread, cut in such a way as you never saw: not through the crust, but in parallel with it (so that if you were lucky you got the whole crust to yourself and the others got no crust at all). They (she, along with representative members of her brood) were for ever on the buses, "going down town". She returned home to eat chocolates. Every night they went to the pictures; every Friday, the Lemonade Lorry (Murray's, from Ness) stopped at the gate and delivered a crate of lemonade. A whole crate! To us, who saw lemonade only at the annual Sunday school picnic, this was mind-blowing.

And every so often in the course of the day she would need to see the children (long after they were children). She would go to the gate, face in the direction of the house they were likely to be visiting and pour forth such a summons as no one has ever heard since: an imperious order laced with such copious swear words as would make even a football-manager blanch. "Thomas, you so-and-so so-and-so, come here at so-and-so once or I'll so-and-so so-and-so your so-and-so so-and-so!"

This was a talent all the family possessed. When I arrived in Laxdale at the tender age of four, I was entirely uninitiated into such mysteries, but the first afternoon I played with Thomas I came back home with such an enhanced vocabulary as was an education to my parents. They then re-educated me.

As often happens with the children of the poor, the Krujers were physically precocious, growing fast and stopping growing early. The fact that they had an uncle, Sammy O'Hara, who was some kind of boxer didn't help, although I think they were even more frightened of him than we were of them. In adulthood they became perfectly harmless. Thomas, sadly, fell victim to some hereditary disease, became totally blind and died young: I once saw him step right in front of a car before my very eyes. Johnny did his National Service in the Pioneer Corps. We thought this was perfectly wonderful. Pioneers! Johnny didn't enlighten us. Danny was put in the Air Force, went off thin as a rake and came back fat as a barrel. Either he made out that he was a cook or we deduced that he was - I can't be sure.

In later years our two families were very close. By Thursday of every week Mrs Fraser's funds would have run out and she would send Danny to borrow ten shillings. Every Tuesday, without fail, it would be paid back. On Thursday, it would be borrowed again.

But Danny was a bonus. Like many Laxdale and Stornoway men, he had good contacts among the dockers and fishermen. In those days, prawns were like silver in the times of King Solomon: worthless. They would be caught in the drift-nets, along with mackerel, and since they were of no interest to curers fishermen saw them as only a nuisance. Danny got them by the boxful and gave them to my mother. And if it wasn't prawns, it was kippers. When Danny worked, it was in the kipper-house. Whether employees were allowed to help themselves or not I don't know, and never thought to ask. But he was certainly a generous supplier, provided you didn't mind the smell. By this time the kippering process involved the generous use of dye, and by the end of the day's work Danny was as impregnated with the essence of kipper as thoroughly as a miner with coal-dust. The kipper-house, however, didn't have baths.

One of the houses which Thomas and his siblings used to visit and at which his mother used to direct her colourful prose was Jeannie's, just across the road from us. Jeannie wasn't unintelligent: sometimes, indeed, she was quite the contrary. She could read and she could write and she could argue and harangue like a Latin-American oratrix. But somewhere there was some slight lack of connection with reality. She certainly succeeded in creating a dysfunctional family. She wasn't married, but she had three children, all from the same father. He seemed to us extremely old and lived with two of his brothers. His name was Cailean, and he lived with his two brothers, Ruairidh and Joseph (we knew the trio as Calan, Oolie and Yoseph, which is what Mondy, Jeannie's oldest boy, called them). They lived in the remains of what had been in its day quite a substantial house. But its day had been a long time ago, and as the elements took their toll the residents had steadily retreated to such bits as they could roof with scrap-pieces of iron sheeting. By my time, most of the building had been abandoned and the three brothers lived in one room offering little more protection than a bus-shelter, with the one important difference that they always had a huge fire.

They also had dogs: dogs beyond number. There were certainly never fewer than seven of them, and one of the rumours that circulated was that when they had a litter they simply threw the pups on the fire. Negotiating this pack of hounds was one of the many hazards of our school day. One of the dogs, named Fanny, was legendary and we treated her with the same respect as we would a wolf. Later, just to make life even more interesting for schoolchildren, their neighbour (their brother and his family, an industrious and productive lot) acquired a flock of geese. These fiends were even worse than the dogs. The thought of going to school was bad enough when all you had to worry about was the teachers. Having to run the gauntlet of a flock of predatory geese turned the unpalatable into the life-threatening (remember that we had the double disadvantage of small bodies and big imaginations). We eventually learned that your only chance was to walk past them sedately as if you hadn't a care in the world. To run was fatal.

All this by way of parenthesis, but while I'm on the parenthesis I may as well note that animals were always a hazard on the way to school. At that time there were still several horses in the village and they used to graze happily by the roadside (the ditches produced luscious grass). My sister was terrified of them; or at least pretended to be. One sight of them and she would sit on the road as determined as a Greenham Common demonstrator. I regard the fact that I got her to school every day as one of my life's major triumphs. She could also, on occasion, be frightened of sheep: an affliction from which my youngest brother also decided to suffer from at an early age. This was no minor ailment. In Lewis you might as well be frightened of fresh air.

With my other brother, it was cows, probably because he had the misfortune of a close encounter with one at a rather early age. When we moved to Laxdale, he three and I four, one of our favourite play-areas was the Brick House (always pronounced "the brick-house"). This was somebody's 'folly': a house begun but never completed. The cavity-walls had risen to four or five feet and hundreds of unused bricks still littered the site. It was a dream playground. You could walk along the top of the wall, you could play hide-and-seek, you could use the spare bricks to build your own house-within-a-house or you could build a fiercely-draughted chimney and light brilliant heather fires.

One day, as we played, Angus gave a shriek of terror. He had seen a cow's head peering round one of the corners. He ran home, hysterical, and all my mother could hear was "Cow! Cow! Cow!" "Did you see a cow?" she asked. "No!" he said, through the tears, "but I nearly saw one!" He was never allowed to forget it and came within a hairsbreadth of having to go through life known as "I-Nearly-Saw-A-Cow". After all, Stornoway already boasted a Murdo-Can-Take-It, a Jessie-Alone and an Annie-Go-Lost. He was lucky.

Back to my original parenthesis: the father of Jeannie's children. The family were known as "the Carolinas": almost certainly because the patriarch had returned from that part of the United States some time towards the end of the 19th century. In the early years of the 20th century, before Newmarket was settled, the house was a landmark for carters travelling between Ness and Stornoway. After they had travelled the nine miles of moorland south-west of Barvas, it must have been a welcome sight to man and beast.

By this man Cailean, Jeannie had three children. Two of them were much younger than I and were taken into care before we really got to know them. Their arrival was the occasion of Jeannie obtaining a pram, and every day she trundled them out the road. This was no aimless journey. About three-quarters of a mile towards Barvas there was a dump and in that dump there was a regular supply of fire-wood. Jeannie piled it on the pram on top of the children, and there they and it might remain for long enough as she made her various calls on the leisurely way home.

And she sang as she went, particularly if she was in a bad mood. The Laxdale Choir had no more loyal or ardent supporter and she had a fair repertoire of Gaelic songs. She also had an outstanding voice. It never graced any platform or concert hall and she probably couldn't have performed to order in any case. On the whole, it was a bad sign if she sang; and when she did, it was out of doors. Many's the summer's night our sleep was broken at 2 o'clock in the morning by the deep, rich voice of Jeannie carrying for miles as she collected peats off her peat-bank, too agitated to sleep or to know what time of day it was. It never irritated; and no-one ever tried to silence her. In different circumstances it would have brought fame and fortune. It remains etched on my memory as one of the definitions of childhood: evocative as the larks which sang above us as we cut peats in blazing summers at Tom Roisneabhat.

Her oldest boy, Mondy, was ages with my brother Angus, and the three of us were inseparable. As often as not, he ate in our house while my mother did her best to protect the two younger children. Many of the night-time arias were the results of vain attempts to persuade Jeannie to change nappies; and many's the time my mother got her character as Jeannie's impassioned eloquence told heaven and earth of the poor quality of today's Christians. But we ate in Mondy's too. There was probably a better supply of goodies and lemonade there. The one problem was that Jeannie's pieces always tasted of the paraffin she used to light her lamps.

Things became more complicated when Jeannie's half-brother returned home with his wife and moved into the other end of the house. We knew him as "Buckie" because his stepfather was from the East Coast. Buckie had served in the paratroopers during the War, or so at least we believed. He had certainly served in something because in my earliest memories of him he was in uniform. A handsome figure he cut, too: fit, dark and virile, with a narrow Errol Flynn moustache. Inevitably, he drank; and when he drank he bawled and fought and shouted. His wife, a gentle, delicate creature, never ventured outside, but she would occasionally put her head out the window, give us half-a-crown and ask us to go and buy her cigarettes. They eventually moved out; and she had the good sense to leave him.

He returned a few years later, a physical and mental wreck. For a few days Jeannie regarded him as a hero, but he quickly became proprietorial and soon they were having pitched

223

battles. The usual scenario was that he would lock her out of the house and she, with much screaming, incantation and lamentation, would throw stones at the door, all the while threatening to appeal to the Land Court. The conflict would eventually subside, but that night there would be great singing on the moor.

On one occasion the exasperated Jeannie decided she had had more than enough and secured the services of some of her more belligerent tinker friends to give Buckie a thorough going over. The first we knew of it was a knock at the door late one evening. It was one of the girls from the Blackwater. I knew her well enough: Bella, a very nice girl, and very pretty, with a face and hair like the baby Princess Anne. She was just a little younger than myself, and her brother, Jimmy, was one of my pals, mainly because he was usually available to play football whenever he was needed.

Bella was in a state, sobbing and terrified and pleading with us to come: "My uncles are killing Buckie!" While my parents yelled at me not to interfere, there was no way I was going to let Bella down, and I gallantly followed her across the road and up the path into Jeannie's house. As usual, it was filled with smoke and the only light came from the dying embers of the fire. Whatever killing had been going on, it had ceased; and whatever tinkers had been hired as assassins, they showed absolutely no interest as I dragged Buckie out and carried him down to our own house. He had certainly suffered something. There was blood, but he was at least semi-conscious, though it was hard to tell whether the 'semi' was the result of a battering or the result of drink. Anyway, his injuries weren't serious.

By the time I had him inside the house, the police had arrived. Bella had gone to another house to seek additional help (rightly calculating that I was hardly the man you would put up against killers). These neighbours were as disinclined to interfere as my parents, but they at least had a telephone (a rare commodity in Lewis in those days) and they had sent for the police. The police were glad of anything to relieve the boredom of their shift, but it was pretty clear that as far as they were concerned Buckie had no rights. He was a drunk and a nuisance, not a person. Battering him had no legal significance. In any case, it must obviously have been his own fault.

I had no quarrel then, and I have no quarrel now, with the fact that there was no prosecution. In those days physical altercations between consenting adults were contained within the community and I wish they were contained there still. But the fact that Buckie was a no-person made a life-long impression.

As Buckie deteriorated he became a persistent public nuisance and found himself more and more more in conflict with the law. He had never been a churchgoer, of course, any more than Jeannie, but for some strange reason he eventually began to make his way towards the Free Church in Stornoway on Sunday evenings. What drove him there we shall never know, but once inside he became abusive and disruptive and the deacons faced the usual dilemma posed by such situations: do you eject a man from church or do you endure his misbehaviour in the hope that somehow the Gospel may get through to him and transform him?

After multiple court appearances, Buckie was certified insane and sent off under escort to Craig Dunain Hospital near Inverness. He soon escaped, and when the news reached Laxdale we all quickly accepted the views of the local pub-lawyers that if he could stay free for a month his certification as insane would have to be cancelled. I can't vouch for it, but it seems fair enough that if a man can support himself for a month without an identity, a job, a bed or any means of support, he must have a reasonable amount of intelligence. It's not a test I would like to face myself.

Buckie escaped, full-stop, and was never seen in Lewis again. Two or three years later, while I was a student in Glasgow, I suddenly bumped into a man on Buchanan Street. There was a flash of instant recognition: Buckie! He moved on without breaking his stride. I did the same. Then, after a few paces, at precisely the same moment, we both stopped and looked back. He sought no help. I offered none.

Did he die, a rough-sleeper, in one of the city's doorways? Or burn his innards with meths and Brasso?

Anyway, time to look after my innards now.

You take care.
Bodach

27 September 2024

Dear Mme Quessaud

Sorry for being so frustrating. I really did think all that stuff about the symbolism in Hebridean churches would prove pretty boring. When your next letter made no reference to it I just thought you wanted to give it a miss. Now, I hope you're not just being nice to an old man.

As you can imagine, a good deal of the symbolism was linked to the Communion Service. I think I mentioned before that when someone took Communion for the first time it was spoken of as "going forward". I was never quite sure about the origin of this phrase. It may have had to do with the fact that communicants had to appear before the Session. Certainly the language was used in that connection. Ministers and elders would be asked after the Session, "Did anyone come forward tonight?" But it was also linked to the fact that at the Communion Service itself people did literally "come forward".

There is, as you know, no altar in a Presbyterian church, for the same reason that Presbyterian clergy are never called priests. A priest's job is to offer sacrifices, and in those Christian traditions which have priests (for example, the Anglican and the Roman Catholic) Communion is seen as a sacrifice: the idea being that the body of Christ is offered up in some way or other. Presbyterians have always regarded this with abhorrence and my own abhorrence-register in this connection is probably higher than most. It was this whole idea of the sacrament as sacrifice that led to the introduction of altars, and when Anglican churches began to ape the Roman Catholic, and Presbyterian churches the Anglican, altars soon made their appearance in Protestant churches as well. In Presbyterian churches, admittedly, these altars were usually called Communion Tables, but that shouldn't have fooled anybody. They certainly weren't for the congregation to sit around. They were shaped like altars, and once they were introduced ministers began to stand apart from the people, consecrating the elements and then serving them. Soon we had naves, robes and everything else. I remember once being in the vestry of one kirk of such tradition and watching the minister prepare to conduct the service (I had the much easier task of merely preaching), and as he put on layer after layer and colour upon colour my mind went back to a day in the early 1950s when I was standing on the pier in Stornoway watching a diver preparing to go under water. I sort of knew the man. At least I knew of him: Peter MacRitchie (Pàdraig Fhionnlaigh). His daughter, Mary Anne, was on my class in school. He put on layer after layer of woolies, then his diving-suit, boots, helmet and oxygen-line. By the time he was satisfied, a full hour must have passed, and when he was ready he looked like Michelin Man; and scarcely able to move. There in the vestry of a posh (very posh) Scottish church I was watching a similar scene; and when it was all over I had the same sense of wonder. How could the man move?

The Scottish Reformers would have no truck with such altars. Nor would they have tholed our modern Communion Tables. They were most insistent on preserving the original character of the sacrament as a meal. For that reason, there had to be a table: a real table around which all the communicants would sit, passing the bread and wine to each other. In fact, they were so insistent on this that when they adopted the Westminster Directory for Public Worship in 1645 they stipulated that it was not a matter of indifference whether or not communicants sat at a table. It was de rigeur. They also made it very plain that they did not approve of "the distributing of the elements by the minister to each communicant and not by the communicants among themselves."

All kinds of ingenious ways were found of providing large "tables" in the old Presbyterian churches, often by designing pews with hinges and other contrivances to allow them to be converted into tables at which worshippers would sit facing each other. In the nature of the case, however, such tables were quite incapable of accommodating the hundreds and sometimes thousands who gathered for the Communion seasons. This is why the old records speak of as many as twenty-four tables being served and the service lasting virtually all day. After each serving the communicants would leave and another group would take their place, until at last everyone had participated. It was for this reason, too, that local ministers had to have the assistance of visiting clergy. Each table required a prayer and one, if not two, addresses.

By my day the practice of seating communicants round real tables had practically ceased: one instance among many of the way that even the strictest Presbyterian churches lost touch with their roots. I might even go further. I've often thought that the Gael had no sense of history. The Lewismen of my young days had no longer historical perspective than the practice of their own grandfathers. That, to them, was ancient tradition. It never occurred to them to question those practices in the light of even more ancient practices. Rev Finlay Cook (died 1858) or Rev Duncan Macbeath (died 1892) was as far back as tradition went. John Calvin, John Knox and George Gillespie didn't figure in it. The inherent conservatism also meant that there was no place for questioning received practice in the light of theological first principles (like, What does the Sacrament actually mean?). In the Sixties of last century some of our church extension charges did began to incorporate George Gillespie's sacramental theology into their architecture. Cumbernauld Free Church, for example, had an integral Communion Table around which the whole congregation could sit. Ironically, traditionalists thought this was a modernist revolution.

In Lewis the word "Table" was still used, but it was something of a fiction. What actually happened was that a certain number of pews towards the front of the church would be marked off by putting a linen strip either on the first of them or on all of them. In the Free Church in Stornoway, the Table, thus defined, would occupy half the area of the church downstairs, but this would not be sufficient to accommodate all the communicants. The first sitting would have to leave to make way for a second. It could have produced chaos, I suppose, and maybe it sometimes did, but I never saw it. While all this movement was taking place the congregation were still singing.

Originally this "Table" was left empty until that point in the service when the sacrament itself was administered. It was then that the minister announced the singing of some verses of a psalm (usually Psalm 118:15ff.) and invited communicants to "come forward" while these verses were being sung. For a while no-one would move. Only when the singing was into the second verse would people begin to rise, one here and then one there, and "go forward". Soon there would be a queue as people lined up to sit at the Table, handing their tokens to the elders, who stood, sentry-like, in the aisles.

At that point a very interesting thing happened. There was something deeply moving about this aspect of a Communion service because it involved a very obvious separation. A wife might leave a husband's side and go forward; or a daughter leave her whole family. Eventually, there would be a very clear and very public separation between those who were "professing the name of Christ" and those who were not. Of course, the practice had no biblical precedent whatever. Certainly no one "went forward" at the first Lord's Supper in the Upper Room. But people "liked" it and thought it was very impressive. Such people were inevitably upset when the practice was discontinued and communicants began instead to take their seats at the "Table" immediately they entered the church.

This reflects a fascinating problem: the tension between puritanism and traditionalism. At first sight they can seem identical. In reality they are mutually contradictory, and this is a huge issue for the conservative mind because it wants to be simultaneously both strictly biblical and also strictly traditional. What happens when there is no biblical mandate for a long-cherished practice? The simple answer, I suppose, is that the "ancient" landmarks always have a profound emotional grip, and anyone who suggests that some of them may not be biblical (or even ancient) is going to have a rough ride. The radical (who calls people back to their roots) will almost always be taken for a moderniser. That's extremely annoying because the radical has behind him the wisdom of the centuries, whereas the moderniser merely idolises the contemporary.

The other distinctive feature of the Presbyterian Communion service was the "fencing" of the Table. I have no doubt that the word "fencing" was originally used in a very specialised technical sense. This appears very clearly in, for example, Samuel Rutherford's famous *Letters*, written in the 17th century. To Rutherford "fencing" was a legal term: to "fence the court" was to constitute it. This was almost certainly the sense in which it was originally applied to the sacrament. To fence it was to formally constitute it (excuse the split infinitive!). But in later practice, unfortunately, it came to be used in its everyday sense, with the result that both ministers and people were genuinely thinking in terms of putting a fence round the Lord's Table to protect it from unworthy intruders.

Of course, some care was necessary. When I was young and active the in-theologians used to argue that there was a huge gulf between John Calvin and later Calvinists; and one aspect of that gulf, they alleged, was concern over admission to the Lord's Table. Only in the late 17th century, they claimed, did Presbyterians become jealous over admission to the Supper.

But that's a piece of nonsense. Calvin's arrangements for the church in Geneva clearly rejected the idea of indiscriminate admission to the Lord's Table. Even the notorious 'Laud's Liturgy' (it was the introduction of this Liturgy into St Giles in 1637 that prompted the legendary Jenny Geddes to throw her stool at the Dean and shout, "How daur ye say Mass in mah lug!") lays down that if any intending communicant be an open evil-liver, the priest is to advise him not in any way to presume to come to the Lord's Table.

The fencing was the first step in the Communion Service as such. What happened was this: after the sermon the minister would announce that they were now coming to the administration of the sacrament and he would then proceed to indicate to whom the privilege of communicating belonged. This would normally be done by way of an address, usually fairly brief, delineating the marks of the true Christian and distinguishing him from the hypocrite. After the address the minister would read Galatians 5:16-26 (a passage which details the fruit of the Spirit on the one hand and the works of the flesh on the other).

This practice obviously afforded considerable scope to any minister who was temperamentally inclined to what was called "searching" preaching or to one who felt it his duty to "strip" Christians of their assurance. I have to say that never in my own experience did I hear this done. By my time ministers had come to see the wisdom of using this part of the service to encourage the weak and hesitant rather than to cut the high-minded down to size. However, when I went to Glasgow in 1970, people in Partick Highland still had a vivid memory of one Communion service when the fencing of the Table was so scathing that when the presiding minister asked the communicants to come forward they were so traumatised that no-one moved. He had to ask them a second time; and even then, I was told, it was touch-and-go that anyone actually went to the Table. In the end, I suspect, they went merely to avoid causing a scene; and the trauma probably included as much resentment against the offending minister as it did spiritual doubt.

I suppose you've heard that very few church attenders actually became communicants? I really don't think Lewis suffered from this to the same extent as other parts of the Highlands. Admittedly, many people attended church regularly who would never have dreamed of taking Comunion, but this is not as odd as it sounds. Many people attended church who did not regard themselves as Christians. This had nothing to do with the doctrine of predestination. It was not that they feared that they were non-elect. Spiritual doubt very seldom assumed that form in the Highlands. What troubled them was whether they were born again. 'Troubled' is probably the wrong word. It would never have occurred to most of the non-communicants that they were born again. They knew perfectly well that they weren't. It was one thing to be baptised and quite another to be a Christian. They also knew Nicodemus. In fact, they probably knew Nicodemus better than they knew any other character in the whole Bible.

Nicodemus was the man who came to Jesus by night and was told in no uncertain terms: "You must be born again!" In the following two thousand years he was the subject of countless sermons. Indeed, in the case of one Moderate minister, as I have already related, he was the subject of his only sermon.

The churchgoers of Lewis knew all about Nicodemus. They knew that he was a fully paid-up member of the Chosen People, a Senior Elder and a Learned Theologian (a "Reverend Professor Doctor", no less), but that none of these qualified him for the kingdom of God. They themselves were in the same position and they were never allowed to forget it. Birth into a Christian family, descent from a long line of believing ancestors, moral blamelessness and regular church attendance were no proof that one was a member of the kingdom. There had to be a Saving Change.

I have no doubt that the standard was pitched too high. Nor have I any doubt that in my early years too much stress was laid on dramatic, Damascus Road conversions. Nor again would I want to deny that this focusing on an experience (the new birth) represented a move away from the Reformation's much more objective stress on divine grace and justification by faith. But, looking back, I have equally little doubt that the vast majority of Christians did take Communion. I mean, of course, real as distinct from nominal Christians; and I realise that it is perilous for us humans to try to make that distinction. Jesus could look into Nicodemus's heart and tell at once that he needed a second birth and a fresh spiritual start. We cannot do that, and I would have been perfectly happy to allow all the baptised to the Lord's Table. But it wasn't the church that decided that those who didn't come forward weren't born again. They decided it themselves; and for the most part they decided right.

There was certainly no kudos to be gained in Lewis, as there was in other parts of the Highlands, by refraining from Communion. Instead, there was a clear expectation that everyone who had undergone a "saving change" would come forward; and most would do so relatively quickly. It is a myth that people would have to wait years. Most of us became communicants within a year of our conversions. A year may sound a long time. But when you bear in mind that Communion was celebrated only twice a year, it means that converts usually went to the Table at an early opportunity. In some instances, indeed, men might be converted, become communicants and commence their studies for the ministry all within a few months. There was never anything remotely resembling a rule (or even an accepted practice) that one must not take Communion too soon.

Nor was there any rule about a minimum age. It might sometimes appear to an outside observer that most communicants were old, but this simply reflected the age-profile of the community. This should not be taken as a dramatic symbol of a population in decline. It is more a symptom of the migration patterns of us islanders. The young leave, the old return (I saw a similar pattern in South African townships, where the men spent their working lives in the great cities and returned as old men to become elders in their churches). In post-war Lewis, and particularly from the 1960s onwards, large numbers of young people became communicants. Many would have been in their mid-teens, but some would have been as young as ten. One granny, having seen the last of her grand-children go forward (and herself not a communicant), was even provoked to remark, "Chan fhada gu 'm bi bhò ag aideachadh!" ("Soon the cow will be taking Communion!").

I never had any problem with children taking Communion, whether by profession of faith or on the same ground as they receive baptism: their covenant link with their parents. But it did raise one difficulty in my mind. In Presbyterianism, full rights of church membership belong to all communicants and it always seemed to me slightly absurd that a child of ten should have, for example, full voting rights in electing elders and ministers and an absolute right to play a full part in a congregational meeting. Fortunately, there was an age-bar on admission to office. You could not be ordained till you were twenty-one! Maybe it was just as well or we'd have been inundated with boy-ministers.

From this particular boy, then, that's enough for now.

Yours till next time
Donald

17 December 2024

Dear Jacqueline

I've done as you said (we modern males are so compliant!) and dropped the formality of "Mme Quessaud". If you have second thoughts, let me know, and I shall become formal as ever.

Anyway, thanks for your letter. It arrived yesterday and, quite apart from its other merits, it gave me at least some momentary contact with the outside world. It brought the postman to my door and he chatted for a minute or two, filling me in on some of the news. Calum Dhonnchaidh, who lived just a bit in the road, died this morning; and one of the young lads out at the Bridge was caught selling Ecstasy on Cromwell Street last night. I won't see the post again, I suppose, till your next letter; or perhaps the electric bill. The home-help, Mary, used to come every morning for an hour and that was a real delight. I knew her granny well. She was only a few years older than myself and was the first person I ever heard use the word 'banana'. That would have been about 1946 and, of course, at that time I had never seen one. I asked her what a banana was and she told me that they were like nothing I had ever tasted. They were "smashing" (another word I had never heard before and which at the age of five I kept confusing with "bashing", until Mary's granny put me right: "'Smashing'", she said authoritatively, "is when something is very, very good; 'bashing' is when you hit somebody.") Mary used to be full of news and cheer, setting and lighting the fire and even leaving a meal which I could cook in the micro. Now, sadly, the Council is too poor, the home-help comes only two days a week and stays for only half an hour. She's harrassed and frustrated and not half the fun she used to be. It's difficult to understand public priorities: lots of subsidies for foreign musicians and ballerinas, but little concern for us old folk. I've never been able to understand why the devotees of culture can't afford to pay for their indulgence, like football supporters and churchgoers. Even less can I understand how artists of all hues can speak so loudly of holding the world and its values in contempt, yet charge exorbitant fees for their work. Maybe if I were younger I could put a few words together on 'The Artist as Mercenary'.

For the most part, I sit in my high-backed chair, strategically positioned so that I can look straight out the window and up to the road. Not a car passes but I see it; and I can tell you, almost to the minute, everyone who walked in or out the road during the hours of daylight. Oddly enough, more are walking than used to some twenty years ago. Why? They're walking their dogs! If one of our childhood neighbours had walked in the road with a dog on a lead, he would never have lived it down. It would have been as bad as carrying an umbrella or wearing a black jacket and pin-stripes: worse, even, than having clean "minister's hands". But nowadays all the neighbours have posh dogs. Laxdale is suburbia.

I haven't yet been reduced to sending Christmas cards to myself, like the old lady I once visited when I was a minister in Edinburgh. It was Christmas-time, and I was delighted to see a card on her mantelpiece. "Oh, Annie," I said, "you've got a card!" I looked inside: "To Annie, from Annie." But the loneliness is hard.

It's a very peculiar thing, the psychology of us elderly. The young elderly are immersed in their children and grandchildren, but as you get older you go the other way and find your thought dwelling on your parents and your own childhood. I would probably panic if I were uprooted. I remember, many years ago, persuading my own mother to come down to Edinburgh on an open-return ticket, hoping she might stay indefinitely. When she arrived, she refused to take so much as a cup of tea till I had booked her return flight in a fortnight's time. I think she thought that I was trying to abduct her and that she might never see her own fireside again. It was hard to understand at the time, but now I understand perfectly. Having your life taken over by others, no matter how well-meaning, is the worst kind of claustrophobia.

Yet we're such a bundle of contradictions. I can hardly claim to have much control over my own life! It's difficult to be independent when you have Parkinson's. The drugs help, of course, but there's been remarkably little improvement in them since the 1980s. They make a huge difference initially, but quickly become less and less effective. It's hard to understand why there have been such enormous advances in nuclear missiles but so little progress in treating a disease which brings misery to almost all the world's elderly.

In my own case, the tremor is not too bad. The worst thing is the way you can't start yourself moving. Sometimes I just freeze, rooted to the spot, and there's nothing I can do about it. When there's nobody around to help, you can remain like that for hours. The other night, I couldn't sleep and got up to make myself a cup of tea. Suddenly, as I was walking towards the kitchen, there was a power-cut and in the pitch-darkness I stopped. I tried to move and couldn't. The hall telephone was only a few feet away: I could see it clearly and I thought I should telephone the home-help. But I remained rooted to the spot. Minutes passed, and then the hours: two hours at least, during which I just stood there, unable to move. Then suddenly the phone began to ring. I still couldn't reach it and in my frustration all I could do was cry. Then I heard the door being opened. It was the home-help! She had wakened up to discover there was a power-cut, and when I didn't answer the phone she had come in at once. God bless her, but I'm still shaking.

I had an even worse experience three months ago. About two o'clock in the morning there was an almighty banging on the door. I was petrified: too frightened even to go to the phone in case whoever it was would hear me. Five minutes later, it started up again; and so it went on all night. The hours passed slowly, but when the day began to break I crept to the phone and phoned Mary (the home-help). She came at once and told me the police were parked at my gate. They'd been there all night and it was they who had been banging my door. Apparently they'd been chasing one of the local boys, but he had given them the slip and was lying snugly in his bed. They had the wrong address, mine instead of his. I've heard nothing from them since: not a word of apology. Mary urged me to complain, but I can't do that. I'm living here all by myself and if these boys take it out on me I'm done for.

Anyway, enough of this moaning. You were asking what we played when we were children and how we passed the time. I often wonder about it. There was no television, of course, and few of us had a wireless. We had one, briefly, after the War, a very plain, box-like thing. Most radios then were powered by accumulators, but this one, for some reason, was powered by a battery. In my imagination, as I look back, the battery was about the size of a shoe-box. I used to have to go to the local wireless shop (D D Morrison's) to buy a replacement battery, and I still remember what I had to say: "A battery for a wireless, please: EverReady No. 3 All Dry". But it doesn't seem to have survived the War long, and until about 1954 we had no radio at all. This was a major drawback because it meant that you never knew the football results till you got to school on Monday morning (and during the holidays you had to wait even longer). This lack didn't seem to have anything to do with being well-off. My pal John Angie had a radio, but his father was paid much less than mine. Another pal who lived with his granny even had a gramophone and there, occasionally, we could hear Gaelic records (and, later, the yodelling of Slim Whitman). He also went to the pictures regularly and regaled me with stories of Roy Rogers (and Trigger), Gene Autrey, Wyatt Earp, Tarzan and the rest. I don't know why, but it was never something I envied. The first time I went to a cinema was in 1950, while attending the National Mod in Edinburgh, and I have absolutely no recollection what the main movie was. I remember only the supporting move ("the wee picture", as it was called): at least, I remember one episode near the beginning. It showed an evil-looking, beturbaned Oriental standing with dagger poised over a baby asleep in a cradle. I was absolutely petrified. He was on the very point of plunging the dagger into the baby's heart when, mercifully, he was interrupted (the story-line was that the baby was a prince, heir to a throne and about to become the victim of a politically motivated assassination). The image gave me nightmares for months and even led to one of my more successful moments in school. Asked to write a composition about a dream, I described what I had seen in the cinema in Edinburgh. It was probably pretty graphic because I was still living it, and the teacher was enormously impressed. But I doubt if the film had any long-term effects. It certainly didn't turn me against Arabs or give me a phobia about turbans. But the sleepless nights were pain enough.

Do you mind if I go off at a tangent, just for a moment? I have very few memories of that first trip to the mainland in 1950, but one has lived with me all my life. Today, children are encouraged to be vocal and articulate and to speak confidently to adults. Our world was very different. In both home and school, a "good boy" was a quiet boy. You never asked a teacher anything, and you lived in the hope that she would ask you nothing either. It was the same at home, particularly if you had visitors. You either left the room to allow old folk to gossip in peace or you sat in a corner and listened in silence. This got to the point where you virtually froze if you were addressed by a grown-up, particularly a stranger. It is one such incident I remember from Edinburgh. I had won some trivial prize in a recitation competition (those who heard me in later life cluttering my words incomprehensibly whenever I was confronted by a script will find this astonishing, but I swear it's true). Afterwards, I was approached by a grey-haired man in a kilt, obviously very important and equally obviously bent on being extremely nice to me. "You've just won a prize, I see." I was very good: I said nothing; and not even the man's best efforts could induce me to change my policy. He might have thought me deaf and dumb were it not that he had heard me speak. Utterly frustrated, he got up and left.

But, to resume: what was there to do? We played football, of course: obsessively and at every opportunity. There's nothing remarkable about that, except that if you could see the terrain around Newmarket you'd wonder where anyone could find a football pitch. To begin with, we played on the road, with stones at each side for goalposts. You could play with just two people, kicking from goal to goal; or you could extend the "pitch" lengthwise and play a team game. It was tough on the goalie, if he had to dive. Traffic wasn't a problem. The few buses came at regular intervals, mainly around teatime; the occasional lorry could be heard half a mile away; and in the whole village there were only two private cars.

It was during my very first such road-match that I had the experience which turned me into a lifelong (well, almost) Rangers supporter. I was standing in the goal and every time the ball was kicked towards me I leapt at it with my feet in a vain attempt to stop it going in. My opponent, Donnie Murray, was very unimpressed. "You're supposed to dive," he said. "What's that?" I asked. "It's what Bobby Brown would do!" "Who's Bobby Brown?" "He's the Rangers goalie!" And that was that: the first goalie and the first football team I ever heard of. I should be thankful. It could quite as easily have been Jimmy Cowan, and then I would have been a Morton supporter. On such accidents do great events hang; and after that interlude I duly practised diving on the tarmacadam road. Later, it came in very handy on the rocky gravel of the school playground.

Besides the road, we had two greens and one pitch. The greens were narrow strips of grass, not much wider than the road. They were probably the legacy of some defunct stream and added a dash of colour to the moor. They sloped away and had the advantage of seldom being waterlogged, but gave little scope for wide players. The "pitch", on the other hand, had some width, but with it came its own inconveniences. It lay at the bottom of the crofts and all the water drained or seeped into it. Keeping it fit for use became an obsession. In the mid-Fifties, we dug a ditch (or at least a drain) round it, and this was some help. We could now play in virtually all weathers, provided we wore wellies. Down there, summer or winter, I was one of the happiest children in Europe, playing with kids two or three years my junior and flourishing as a dominating central defender. It was not quite the same playing against those of my own age, all of them physically precocious.

There's no point in going looking for these venues today. They don't exist. "Developed?" you might ask. No! Nature's work entirely, and a powerful commentary on the treachery of landscape. You can stand on these spots today and wonder that anyone ever played anything there. The greens have disappeared in the heather. The pitch is a bog where even the sheep don't venture. Streams where once there were trout are dried up; little pools, and even lochs, filled in. Hummocks which once served as landmarks are no more. Pits where we burrowed for clay to load on to our toy lorries are lost even to the imagination. Gravity and water make the land play traitor to our childhood.

One of my most vivid childhood memories is related in an almost Wordsworthian way to one of these clay-pits. It was so insignificant that I can hardly describe it. As you travel north from Stornoway to Barvas through Newmarket, the road falls away sharply to your right (the east). There was one particular spot, just outside our house, where the soil adjacent to the road was a soft clay. We had begun to play lorries there, digging and scraping until our crude little miniatures had a full load and then driving off (making the appropriate engine-noises) to dump them. None of the loads amounted to much, but there is no doubt that the accumulated effect was considerable. Our quarry ate further and further into the roadside verge and the grown-ups began to warn us that if we didn't stop "the roadmen" would come. We didn't know then that roadmen had no interest in anything except making tea, avoiding work and keeping dry. Judging from the tones used by our parents, the roadmen were worse than the Germans. But not menacing enough to make us stop operations.

Until one day. My father was at work and mother ("the ole lady", as we would have called her among our peers) had gone down town for the messages. In those days, no-one worried about leaving children alone in the house: at least not in Lewis; and certainly not with an eldest child as wise as me to look after them. But my mother was late coming home: dreadfully late, probably because she missed the bus. It was a dark, forbidding day, grey and ominous and somehow doom-laden, and as the minutes ticked by we were gripped by mounting panic. Just then, our worst nightmare materialised: the roadmen, in their enormous boots and tar-stained dungarees, wielding their shovels with a skill born of long years in the Home Guard and probing away suspiciously at the enormous, planet-threatening hole we had made in their road, endangering every vehicle and pedestrian in the world. They looked and looked, left and returned, retired and regrouped, and arranged and rearranged their tools in a manner thoroughly business-like and menacing. Any moment now, they would be down to take us away and we would never see our mother again. We howled and howled; and we never played "in the clay" again. The emotion (a pure terror which cast the roadmen as otherworldly avengers of wrath) made the experience unforgettable. Fortunately, I lived to recollect it in tranquillity.

There were many days, of course, when you couldn't play outside because of the weather; and other days when you couldn't find anyone to play with. Those days, I played indoors, rearranging the furniture in the bedroom to allow me to slam the ball against the wall, trap it, head it, lob it and whatever. I became pretty adept at such things. Later, I would learn, of course, that football, as men played it, was a physical and contact sport in which the ball spent most of its time up in the air. That particular game, I suppose, I never played. But isn't it remarkable what parents let you off with? Equally, isn't it interesting that when the old house began to deteriorate the floor I played on was the first part to give way. It had had a tough time.

In the summer we played cricket, boys and girls together. Whenever I used to mention this, I met with incredulity. Cricket in the Hebrides? It was probably confined to our part of Laxdale, but it certainly wasn't I who introduced it. That honour would probably go to Donnie Murray, two or three years my senior. The idea came, I'm sure, from what we called "the comics": the *Wizard* and *Adventure*, the *Rover* and the *Hotspur*. Comics they certainly were not. They offered unrelieved double-column print and regaled us with serialised stories of war, the Wild West, detectives, football, athletics and English public schools (the instalments always ending at the most dramatic moment, followed by an editorial commercial: "What happens next? Don't miss next week!). It was from these last, I suspect, that we learned about cricket, particularly from a series called 'Smith of the Lower Third'. We played the game with total respect. We had wicket-keepers, overs, catches, lbws and one or two more rules of our own, the most important of which was that the batsman wasn't allowed to hit the ball twice (I've often wondered about this when watching Test batsmen prodding and scraping the ball away from their stumps after a mishit). To begin with, we bowled only underarm. We knew that wasn't quite proper and repeatedly tried overarm, but that made things all too easy for the batsman as almost all our early efforts at overarm ended up as half-volleys or full tosses and could be hit for miles. As Greg Chappel remembered during an infamous one-day match in Australia, it's almost impossible to score off under-arm bowling ("daisy-cutters", we used to call them). On the other hand, it's almost equally impossible to bowl someone out. The batsman can stonewall every delivery. Eventually, we got the hang of the real thing, and I quickly showed my usual talent for mastering basic techniques, reaching a level of competent mediocrity and then developing no further.

Our equipment was below basic. It was primitive. I saw neither a real cricket bat nor a real cricket ball till I was about fifteen. We played with a tennis ball or a similar sized sponge-ball and we made our own bats. For the most part, I suppose, I made them, being always the most desperate for a game. Initially, I simply cut a piece of flooring or some such timber to the right length and sawed out a handle. Later, having seen my father use an axe as an adze, I could take a substantial block of timber, chip away at it and produce a shape much more like the real thing, with a ridged back thickening towards the bottom before tapering away again. With one of these you could thump a soft-ball enormous distances. I longed to try it on a real cricket ball. Sadly, when the great moment arrived, the handle broke on impact with the very first ball. No-one had told me it needed to be spliced.

During our fourth year at the Nicolson, a bunch of us, led by the Laxdale boys, began to play more seriously, at least to the extent that during the lunch-break we played with real bats, real balls and at ferocious pace. Two of the taller guys, John Angie and TS (Norman Thomas Shaw Mackay, a Valtos boy who emigrated to Australia with his family a year or so afterwards), were fearsome, and it's a miracle that no one ever received even a minor injury. We wore neither pads nor boxes, the pitch was wet, muddy and bumpy and we played flat-out.

After school, cricket ceased until I began to attend the Free Church School in Theology, which used to meet at Carronvale, Larbert, every September. The theology was OK, but the main draw was the cricket, and I discovered that at this particular level my bowling was pretty fast. Most of the rest had never played cricket in their lives.

You can draw your own conclusions about human pretentiousness from what follows. I thought a lot about my cricket. When I was minister in Kilmallie, I used to practise batting against the wall of the church. In Glasgow and later in Edinburgh I begged the kids to play with me. And all the time I thought about spin-bowling. In fact, I did more than think about it. I practised it; and the only result was that it ruined my fast bowling, putting my action completely haywire (basically because I was trying to spin even the fast ones). Eventually, I had so little control when I tried to bowl fast that I was frightened to let the ball go in case I killed the man at the other end. Cricket doesn't know what it missed: a moody obsessive more concerned to emulate skills he didn't possess than to develop those he had. But it's given me lifelong pleasure and kept me paying my TV licence when all the nonsense of game shows, horror movies, jersey-pulling footballers and sheer mind-blowing inananity screamed at me to give it up. My heart still leaps at the mention of Denis Compton, Cyril Washbrook, Freddie Trueman, Jim Laker, Peter May, Garfield Sobers, Keith Miller, Ray Lindwall, David Gower, Viv Richards and Ian Botham. Some of them I never saw, even on television, but we heard them playing on the radio through the mellifluous tones of Rex Alston, John Arlott and Brian Johnson. These cricketers had no life outside the commentaries, and if they had flawed private lives, we knew nothing about them. They were their batting and bowling averages.

In the Lewis winter, as you know, the darkness comes early, and by the time you're home from school there's no light for play. In fact, in my early years the schoolday itself was cut short in winter. We had no electricity till about 1950. I cannot remember the school having even basic oil-filled lamps, though there must surely have been something for emergencies, but in the years immediately after the War we didn't begin school till ten in the morning and we finished around three. The weather could even provide further bonuses. In the event of a storm, the whole school closed early so that the older pupils could escort the younger children home: a magnificent arrangement, considering that there is a gale-force wind in Lewis on 200 days in every year! We didn't have the problem then of mothers all working and insisting that the school looked after their children for the whole day. Parents knew nothing of the early closing till we suddenly (and delightedly) appeared.

But the darkness couldn't stop you playing, especially if there was frost or snow. I doubt if the moon shone on every frosty night. But that is the memory: no lights but those from the neighbours' windows and a dozen children, boys and girls, locked in what they thought was an eternal companionship of life and fun.

It didn't take emigration to sever us. Adolescence was enough. Emigration merely confirmed it. There was never any formal parting or laboured farewell. One minute we were daily companions, eating pieces in each other's homes. Goodnight! Then nothing. You hear that one is married (had to), another is working and another is with his pals down town. Strangers: the social landscape as disloyal as the moor.

Snow was magic: to waken up one morning and see the whole landscape covered in white and framed by the angry grey of the sea and the clear, cold blue of the sky; or to stand at the window and watch it falling, your eye trying to focus on individual flakes as they twirled slowly downwards and disappeared into the white blanket beneath. And sometimes it was awesome: especially when there was cabhadh-làir (literally "a snowstorm from the floor"), and the wind lifted the snow from the ground and drove it relentlessly against your face, taking your breath away; or against a fence or a house or any other fixed object, causing massive drifts. These last twenty years, due, I suppose, to global warming, snow is as rare in these islands as earthquakes, but in those days blizzards were regular winter occurrences. In 1947 many of those who went to the March Communion in Ness were stranded there for days by a snowstorm. In 1955, we were off school for two whole weeks. Of course, if we had made a "superhuman" effort, we could have managed, at least after the first few days. It wasn't that far to walk (two and a bit miles), but attending school could never justify such heroics. As for food, we had a good supply of potatoes and a barrel of salt herring in the cellar. I can still feel the romance of it: the dim light, the meagre provisions, the vague sense of crisis, the grandeur of the elements outside and the warm security of the environment within.

But don't over-romanticise it. In these conditions, the peats froze and stuck together like solid blocks of ice: so solid you had to strike them apart with a hammer before you could put them on the fire. At that point they seemed hard and dry, but once on the fire they thawed out and turned soft and soggy. "By the peat-fire flame" is not quite the same when you're sitting, shivering, with nothing to warm you but smoke.

I remember another odd thing, too. For several days we had no milk: instead, we sprinkled oatmeal on our tea. It had the effect, at least, of making it look milky. It didn't seem to be a measure adopted in desperation, but a practice which my parents deemed perfectly natural in the circumstances. I don't have the same nauseous vibes about it as I have about another practice I sometimes saw: putting tea-leaves into a pipe instead of tobacco. I have absolutely no doubt about that memory. What I'm not clear about is whether it was resorted to in the absence of tobacco or whether it was a substitute for those too young to smoke. Whichever it was, it tasted vile.

But the whole point of this rambling excursus about snow is that it provided us with our greatest annual thrill: sledging. In those days Lewis was much more open than it is now. The passion for fencing everything off developed only later (largely driven by EU grants), and in any case many of the allotments in Newmarket were vacant. We had vacant, open lots ("loats", we called them, probably because we thought "lot" was Gaelic) on each side of us, sloping steeply at the top and levelling off at the bottom. Today, they're magnificent private gardens. In those days they were magnificent sledge-runs and many's the day we careered down and trudged back from early in the morning till long after nightfall. At night, the clear sky brought hard frost and our clothes, sodden with snow, then became hard and stiff. We wore dungarees (or some home-made equivalent) and by the day's end our trouser-legs were as firm as stove-pipes.

The sledges were home-made and the quest for the perfect sledge followed me right through childhood. The odd thing was that the perfect sledge already existed. In fact, it was the finest sledge I ever saw and it was the property of Angie MacLennan, who lived next door and who had already left school by the time I arrived in Laxdale at the age of five. Angie's sledge was the one everyone wanted to have. It flew over the snow in a straight line and responded at once to even the slightest tug on the steering-rope. It had many imitators, but no equals. But what made it perfect?

We thought we had a fairly good idea. The runners were the important thing. These were the two parallel pieces which were in direct contact with the snow and performed more or less like skis. They had to be smooth; they had to be exactly parallel (though we didn't know that word then); they had to be aligned in such a way that they moved with the grain; and they had to be angled at the front like the bow of a ship (if they had square ends they would plough into the snow and dig into the soil).

I designed them in my dreams and worked them out perfectly, but between the conception and the execution there was an unbridgeable gulf. Angie Maclennan's runners probably began life as 2"x2" timbers. When we tried these, our sledges wouldn't move because they sank so far into the snow that the crossboards were digging into it and blocking all progress. We tried deeper, narrower runners (pieces of flooring and the like, 4"x1") and these were fairly satisfactory till they eventually buckled. Later, we found that the uprights of dining-room chairs made excellent runners, but they never matched Angie MacLennan's. Nothing did, though Angie could never have told you the secret of his, even if he had wanted to. No child today, with his shop-bought toboggan for the occasional flurry of snow, could understand the torment of our quest. The wonder is that between the breakdowns, collapses and utterly useless prototypes, we had any pleasure at all. But we had, in abundance, boys and girls together, two or three sledges between the dozen of us, till exhaustion or the calls of our parents brought proceedings to a halt. The saddest days of childhood were the days when the thaw set in and all the pure, sparkling snow turned to grey, messy slush.

But I suppose that happens in Quebec too.

Take care
Bodach

Beinn Roisneabhat Nursing Home
STORNOWAY
Isle of Lewis

18 May 2025

Dear Jacqueline

As you can see, I've changed my address. I keep thinking to myself that I've been taken into care, but I suppose that's the wrong word. It's for children, isn't it? But then, isn't that what I am now: a child all over again? When I was a boy, playing football and learning to ride a bike, my grandfather used to say, in his good Buckie English, "You're always felling!" Well, that's how it was with me these last few months at home: always falling. Maybe it's the drugs, though I feel all right at the moment. Sometimes, from what the home-help was saying, I think I was all confused about night and day. It seems I was getting up at all sorts of hours, falling, and lying there till she would find me on the floor in the morning. If I had fallen behind the door, she wouldn't have got in at all.

And now, here I am. I'll be less of a nuisance to everyone now. It's a room, with an en-suite bathroom, and a nice view over a farm and an airfield. There's a better view of the aircraft taking off and landing than I had in Laxdale, and the cows are always interesting. The staff tell me that this is now my home, and that I must give it some personal touches to suit myself. I've hung a few photos on the wall. It's too small for paintings, and I've left these behind, including my favourite: a large painting showing a baby sleeping among autumn leaves against the background of the ruins of a church and the yellow-orange light of an autumn twilight. I bought it forty years ago from a Free Church girl who was studying at Edinburgh School of Art and it hung in my office at College almost all the time I was there. My motives for hanging it there weren't, perhaps, of the purest. I took a kind of perverse delight in the fact that almost every visitor would ask, "What does it mean?" and an even more perverse delight in replying, "You mean, 'What does it mean in words?' You can't put it in words. It's a painting."

But there are no paintings here, just a few family photos (plus one of Hugh Miller and another of the Faculty of the Free Church College in the 1840s). Visitors (I've already had a few) find them rather eerie, I think, and just about everyone asks how I can sleep with all these bearded ghosts looking down on me. So far, they've done me no harm.

And to the best of my knowledge I've done no harm myself. I mention that because when one of my neighbours heard I was going into a home he remarked that it wouldn't be fair on the other residents. There were enough ministers coming into the place already, he said. Besides, I'd be going about singing Gaelic songs; and what's more, I wouldn't be in the place a month before I'd be proposing some structural changes. You would think I had a reputation.

Anyway, whether it's home or not, this is my last posting. It's warm, it's secure and there are other people around twenty-four hours a day. Not to mention, of course, three meals a day, although the dining room is so far away I have to be taken in a wheelchair. Which is just as well. If I didn't have the wheelchair, I'd need a navigator.

All this by way of excuse for not writing you a decent letter. Once I settle down you'll get something, I promise.

Yours
Old Crock

20 June 2025

Dear Jacqueline

It's me, back. I've been in the Home a month now and on the whole I'm settling down fine, even though I had a bad day yesterday. It could have been too much coffee (or too little), but I'm inclined to blame the wedding. I don't get asked to many nowadays, and when I do I usually manage to persuade everyone that it is quite impossible, absurd and unthinkable that I should go, and that no-one with the tiniest modicum of intelligence or charity would expect me to do such a thing. But this time it didn't work. The bride was the great-grand-daughter of one of my Sunday School teachers, and as if that weren't enough, I had known her granny when she was a young teacher in Edinburgh. Everyone took my attendance for granted: seventeen generations, remarkable connections, evocative memories and all that. I went, compliant as ever, dressed up and smoothed down and hand-finished by the staff here. For the first couple of hours I gave a fairly good impression of being alive. After that people must have found it hard to suspend their disbelief, although, as far as I can recall, no-one actually pricked me just to make sure.

I've never been able to understand these modern weddings. They offer an obvious opportunity to meet up with people you haven't seen for decades and to relax with people you see every day. But this, apparently, is against some Act of Parliament. You have to sit with people you've never met in your life (so that you'll 'mix'), and just when you think that's over and you can blether away with some old friend, the dancing starts: or should I say all hell breaks loose. I came to the conclusion fifty years ago that all modern singers and dancers are stone-deaf and can't hear a thing unless they're surrounded by enormous amplifiers. It's literally pandemonium: an orchestra of demons engaged in a decibel competition. They should be metered, these things, and the organisers arrested if the band is more than three times over the limit.

You'll probably tell me that you love such events and that the music is just a matter of idiom and taste. It's not that I mind volume, so long as it's natural. But the distortion and exaggeration are unforgivable. In fact, as I sat there pressed up against the back of my chair last Friday, I remembered a moment in my childhood. I was about five or six at the time and I was standing on the pier at Stornoway, probably with my father, watching an old steam-trawler about to slip her moorings. Everything was quiet and peaceful in the calm, unhurried manner of seafarers. Suddenly, the skipper blew the siren. I was only a few feet away. Behind me was a huge shed, before me only the sea. Ear-splitting, doleful, inescapable and sinister, it was the theme-music of all my fears: the last trump, the atom bomb and my mother's funeral in one endless single note. Give me quiet, dear Lord.

I have few memories of old Lewis weddings, probably because all the relevant aunties and uncles were married before I was born and I wasn't invited. The exception was my Auntie Kate, who married in 1946. My memories of that are very odd. I have absolutely no recollection of any kind of religious service. If I was in church, I don't remember. If there was a minister, he's fallen through a hole in my memory. I do know what I was wearing, however, because I still have the wedding photo: an extraordinary document. The bride had forgotten her bouquet and her arm hangs, elegantly enough, by her side. My mother had broken her arm and is hiding it behind someone's back. And I'm there in the very front row, wearing (or sort of wearing) an ill-fitting kilt, a kilt jacket, a waistcoat, a Glengarry bonnet and stockings which are trying to make up their minds whether to stay up or fall down. I am not at all happy. My hate affair with weddings (and cameras) has already begun, and disenchantment and misery are written all over my face. Why should anyone have to wear a kilt?

The reception was held in our house and I haven't the faintest recollection what we ate or drank. But I do remember the dancing, probably because I had never before seen such ridiculous behaviour, even from adults. It took place in our front room, a confined space some fifteen feet by twelve, and among the dancers was our neighbour, Dòmhnall Ruairidh, recently demobbed from the Royal Navy after distinguished War service. My abiding memory is of his head hitting the Tilley lamp which hung suspended from the ceiling, and of the thing swinging precariously for a second or two before deciding not to precipitate a disaster.

Your mother probably told you of the old style Lewis weddings with their rèiteachs and so on. She probably had much more first-hand experience of them than I had, but from all you've said about her she seems to have put her Lewis culture very much out of mind once she went to Canada. That's not surprising. After all, she had to build not just one but two new lives. I suspect, too, that unlike me she found the whole culture repressive, and rather than reject bits of it (the church bits), she found it easier to forget it all. But it's still annoying. She was a first class Gaelic scholar, far better equipped than I to make a serious contribution to the Gàidhealtachd. Had I dared to suggest to her when I last saw her that day in 1961 that she would end up a total culture buff and an aficionado of the opera - well, I can't imagine her doing or saying anything violent, but she would at least have laughed.

Anyway, by my time the *rèiteachs* had died out and I knew of them only by hearsay. They were very much cases of self-catering, the immediate family supplying the necessary sheep and every house in the village providing a chicken. Not that they were called chickens then, of course. They were hens, past laying. No one killed chickens or productive birds. Indeed, to kill a hen on suspicion that it wasn't laying its weight and then find eggs inside it was regarded as a minor disaster: certainly something worth reporting to Seonag Ailein on her next ceilidh. I have heard tell of one shrewd old lady who always offered a diseased or dying bird for the *rèiteach*. That might have raised a few eyebrows: it certainly lived in village folklore. But the merely old bird was perfectly fine for soup, as any Arab will tell you.

I say, 'Arab', because of something that happened one day in the 1990s when I was on a visit to Jerusalem with a party from Lewis. The women, enjoying a rare travel-free afternoon, were sitting outside the hotel flirting with a group of young Arabs, probably hotel staff. Soon the proposals of marriage were flowing freely. One lady, greatly enjoying the interchange, dismissed a proposal on the ground that she was too old. "Old birds make the best soup!" said the Arab, quick as a flash. The lady decided she didn't want to be in the soup.

But I'd better address your question: the tinkers. The word became politically incorrect some time in the Eighties of last century, as if it were somehow derogatory. We began to call them 'travelling people' instead. Whether that changed either their status or public perception of them I could never be sure.

In my early schooldays there were three tinker encampments round Stornoway: one in Marybank, one at Tong Bridge and one at the Blackwater, about three hundred yards from our home. They lived in large tents consisting of a sheet of canvas supported by long willow branches bound and bent in the shape of a Nissen hut and big enough for a family. Each tent had a stove in the middle with a vertical pipe going through the roof. The encampments were fairly permanent, but periodically the Blackwater tents would be dismantled and loaded onto a cart, and off the tinkers would go. Where, we never knew, although when they returned to school they tended to say they had been to Uist or Skye.

To us, tinkers had enviable skills. They could make hooks with safety-pins and catch fish without even bothering with worms. And they were great horsemen. Each family had a horse and a spring-cart. For some reason we always pronounced the latter with the emphasis on the first word: 'spreeng-cart'. Presumably they were so called because, unlike ordinary crofters' carts, they had springs. As far as we were concerned, they were unique to tinkers, although they probably had had some prior existence in a more aristocratic environment.

The horses themselves were pretty lively creatures, with a reputation for bolting. Maintenance wasn't a problem. They were simply left to roam the moor which formed the Common Grazings. This was occasionally supplemented with hay which was sold by one enterprising local crofter who charged half a crown a bag. A bag, of course, is the same size as a piece of string, and the tinkers were adept at getting value for money. The same entrepreneur also sold paraffin, and although a horseless family such as ours had little need of hay, we did need paraffin. We used to dread being sent for this stuff. It was no fun at all carrying a gallon of it for half a mile, your hands numb and your rain-lashed legs rubbing against the heavy steel can. But when it was your turn, you went, and I remember on one of my visits being witness to a sharp altercation between the supplier of hay and a tinker. The quantity of hay you can take away in a bag depends not only on the size of the bag but on your skill as a packer, and on this occasion the supplier was very much of the view that the packer's skill was beyond the bounds of commercial propriety. The tinker, John Angus, was a boy of just about my own age, but he stuck to his position. He had come for a bagful; and the bag wasn't yet full. I suspect he was much more frightened of his father and older brothers than he was of the purveyor of hay, who watched helpless as almost the whole of the year's crop disappeared into the one tinker's bag.

The tinkers were the only people in the Lewis of those days to produce their own foals, and I can still recall my many futile attempts to persuade my grandfather to explain to me how foals were made. He kept talking about 'the stallion': a concept with which I wasn't familiar (presumably because most crofters' horses were geldings. As you can see, I have learned a few things since I grew up). Anyway, he always changed the subject: either to 'the Martyrs' or to his own version of 'The Rime of the Ancient Mariner'.

But far the most spectacular thing to us was the sight of the young tinkers riding bareback, often with nothing to cling to but the horse's mane. Crofters' horses never galloped, although the milkman's and the fish-cadgers' sometimes trotted. Remember I told you before that no command, coercion or coaxing could ever persuade my grandfather's mare, Maggie, to gallop, or even to trot? She had evolved only to the point of walking. But the tinkers' horses galloped, sometimes on command and sometimes despite it, and no rodeo ever provided more spectacular entertainment than the sight of a horse careering over the moor with John Angie or Coll or Peter or Jacob hanging on; or falling off, chasing it and leaping back on. Pure magic: and almost the closest we could get to real live cowboys.

I say "almost" because every so often a mysterious figure called 'The Cowboy' would appear among the Blackwater tinkers: a swarthy, hatted gentleman, all the more mysterious (and sinister) because he was dumb. His reputation may have been based on nothing other than his dress, but I doubt it. His appearance and body-language were different from those of the tinkers and such whispers as went around suggested that he came from South America. I pictured him riding the pampas of Argentina swinging his bolas (and we made bolases, too). But his real habitat, I suspect, was the sheep-country of Patagonia. After the rigours of Tierra del Fuego, life in a tinker's tent must have rated as luxury.

The tinkers' prowess wasn't confined to horsemanship. They were also outstanding schoolboy athletes, excelling as both footballers and runners. I may have mentioned earlier that they often played without shoes, boots or any form of footwear - and this on a stony, gravel-covered playground. The school may have ignored them educationally, but it was more than happy to have them in its football or sports team.

These tinkers were no mere beggars or scroungers. They still plied their trade as tinsmiths and went round the houses selling their pails and milking-jugs (*muga-seipein* in Gaelic). The womenfolk also operated as pedlars. Many's the day I remember these bent, wizened, mysterious old women coming to the door and addressing my mother most respectfully as Bean Dhòmhnaill. They carried their wares in a huge bag-like thing on their backs. It wasn't actually a sack. It was more a large square of sacking folded in a way that must have been a trade secret and forming what was known as a *màileid*. The lady would be given tea, the *màileid* opened in front of the fire and the wares offered to my mother, who kept on saying, "Gheibh mi nas saoire a's na Woolies e" ("I can get it cheaper in Woolworth's"). I don't recall the tinkers pointing out that, yes, that might be true, but she'd have to go on the bus to get it, and here it was, coming to her. What was undoubtedly true is that most of the wares did come from Woolworth's: an assortment of needles, reels, hair-nets, grips, clasps and utensils, all marked up more or less significantly. Whatever the haggling, the tinker never left without making a sale and uttering a blessing.

The Marybank tinkers eventually branched out into what proved for them a very lucrative line of business: collecting *fuigheagan* (wool-waste), which every loom-shed had in abundance and for which in these days there was a ready market (by the end of the century you almost had to pay someone to take away the fleece, let alone the waste). They prospered, bought vans and pick-ups and began the slow process of absorption into the wider community. Initially (and to the consternation of the Stornoway Trust) they built permanent houses on the site of their encampments, but soon they were buying property in the town itself or moving into council houses.

To what extent did we mix? We seldom visited the tents, but we certainly drafted them into every football game or any other game that was going; and I remember once getting into awful trouble with my mother for fighting with one of them, Jimmy, the best footballer of the lot. I knew he'd been ill, but I didn't know he had a brain tumour. He had a sister, Bella (the one who came to our house one night to tell us her uncles were killing Buckie). In her early teens she married one of her cousins at Tong Bridge and the story went around that when one of her family was asked whether there would be many guests the reply was "No-one but Angie Òg (their nearest neighbour) and the 'revelations'." I wouldn't vouch for it: Bella was my pal. Nor would I vouch for the other wedding story, according to which the minister went up to the obvious suspect and asked him, "Are you the bridegroom?" "No," he said. "I'm only the man who's getting married."

It's probably fifty years since I last had any contact with these MacDonalds, Stewarts and Drummonds, although I suspect I've unwittingly spoken to their grandchildren many times. It's odd the things you remember. I remember Archie Drummond, a rotund, cherubic blond who probably made more money trading in *fuigheagan* than I could ever dream of. Our assistant headteacher in Laxdale, John Murdo MacMillan, an incorrigible humorist (and much else) used to delight in asking young Drummond, "Who do you think you are?" and young Drummond delighted even more in replying, "I think I'm Archie, sir!" And I remember Evan Stewart, who risked his life one lunchtime going to the rescue of a sheep which had fallen through the ice into the deepest pool on the Laxdale River; Jimmy Stewart, whom a sheriff banished from the island for some felony; Dolly and Bella Drummond; Jimsy and Dolly Mary Stewart; and Hannah.

Especially Hannah. Hannah was the last of a large family born to Clemag. Clemag had a husband, of course, Joseph by name, but I have no memories of him. Well, few memories. I remember the time of his death in the late 1940s. Death was an unusual event in our childhood, since everyone in the neighbourhood was relatively young (I think I've told you this before:

remember, I'm in a Home), and I can still remember looking with mingled pity and awe at Hannah and her brothers and wondering how they felt. But the main reason I remember little of Joseph is that his wife, Mrs Clementina MacDonald, was a huge personality: the Queen of the Lewis tinkers, liable at any moment to start a fight with her own shadow, talking like an angel when she visited your house with her *màileid*, exuding the aura of another (and sometimes a nether) world, and in her latter years taking her place with the saints in the weekly prayer meeting. Along with her two sisters, Chirsty and Doileag, she provided the core families of the Blackwater community.

Hannah, as I said, was her youngest daughter, exactly my own age and on my class at school. She was a spare, lean, dignified girl, drawing no attention to herself and never in trouble (a feature of all the tinker girls; and as far as the Blackwater boys were concerned the only trouble they were ever in was being late for school: something that was no fault of their own). Hannah functioned as a kind of calming, mother-like influence among the rest of us.

When I left Laxdale School for the Nicolson in 1953, I gradually lost touch with Hannah. That may seem odd, but in a Lewis winter there's little time for play after school; and Hannah had her own network of relationships. But she clearly didn't forget me. My first charge after my ordination to the ministry in 1964 was Kilmallie, a parish adjacent to Fort William. Soon after I settled there, I boarded a crowded bus for the return journey from the town to Corpach, where the manse was. I was dressed in clerical finery, as ministers were in those far-off days. Suddenly there was a piercing, delighted yell: "Hello, Donnie!" Every head turned, my wife's face fell and I blushed as only I could. "Hi, Hannah!"

Hannah was visiting her sister, who with some other members of the Laxdale clan had joined the encampment at Annan on Lochiel, near the site of the ill-fated pulp mill. I never saw her again. She will never grow old.

I mentioned that Clemag had about her something of the aura of another world. Always dressed in black, she was a small, wiry little woman, with a long, sharp nose, and it was easy for us kids to think of her as a witch: all the easier because of her association with Jeannie. Jeannie often visited the tinkers, and Jeannie, by her own way of it, was heavily into *buidseachd*. She was probably frightened by it and was certainly not above using it to frighten others. In those days, remember, there were no horror movies - at least, not in Laxdale.

Sadly, I have long since forgotten all her tales, except one. It was the story of a couple of churchgoing women, one of them the wife of an elder, who were suspected of practising *buidseachd*. One night, a traveller on the road to Barvas suddenly saw a group of women dancing and cavorting on the moor. He instinctively stopped and watched. The women saw him and immediately disappeared; or sort of disappeared. In their place was a pack of cats fleeing at high speed across the moor. One of the cats suddenly tumbled, fell on the ground and lay still. The following morning news went round that the elder's wife had broken her leg.

Yes, I know what you're going to say. That story, with local variations, is told all over Scotland. But I didn't know this until, many years later, I read Edwin Muir's autobiography and came across the Orkney version, according to which 'a Sanday farmer, coming back for his dinner, saw the local witch's black cat slinking out of his house. He rushed in, snatched up his gun, and let fly at it. The cat was leaping over a stone dyke when he fired; it stumbled and gave a great screech, then ran away, dragging one hind-leg after it. Next day the witch sent for the doctor to set her leg.' The core of the story is the same, but trust the Lewis version to be anti-clerical or at least anti-church!

But such stories were confined to Jeannie and her circle, although just occasionally references would be made to people of a past generation who were reputed to have 'the eye' (*an t-sùil*, as it was in Gaelic) and to have used it to make their neighbour's cow go dry. And I remember, just vaguely, that in my early days in the ministry memories were still alive of a Communion service in Lewis when the minister fencing the table laid great stress on *draoidheachd* (witchcraft), one of the 'works of the flesh' listed in Galatians 5: 19-21 (the passage which was always read in connection with fencing the Table). He warned in the most solemn terms that no-one involved in *buidseachd* should sit at the Table; and the story was that at that point a woman got up, left the church and never took Communion again.

That was about the extent of my contact with stories of the occult, and I've no regrets about it. The occult, as far as I can see, is a very minor Office of Pandemonium, and probably its main function is diversionary, to draw attention away from more important operations. After the Holocaust, the Congo, Rwanda, Kosovo and Dunblane it was difficult to get excited about cats breaking their legs.

Forgive me. The old folk always said the Devil wasn't worth talking about and they were absolutely right. But I'm sure he has a kind of Press Monitoring Service which carefully logs every column-inch and soundbite devoted to him. Why should I pander to his vanity?

Walk slowly
Donald

5 September 2025

Beinn Roisneabhat Nursing Home
Stornoway
Isle of Lewis.

Dear Jacqueline

I don't know if I told you before, but I'm no longer living in my old house. They tell me I can still go and see it whenever I want (it's empty), but it was still hard, turning the key in the lock for the last time. Anyway, how can I go there "any time"? I certainly can't walk. Neither can I drive. Will I fly?

Everybody is nice, except that they all have such loud voices. Sometimes I think they think I'm deaf, but I don't see why they should think that. Maybe I should shout back. Most of the nurses are foreigners: beautiful girls, but hardly any English. "You likee soup?" they say (or something like that). It's very infectious. I began to mimic them a few days ago. "Me going to sleep now," I said to my visitors. "Me not happy!" They looked at each other, very solemnly. I'm sure they went off and reported they had seen a big change in me. I can almost hear them: "He's failing. He's not himself." I've not been myself for forty years. I'm not even sure I'd know how to be myself; or want to be.

The days are very strange. Sometimes the place is full of hustle and bustle: cleaners, breakfast, lunch, dinner, nurses, doctors. On Sundays, elders (or aspiring elders) come, often from all the churches at once. You can have two or three in one day. They're very interesting. They walk in as if they were doctors and then after a little chit-chat anounce they're going to pray. Sometimes, their prayers lift me up. Other times I feel like saying, "It's my house and you can't walk in here and take it over, just like that." I've been very nice, so far, and haven't said a single nasty thing. And anyway, you sort of miss them when they go, because you may not see anyone else for the rest of the day. Four walls make a small world. Even reading is hard. The books seem so heavy now and, anyway, since I moved to this new house I can't find anything.

I don't suppose I have much of a future now, and even though I have a lot of past it's no longer of any use to anyone. You know most of it, and I am so grateful to you for taking such an interest. Maybe you'll be its custodian (for what it's worth), and I hope you can be kind to it without being dishonest or untrue to yourself. So much of what's been written about our island and its way of life has been hostile. I used to say to my car-dealer, "I don't want a bargain, just a fair deal." That goes for Lewis too.

You know, it's odd, too, that you've never called me "Donald". Here youngsters I've never met in my life speak to me as if they were my auntie.

There's another odd thing, too: how the past makes you think of progress. Do we ever really progress? Here am I in my old age surrounded by comforts our forebears could never have dreamed of. But they had one thing: they died with their families around them. They had no central heating, no carpets, no orthopaedic beds, no loos, no showers. They didn't even have Zimmers (or hearing-aids). But they had their daughters (or daughters-in-law) to tend them till their dying breath. Weren't these "great Victorians" lucky: "died in the bosom of his family".

It would be lovely to hear from you again, even though I've nothing more that would help with your research. I hope I amn't too depressing. You must make allowances for my Thomson genes. My grandfather said to me every summer for twenty years, "Beannachd leat is turas math. Chan fhaic thu mise tuilleadh" ("God bless you, and a safe journey. You won't see me again"). If my next letter says, "You won't hear from me again," don't take me too seriously.

God bless you
Donald

Beinn Roisneabhat Nursing Home
Stornoway
Isle of Lewis

Dear Mme Quessaud

I'm living in a new house now, though I can't quite remember when I moved. The house is very good. There's a lot of home-helps and they seem to stay all day long. The only thing is, I've been in hospital. Twice, I think, though I'm not sure why. I think the first time was because I fell and broke my leg. The second time, they told me, was for an experiment. My tremor was getting worse, and very tiring (and very messy). The cardiologist (I'm sure that's what he said) strapped a small black box to me and said "Slow release." But I think the experiment didn't work and they sent me home (without the black box). It was great to get back home. I was in a ward with lots of old people and they didn't seem to have any sense, especially in the middle of the night when they were moaning and groaning non-stop.

There are lots of visitors in this house and sometimes it's very noisy at mealtimes. One day, they started without saying the grace. Another day, they started eating before Seanair had started.

I spend much of my time painting a bottle. Long, long ago, on my first job, my boss told me he had never seen anyone paint a bottle as well as me.

The other day a man came in dressed like a minister. I knew he was wicked and screamed and screamed till he left.

It's good here and I'm very happy in myself because I don't have to worry about a thing. In fact, it's very funny how being old can make you happy. There's a lot of people in the corridor just outside my door, all laughing and bubbly and happy as the day is long.

Love
Donald